Claiming the Blame

by

S Ben Hawksworth

Grosvenor House
Publishing Limited

This book is published by
Grosvenor House Publishing Ltd
Link House
140 The Broadway, Tolworth, Surrey, KT6 7HT.
www.grosvenorhousepublishing.co.uk

A CIP record for this book
is available from the British Library

ISBN 978-1-83615-010-7

To those who take the time to listen

CHAPTER ONE

Two and three-quarter seconds. He had calculated that when he jumped, that's how long it would take before he hit the muddy waters of the river below. He had made up his mind to do it, but how should he actually do it? It would be easy to scramble up onto the top of the guard rail above the pedestrian walkway, but what then? Should he just sort of flop over and then plummet down, arms and legs flailing like some unstrung marionette? That would be a bit ungainly, and that just was not on. He wanted to make a dignified exit. Perhaps he should clamber on top of the guard rail, stand there for a brief moment and then make a majestic swallow dive like those South Sea Islanders who dive off high cliffs? An appealing idea, but he wasn't much good at diving; he had tried it once in the local swimming baths from the high board and it had hurt. He didn't want to hurt himself now. It was a moment or two before it dawned on him that this was more than a little irrational. Whichever way he did it, it was going to hurt.

This needed a bit more thought. Terry felt that he had planned most of his exit very carefully. He stood there on the bridge, dressed in his best suit, the one he had bought for his gran's funeral. It had seemed appropriate. He had even given his shoes a good shine for the first time in years. The sun was newly risen, and it looked like it was going to be a warm day. Below him, the wide expanse of the Humber went about its muddy business, but much of this was lost on Terry as he was engrossed in the process of finalising his plan; this was far too important to get wrong.

"You don't want to do that," came a voice from behind him, and he turned abruptly to see the source of this unsought advice. He was surprised to see a stranger standing beside him on the path; a shabbily dressed young man in a well-worn brown suit with a collarless shirt and a grubby handkerchief around his neck.

"Do what?" asked Terry.

"Jump," said the stranger. "You don't want to jump."

"You can't stop me," protested Terry, taking half a step towards the side of the path.

I know. I can't stop you doing anything," said the new arrival in a resigned way.

"So why are you just standing there?" asked Terry, becoming just a little annoyed at this unwarranted intrusion into his big day.

"I spend a lot of time here," said the stranger, staring down the river and apparently singularly unimpressed with the fact that Terry was intending to throw himself off the bridge.

"So why don't you just go back to wherever you came from and leave me in peace?" suggested Terry.

"That's a bit complicated, you see, I'm from the other side."

"The Lincolnshire side?" asked Terry, gesturing southwards.

"No. The other side."

"The Yorkshire side!" offered Terry with ill-concealed annoyance.

"No. The other side. I don't live anywhere. I'm dead."

"That's just bloody great! I come here for a bit of quiet contemplation with a view to ending my problems, and I meet some nutter who says he's dead. Well. Look here, pal. I was here first, and I have no intention of doing a tandem jump, so go and find your own bit of bridge and leave me to mine."

"As I said, I can't stop you. It's just that it's not a good time to jump."

2

"A good time? What the devil are you talking about? Is this some home-spun Feng shui from the mystical East of England? Are my stars aligned in some unpropitious way, or are you just intent on being a pain in the arse?"

"It's an hour before high water. The tide is still on the flood. If you jump now, you will be swept away and may end up in a reed bed somewhere upriver with a strong probability that your body will eventually be found by some poor dog-walker or the like with a fair chance of putting at least one of them off their breakfast. In a couple of hours or so, the water will be on the ebb, and there is a good chance you will be swept out to sea where your remains won't upset the crabs. In fact, they'd welcome you," explained the stranger in a matter-of-fact sort of way.

"I note your concern for the sensitivity of dog walkers, but, the way my life has been going, this is a good time for me to jump. I've got my own problems."

"I can see that. Contemplating a fall of over one hundred feet into cold, muddy water is bound to hurt; that would never have been my way out, but each to his own." The stranger paused for a while before asking, "So what made you decide to come over to our side?"

Terry's natural inclination was to tell the stranger, in no uncertain terms, to go away. But for some strange reason, he felt an irrational compulsion to share his recent experiences with someone else as if to justify what he was doing there. He reckoned that it wouldn't do any harm to tell him what had led to this moment. He hadn't had the opportunity to discuss it with anyone else, and in some ways, it seemed less intimidating to tell a stranger, somehow less embarrassing.

"My life is a mess. My girlfriend suddenly announced she was leaving me, and as I was getting over that, I lost my job. All that mattered to me was gone," explained Terry.

"She must have meant a lot to you."

"She was the centre of my life, and then she just said she was leaving. We never had rows; Lizzie's experience as a social worker meant that we never argued. We simply 'saw things from a different perspective' or 'held differing views'. We never had problems, we had 'situations', 'challenges', 'concerns' or 'issues'. Perhaps we should have had problems and argued about them rather than just trundle along as though everything was perfect. One minute, we seemed to be doing fine, and then she suddenly accused me of being selfish and not thinking of her."

"What caused her to think that?"

"No idea. For months she has talked about wanting to go on holiday, and then when I go to the trouble of booking something, she ups and says I'm selfish and she's leaving. There's no pleasing some people," asserted Terry and then, after a short pause, he added, "But I still miss her."

"I miss my wife too," added the stranger.

"So, did she leave you?"

"In a way, yes, but in a way she's always with me. She died. She drowned somewhere down there."

Terry found himself following the stranger's gaze down to the water below, and the two stood in silence for a few minutes before Terry broke the reverie by asking, "So did she jump from here?"

"Oh no. This thing wasn't even built then. No, she was looking for our young son on the banks over there. It was assumed at the inquest that they had been cut off by the incoming tide. He was only two, our George. I was away at the time. I should have been here; it might have made a difference."

Terry began to recognise that the visitor's confused state might well be the result of having lost his wife and son so tragically. He was probably just a little bit 'unhinged'. Terry would be the first to accept that a sudden loss could turn one's world upside down and make one do irrational things, like contemplating jumping off large structures into murky water.

"So sorry to hear about your loss. I'm Terry Henderson, by the way," he continued, holding out his hand.

"I'm Michael Lampeter Hodge," replied the stranger in a strangely formal manner while politely ignoring the outstretched hand.

For a few minutes, the couple stared silently in the general direction downstream where the tragedy had occurred before Michael broke the silence.

"It was always something I regretted; being away when they died, I just couldn't help," and then, after a lengthy pause, he continued, "Bright as a button was our George. The crew of a barge found them floating downriver. I like to think they went together; I hate to think that he might have died alone. He was only two, our George. Mary would have tried to be with him; she knew the risks, but she would have tried."

Terry had to concede that Michael was an accomplished storyteller. The man was obviously confused, but he told a coherent story that made it hard for Terry to openly accuse him of making it all up.

"Anyway, they're both together now in the village," continued Michael, nodding in the general direction of a small group of houses that Terry recognised as Barton Saint Martin.

"So where were you when all this happened?" asked Terry, who had now recognised that the stranger was not going to go off and leave him to his jump.

"In France."

"On holiday?"

"No, I'd signed up for the duration. I was in hospital with shrapnel wounds."

Despite himself, Terry was becoming increasingly interested in the story that was unfolding. He found he had unwittingly suspended his disbelief and was becoming quite interested in what the stranger had to say. He found himself asking, "So when exactly did you go to France?"

"Nineteen sixteen. My job maintaining the dykes around here was important work, but evidently they needed the same skills in Flanders. I didn't want to leave Mary and young George, but I had to do my bit for the country. I considered myself lucky as I wasn't sent up to the front where all the scrapping went on. It should have been a nice cushy job out of harm's way for the main part, but a stray shell, one of theirs or one of ours, soon changed that. It took a lump out of my side the size of a football."

"So that was how you died?"

"No, they patched me up first at a field hospital near Saint-Omer before shipping me back to a huge hospital near Southampton. They did a first-rate job, but I wasn't fit for active service, so they sent me home. But, without the family here, it wasn't worth coming home. We'd had such wonderful times; we married in 1904, but it was ten years before young George came along. We thought it wasn't going to happen; we'd always been happy, but the baby just made it perfect. We felt like a real family and thought we might even be able to have more children. We had such plans. George wasn't going to dig drains for a living; Mary would teach him to read just like she taught me, and he would have a better life, become a gentleman and live in a house with an indoor toilet. That was what we wanted, what we planned, but it never worked out that way."

Terry knew it was irrational, but he felt sorry for this man's apparent plight and asked, "So when exactly did you die?"

"I don't recall exactly."

"You don't recall?" asked Terry, unable to hide his incredulity. "I would have thought that the day you die is pretty important."

"Oh yes, to the living it is, but when you've passed over, well, it's just the start of eternity, and that doesn't have a specific time frame," pointed out Michael.

"Surely, apart from your date of birth, it is the most important event in your life?"

"Oh no, I remember the most important times; meeting Mary, our months of courting, much of which was in the reed beds over yonder," he added with a mischievous grin. "Then there was our wedding day, of course. Saint Martin's was packed with all our friends and family, and afterwards we had a grand wedding breakfast that the ladies of the village contributed to. I'd never seen so much food and we got two barrels of beer provided by one of the local bigwigs. It was a right good party, and people talked about it for years," he added with a broad grin as his memories flooded back. "Then after years of trying and eventually giving up, we were blessed with George; those are the important things in life, and I cherish every single memory, but dying is just stepping through a door to another place."

Terry was aware that he had been prepared to go along with this fantastic story, but this was just too much to be asked to believe, and he found his natural scepticism returning.

"So now you're dead?"

"Yes."

"So what is it like, being dead? Have you met God?"

"Have you been to London?" replied Michael in a matter-of-fact way.

Terry was momentarily stunned by this apparent non sequitur and replied, "Yes. But what has that got to do with it?"

"Did you meet the Lord Mayor?"

"No. London is a big place, you know. It's full of people."

"The other side is rather a big place too, and there are lots of residents; you can't expect to meet every celebrity. Anyway, I like to keep myself to myself."

Terry got the distinct impression that he was now being humoured but considered that the flippant nature of his question meant that he deserved it.

"It's not like some great big social club on the other side," continued Michael. "And if it is, it's the least exclusive club that ever met. They let anybody in. In fact, everyone gets to join eventually. We don't just sit about on clouds chatting or singing in the choir celestial. Death isn't a communal thing; we all die alone."

"So how did you die?" asked Terry, conscious of the fact that it was a strange question to ask of someone but trying to sound genuinely interested. "Was it in France?"

"No, I never went back. My injuries made me unfit for active service, particularly something like canal work. I had some infection shortly after I got home, possibly aggravated by my injuries or perhaps it was the flu, and I just died. I never really think about it. It wasn't some heroic death on the battlefield. I just died."

For a few minutes, the pair stood and looked down at the river, which continued to flow along, apparently indifferent to the drama that was going on above it. Michael broke the silence by remarking, "Your Lizzie sounds like an interesting woman."

"Yes. She does some strange things at times, like the way she just walked out of my life. Neither rhyme nor reason, but I still miss her. She was very understanding when I told her about being sacked. She had come round to collect some of her things and was a bit surprised to find I wasn't at work. Typical of Lizzie, she pointed out that I hadn't lost my job, I just had a new opportunity to explore new areas and 'another door would open'. For a while I believed her; at least she had faith in my ability, but when I sat down on my own later, I realised just how hopeless it all was."

"So that's why you were considering the big jump?"

"Yes. I just felt crushed. One minute I was in a job that I was bloody good at and coming home to a woman who loved me, and the next it was all gone. My job is now 'computerised'. Don't get me wrong; I'm no technophobic Luddite, but I ran that storeroom as efficiently as any you would wish to find. Even the boss accepted that I was a great asset, but the company had to move on."

"I see," said Michael, more out of politeness than to express any real understanding.

For a few more minutes, the two stood in silence looking down at the river before Michael absent-mindedly commented, "It looks cold down there."

"Yes. Perhaps I'll wait for a warmer day."

"Good idea. It will give you a bit of time to think it over. It's always good to think things through carefully before making big decisions."

"Yes. I was probably being a bit hasty," suggested Terry before adding, "I think I'd better be getting back home."

"I'll just hang around here and take in the view for a while. Look after yourself." The last comment was uttered with a degree of obvious sincerity that was not lost on Terry as he turned and headed back for the north bank.

After he had walked some distance, it suddenly occurred to Terry who the mysterious visitor was. He was obviously one of those Samaritans who frequent recognised suicide spots to dissuade people from ending it all. His methods were unorthodox, but they obviously worked. Terry turned to wave at the stranger, but he had gone.

"Obviously gone back to 'the other side'," mused Terry as a bizarre question entered his head. "If you do go over to the other side when you die, does everyone who dies in Hull end up in Lincolnshire?" Terry chuckled to himself and increased his pace as he became aware that it was still quite cool. The day was warming up slowly, but there was a cold wind blowing down the river.

CHAPTER TWO

Terry made his way back to the car park at the viewing point, and as he approached his car, he instinctively put his hand in his pocket to find his car keys but remembered that he had left the car unlocked with the keys in the ignition. There had seemed little point in taking his keys to the bottom of the river with him. He quickly got into the car and started the engine. He put the heater on and sat for a moment, getting warmed through as he looked out over the river. The high tide concealed the mud flats, and the river was at its most majestic. The tide would be turning soon, and the time was approaching when the stranger on the bridge had suggested it might be more convenient to jump. Terry felt a sudden shiver, but it was not the cold. Deep inside him, he felt that it had probably never been his intention to jump, but there was that frightening thought that he had even considered it. One way or another, the enigmatic Mr Hodge had probably done him a favour. Meanwhile the river went on with its business, unaware and no doubt unconcerned that there was one less object it had to carry with it today.

Terry suddenly felt very hungry, and his thoughts immediately turned to a local mobile café that he visited frequently on his many trips to the bridge. The term 'mobile' café was an apt one as its location changed from time to time as the owner played a cat-and-mouse game with the local authorities who repeatedly moved him on from his chosen sites. It only took Terry a few minutes to find the most recent pitch for the Red Star Café, and from the alluring smell of frying bacon, he was delighted to find that his old friend was open to catch the early morning breakfast trade. The only other people in the area were two traffic police officers who were sitting in their car. At first, Terry was afraid that the officers were there to move the café on, but a closer observation showed that they were simply having a bite of breakfast. This might be an illicit site, but the bacon sandwiches were enough to encourage the local constabulary not to be too officious.

Terry wandered over to the counter to be met by the salutation, "Morning, comrade Terry, and what can we do for you on this beautiful morning? The usual?"

"Yes please, Lenin."

The proprietor busied himself putting bacon onto a griddle and poured a mug of tea from a huge teapot. Terry watched the flawless efficiency with which the meal was prepared. The café owner had long been known as Lenin, and his outfit indicated his supposed political allegiance. He wore a loose-fitting olive-coloured fatigue jacket with a selection of small badges showing red stars and the classic hammer and sickle. The outfit was topped by a baggy red army cap with obligatory red star. A military purist might have pointed out that the outfit owed more to Chinese communism than Russian, but the café owner found it easier to adopt the former Russian leader's name than that of Mao Zedong, which he found difficult to pronounce and impossible to spell. The outfit was theatrical rather than political, and the proprietor wore it as some sort of marketing gimmick. Within minutes the feast was prepared. Two thick slices of white bread laden with a generous serving of bacon, which projected enticingly from all sides of the sandwich.

"That will be two pounds fifty of your filthy capitalist money," prompted the owner.

Instinctively, Terry went for his money but remembered with some horror that he hadn't got any with him. It hadn't seemed necessary that morning. He hadn't expected to need it on the bottom of the river, and he recalled how it presently resided on his bedside table next to his perfectly made-up bed in his immaculately clean room.

"Sorry, Lenin. I'm afraid I've come out without any money."

"Bloody capitalists, taking advantage of the proletariat, as ever! Never mind, I'll catch you next time."

"Sorry, Lenin," he repeated. "My money is all in my other outfit."

"I thought you looked strange. Are you going to a funeral?"

"Nearly," he said, with an involuntary look in the direction of the river before quickly adding, "Well, this is my funeral suit."

"Oh hell! Lord Leonard hasn't died, has he?"

"No. Well, he was OK yesterday when I visited him."

The café owner was visibly relieved and added, "Thank goodness for that. He's one of my better class of customers. One of my few regulars who asks for a serviette, and not just to blow his nose on. If they were all like him, I wouldn't have to keep the sugar spoon on a chain. I'll miss him when he does go."

"Strangely enough, he was talking about you yesterday," added Terry. "He likes his trips down here to see you. He says it makes a nice change to get away from the residential home and to meet real people. The staff can't do enough for him; they mean well, but they do tend to fuss a bit."

"I know, and he gets pig sick of them enquiring after his toilet habits. Evidently they are not happy until they have found out if he has 'performed' that day. Compared to them, he is an intellectual giant, but they have their little routines to follow."

Terry picked up his bacon sandwich and his mug of tea and wandered over to the little plastic picnic table that the proprietor put out for his customers. He looked over in the general direction of the bridge. He couldn't see the roadway, but the towers soared up over the trees in the foreground. Terry reflected that it was good to be able to see them. He was glad to be able to see them at all after what he had planned for the day. His thoughts were interrupted by Lenin, who had come over with a mug of tea and sat on one of the plastic chairs next to him.

"So how's things with you, comrade?" asked the café owner in a cheery manner.

"So-so. Things have been better. I lost my job at Enderby's; they've decided they can do without me."

"They can't do that. You've been there since you left school. No bloody loyalty, the managerial classes. Is the company going bust or something?"

"No, they've put in a computerised system in the store. All you have to do is type in a keyword or code, and the computer tells you exactly where in the stores the item can be located."

"But you know that store like the back of your hand; what the hell do they want to put a computer in for?" asked Lenin incredulously.

"I tried to reason with them. I pointed out that you can't just go to the computer and ask for 'one of those little brass things about the size of my thumb with a 15-millimetre screw that connects to the boiler outlet'. The computer couldn't recognise such a vague description, but I'd go straight to shed three, aisle 10, section B, lower shelf. It's easy when you know the place and the stock as well as I do."

"Exactly! So why the computer system?"

"The boss saw my point, but he pointed out that other members of the store room staff don't share my gift, and when I'm not on duty, it can take ages to find items, so the computer is in and I'm out."

"They can't just throw you out after all those years. You've got your rights, comrade. You should take them to a tribunal, brother, unfair dismissal and all that."

"To be fair, they didn't just throw me out onto the street. They did offer me another position, no loss of salary or anything, but I told them what to do with their poxy job and even told them the location of the appropriate piece of apparatus in the stores which would help them stuff the job exactly where I had suggested."

"So you didn't ask for time to consider the offer?"

"Correct."

"You didn't need that job; you were wasted in that place. You've got talents they wouldn't even guess at. After all, you are Terry the Car Boot King. You can spot a bargain and turn a profit just like that."

"Thanks," responded Terry. "But I'm still learning some of the restoration skills, and the big profits you see on the antique programmes can be a bit illusive."

"You did very well on that little cabinet you bought for twenty quid. A quick cleaning and waxing, and you got eighty for it."

"True, but as Lizzie is quick to point out, I don't always do so well. I bought an old exterior lantern for a fiver and sold it for twenty but, as she reminded me, I spent thirteen pounds on paint and glass, and it took me four hours to tart it up. That makes a rate of pay of fifty pence per hour. Hardly a strong commercial proposition, and on occasion I have made a loss or been unable to sell on my goods at all. My house is full of items that I bought to sell but which didn't prove attractive to any customers. Lizzie wasn't too pleased about that either."

"But you enjoy the car booties."

"Yes. It's a great hobby but not a reliable career option. I have been trying to get into true antiques, to go upmarket a bit, but it's not as easy as it is on the telly. I never miss an edition of any of the antiques programmes, and I can hazard a good guess at some of the valuations, but it's such a vast area. You need to have some specialist area of expertise and a group of clients you can sell to as well, so you only buy what you know you have a fair chance of selling."

"So what are you going to do in the short term?" asked the café owner, trying to be practical.

"I don't know. I need time to think, to get a proper plan."

"What you need is a holiday, comrade."

"Don't you start."

"Start what?"

"Has Lizzie been talking to you?"

"I haven't seen the lovely Lizzie Barker for a few days – sadly – she's a very decorative addition to my establishment when she calls round. She particularly likes it when I can get a site with a view of the river. She spends hours just watching it in all its moods. Sometimes, because of her erratic shifts, she would come down for a sandwich or the like, and she always pays!" he added pointedly before continuing. "Anyway, what's that got to do with you needing a holiday?"

"She's left me."

"Is she looking around for someone new? A debonair mogul from the catering trade?"

"No, she is not," retorted Terry, who sounded more than a little irate.

"Only joking, mate. Anyway, my wife wouldn't allow me to keep a pet. She hasn't really left you, surely? What brought it all on?"

"For months now, Lizzie has been dropping big hints to suggest we needed a holiday. Now I'm not at all keen on holidays, all that expense, often involving being herded around airport lounges and kept waiting long enough so that being crammed together on a plane almost seems like an attractive proposition. Then after two weeks simmering on some crowded beach somewhere, you have to face up to the trials of the return journey. I knew Lizzie was becoming a bit emphatic about the need to get away, so I suggested a trip to Oxford for us. I was flavour of the month for coming up with that idea, and I said I would do all the arrangements as a surprise. I gave her the date we would leave and went about booking the whole thing. It certainly proved to be a surprise. It turned out she had assumed we would be having a week's break and had managed to book some of her precious leave time. She was looking forward to a week in Oxford with all the culture, the architecture and the Morse experience while I had booked a night in a hotel near Oxford with the possibility of half a day in the town to do a bit of shopping – women like shopping. There was also an antiques auction that I had intended to go to, but she wasn't keen."

"A bit of a misunderstanding then?"

"No. The English Civil War was a bit of a misunderstanding; this was much worse."

"So she's left you? Just because of a holiday?" asked Lenin, attempting to show some support.

"It appears there was more to it than that. She had one or two things to say about my lifestyle, and she was uncharacteristically hostile in her tone; in fact, she was positively aggressive. Apparently, she was dissatisfied by the fact that my life was going nowhere. She didn't like living in a house littered with my unfinished projects – she compared it to Steptoe's scrap yard – and apparently, she has kept an extensive inventory of all of my unsuccessful trading efforts since the day we met. She was almost savage in her attack on what she thought were my shortcomings."

"She was always a bit different, your Lizzie. She was always a smart, practical, sociable sort of woman while you…"

There was a short pause before Lenin continued, "Well, you. Sort of, well, live in your own world, more sort of independently minded, not bothering too much about what others think of you."

"So! It's character assassination time now. Go on, hit me while I'm down, why don't you? Job gone, girl gone! What next?"

"I didn't mean anything by it, comrade. It's just that she was so easy to get on with; everyone liked her."

"You're not helping here, pal."

Conscious of the fact that his attempts at consoling his friend were not going too well, Lenin opted for a lengthy diplomatic pause before saying, "Perhaps it was just not meant to be? But it does seem strange; she must have been with you for two years now. You just went together so well, like a pair of book ends."

"Two years and eight months ago, she moved in. I thought my life was sorted. I even contemplated marriage, but each time I managed to steer the conversation round to it, she would go on about all the wrecked marriages she had witnessed in her clients. It sort of spoiled the moment; it's hard to create the right romantic ambience when she is going on about all the scenes of domestic violence she has witnessed. Not that she ever discussed the cases in any detail, but it was obvious that they showed up many marriages in a very bad light."

"So how did you two come to meet?"

"Lord Leonard was living next door to me at the time, and after his wife died, I used to look in on him occasionally. He's a very intelligent man, but he's never been domesticated in the sense of being able to look after himself. When his wife was alive, she was the organiser; he would willingly do his fair share of the chores around the house, but cooking was not his forte. He always said he was designed to eat food but not to cook it. He was bright enough to acknowledge that he needed some support, and he was glad of the visits from Lizzie at the social services department. That was in the days when she was a general social worker, before she joined the special cases team. One day, he forgot that he had asked me to collect his suit from the dry cleaners and he sent Lizzie as well. We met in the dry cleaners, and that was the start of our relationship. After that, we both kept an eye on him until he decided he wanted to go into some kind of residential setting. He has no family to help out, so we helped him look round a number of retirement and nursing homes. He chose Tranby Manor because they served sherry before dinner, not good sherry, but sherry, nevertheless. He seems very settled and happy there now."

"I forgot that you had lived next door to him. Did he have a stately home?"

"No, just a rather nice, detached house, nothing palatial. Why?"

"It's just with him being a Lord and all."

"No, you prawn. 'Lord' is his forename, not his title. He's not landed gentry. His full name is Lord Balaclava Leonard; I think it was his great grandfather or some such relative who was injured in the battle of Balaclava," he added by way of explanation.

"He always seemed a bit posh. I just assumed he was a toff."

"He was an officer during the war, a captain I think. That might explain the way that he always seemed authoritative. Even in his more confused moments, he sounds like he knows what he's doing, typical officer material. He had a distinguished career in Europe after D-Day, but he never talked about it. Mrs Leonard once showed me a photo of him as a young man. He had a chest full of medals."

"So he isn't one of your actual landed gentry?" pressed Lenin, who seemed unable to comprehend that his old friend was really just Mr Leonard.

"Just one of us regular guys."

There was a lengthy pause, during which the café owner appeared to be trying to come to terms with this recent disclosure, but after a while he stood up briskly and asked, "Another tea? On the house."

"Thanks, and then I've got to get down to some serious thinking as to where I go from here. I need to check the papers to get a new job for a start, and then I will have to arrange with Lizzie so she can pick up the rest of her things. I told her there was no rush, but she wants to get it all sorted, make a clean break and all that. She's coming to the house tomorrow to 'talk things through'. Talking of which, I'd better get back and tidy up before she comes over."

CHAPTER THREE

Terry parked his car outside his house and looked up at it. From the outside, it looked much the same as when his gran had left it to him. It was a small, detached house in a pleasant residential area, and Terry had always been fully aware of his good fortune. Here he was, not yet 30, with a place of his own. He couldn't help the feeling that it was strange to be back as he had never planned to return.

Terry let himself in at the back door and stood for a while in the kitchen. It was uncharacteristically tidy. He had lied to Lenin in suggesting he needed to tidy up before Lizzie arrived. He had spent the entire previous day making sure that the house was clean; he hadn't wanted to leave a mess for others. His real reason for wanting to get back was to remove an envelope he had left on the work surface next to the kettle. This was the place where he and Lizzie left messages for each other, knowing that each of them usually made a cup of tea when they got in. He was extremely relieved to see the envelope was still there. Terry picked it up and wandered through to the lounge. He sat in his favourite chair and opened the envelope that was addressed to Lizzie. Inside was a letter and another sealed envelope with the words *Last Will and Testament* printed in large Gothic script.

Terry unfolded the letter and read it out aloud,

"Dearest Lizzie,

I'm sorry to have to leave you this note, but I just wanted to explain my actions to you. I suppose I've realised that life without you is unbearable. I've arranged for you to get the house by drawing up my will and getting Lord Leonard and the manager of his residential home to witness it for me. I realise I was a disappointment to you, and I didn't show you how much you meant to me. I guess I was never good at that sort of thing.

Please don't feel too bad about this. I guess I was just not up to the challenge when things got a bit tough for me. I hope you will be very happy in the house and don't think too badly of me.

Ever yours, Terry"

Terry couldn't escape the feeling that as dramatic last messages go, it was pretty average. It struck him that the letter was strewn with references to 'I' and to 'me', which might not have been surprising as a suicide note, by its very nature, does tend to be personal, but this note went beyond that to become a rather selfish message. Not for the first time that day, Terry was grateful to the Samaritan for dissuading him from taking his early morning dip. Come to think of it, he hadn't taken much persuading to rethink his plan. Perhaps he had never really intended to jump? Perhaps it was the proverbial cry for help? Terry couldn't escape the feeling that it was a good thing that Michael Lampeter Hodge had been there to listen to that cry, and for a brief moment, he wondered how many other desperate individuals had reached such crisis points without having the lifeline of someone with whom to talk through their problems. Even if his response had been somewhat unconventional, Michael had offered him the luxury of time to think.

Terry took the opened envelope and the letter and placed them in the grate before putting a match to them. As they burned, he looked at the unopened will and considered what to do with it. He still felt that Lizzie was the only person in his life who he would like to inherit his house, even if his current plans no longer decreed that she would inherit it immediately. He looked at the small group of photographs on the mantelpiece. His entire immediate family, or what he knew of them, was portrayed here. There was an impressive, framed photograph of his grandfather, who had that distinguished air of someone who had done reasonably well in life. It was a very formal posed image that was in keeping with his grandfather, who had always been a somewhat distant figure. He had never really known how to talk to Terry, who was still at junior school when his grandfather died. Next to his photograph was a smaller one of Terry's gran. It had never seemed strange to Terry that his grandparents had always been shown in separate pictures; there were no pictures of the happy couple on display but then they had never been close in that way. Terry had always felt that his grandparents had been content rather than happy; Grandad provided a comfortable home, and Gran looked after it well, but there were few signs of endearment, no romance. Theirs was a comfortable rather than overtly loving relationship. Terry's grandparents had looked after him well when his mother had left, but there was little observable affection shown. By the time his grandfather had died, Terry's mother was a very infrequent visitor, and his last memory of her was as someone who turned up briefly at the funeral.

Terry's eyes moved on to the picture of his mum, Janice, an attractive young woman at the time, in the fashionable clothes of the seventies. She had made no secret of the fact that motherhood was not for her. Perhaps as a result of the staid upbringing by her parents, she had rebelled at an early age and made it clear that she was out to enjoy life. She had a devil-may-care attitude, which was a contributory factor for the lack of a picture of Terry's father in the collection. The identity of Terry's father had always been a mystery. Janice always maintained that he was the bass guitarist in a very well-known band that was enjoying considerable fame at the time, but Terry felt that a group of such status would have been unlikely to have been playing any of the village dances or small clubs that were Janice's haunts in her youth, and her parents would never have let her go off to the bright lights in Hull where the more famous groups might occasionally put on concerts. Janice had never taken to motherhood, not that Terry felt that she had tried too hard, and he was still young when she had left him in the care of his grandparents. Originally, she had claimed that she was having to move away temporarily to secure work, but her return visits became increasingly rare, and by the time Terry was 11 she was effectively out of his life for good. He had a Christmas card each year with a gift token, and the odd birthday card, but no visits and no return address.

Latterly, life with Gran had been pleasant enough, and Terry never went without the material necessities. On the contrary, he had wanted for nothing, perhaps even been over-indulged, but his emotional needs were largely unrecognised. When his gran died he was sad, but he never experienced any of the grief that he felt he ought to. He attributed his lack of emotion to the fact that he never wore his heart on his sleeve; that just wasn't the British way to do things after all. Obviously, he had cared for her, but he didn't feel the need to show it. However, he somehow couldn't avoid the niggling question of how he ought to have shown it. Janice had not turned up for her mother's funeral, which was a surprise to Terry rather than a major disappointment.

Terry looked down at the brown envelope in his hand. What was he going to do with it? The instructions in it had been a bit hurried, but he still felt that his decision to leave the bulk of his estate to Lizzie had been a sound one. True, she had left him, and he still didn't entirely understand why, but she had been the only person he had ever met who had shown she actually loved him. For a while, he had put her ability to demonstrate affection down to her job; she must have learned how to show people that she cared for them; surely, that's what social workers have to do? It was a while before he had noticed that Lizzie was not just demonstrating some intellectual skill; she really did care. This feeling was reinforced when he had met some of Lizzie's colleagues, for many of whom affection was purely an affectation; it was part of their professional role to show concern for clients, but it was merely a persona they adopted as part of their job.

After a few moments walking around with the will in his hand, looking for somewhere to put it, he decided to place it in his gran's bureau. Glad to have resolved the issue, he paused for a while to decide what to do next. Lenin's bacon sandwich had been good, but Terry was aware that he was hungry again. Instinctively he went to the fridge, only to be reminded that he had cleared it out and put the contents in the bin. The assortment of tinned and dry food in the cupboards didn't immediately suggest any lunch menu to him, and he didn't even have a drop of milk for a cup of tea; he was beginning to regret his zeal for tidying everything in preparation for his final exit. The solution was quick to emerge; he would go out for lunch, and furthermore he would invite his old friend Lord Leonard to accompany him.

Terry arrived at Tranby Manor to see that the dining room was already being set out for lunch, so he quickly went to speak with the manager to check that it wouldn't inconvenience them too much if Lord were to eat out. Terry found his friend sitting in one of the comfortable lounges within which he often chose to spend his mornings.

"Morning, Lord," said Terry, seating himself in an armchair next to his old friend. "Lovely day, too nice to be staying in."

"My word," exclaimed Lord, "it's good to see you back in a better state of mind. Last time you came you were moping around like a wet weekend, and asking me to witness your will didn't brighten up the day either. I thought you must have learned that you only had a few weeks to live or something."

"No. Not at all. I just felt it was about time I put my things in order; I'm absolutely fine. I must admit that I haven't exactly been all singing and dancing over the last few days, but I feel better now."

"Writing a will at your age; it's unnatural."

"We, none of us know when we will be called, Lord."

"I know that I'm called Lord."

"You know what I mean. None of us knows when we will pass away."

"If you mean none of us knows when we will die, then why don't you say so? By the time you get to my age, you have more or less come to terms with the fact that death can't be far off. I don't say it's an attractive proposition, but refusing to mention it does not mean it will go away."

"Sorry for being super sensitive," said Terry lowering his voice, "but I don't like to mention death in here."

"Don't worry," said Lord, looking around the room, "most of this lot probably can't hear you, and those that do will probably forget what you've said within a few minutes. On the subject of wills, I've got mine sorted now."

Terry was glad that the conversation had moved away from the frailties of the other residents, so he asked, "Again? Didn't you only rewrite it a couple of months ago?"

"True, but I changed my mind. I've decided that a bequest now goes to Dorothy over there." He indicated a smartly dressed elderly lady who was going in to lunch. "She's as giddy as a kipper, but she has a firmer grasp of reality than many of us. Most of the group here are absolutely scatty, well-meaning and harmless but top-weight scatty, and that goes double for the staff." The conversation was a return to one of Lord's favourite topics, being the appraisal of the people in Tranby Manor, and Terry was more than a little worried when Lord got on to a specific topic which had become a recurring theme in his good-hearted criticism of Tranby Manor.

"The lavatory and its attendant uses," continued Lord. "Most of the staff are obsessed with the topic but seem unable to mention the room or its purposes by name. Betty, the assistant manager, has at least a dozen ways of asking about my toilet habits. If I ever did have problems in that area, she would be as likely to call a plumber as a doctor. I swear that sometimes it takes me a few minutes to work out what it is she's enquiring about when she asks about 'movements', ' waterworks' and 'performing'. She was a bit surprised when she asked me if I was 'regular', and I told her that I had been in the regular army for a while but that I had not been a regular person for over 50 years."

By this time, the rest of the residents had gone in to lunch, so Terry felt a little more comfortable as the prospect of Lord being overheard was no longer a problem, and he ventured to say, "One day you'll get yourself in to hot water by being so outspoken."

"They all know I'm harmless; besides, they no doubt talk about me as well. I know my memory isn't as good as it used to be," confided Lord, who gave a sly smile before continuing, "Latterly, when I was at home, I lost my car keys at least once a week, but old Mrs Price in the room next to me lost her car! She went out for a drive one day, came back on the bus and a couple of hours later she hadn't the faintest idea where she had left the car. Not where in the car park, or even which car park, but which town she had left it in. It took the police hours to find it."

"That must have upset Mrs Price."

"No, she saw the funny side, and the police were very understanding, but shortly afterwards she did give up driving, thank goodness. She always said there were just too many idiots on the roads and that her giving up would at least reduce the number by one."

Terry looked at his elderly friend who, for all his displays of rebelliousness, was very happy in Tranby Manor. All the domestic arrangements were catered for, leaving Lord plenty of time to carry out his mildly subversive but entirely harmless activities. Having left the army, he had taken up a senior post with the electricity board where he had been able to use his not inconsiderable intellectual skills. His intellect, which by his own admission was not quite what it had been, was still considerably greater than any of the staff, and at first he had resented their patronizing comments, but he soon realised that his tormentors meant well. He had learned to withstand their misguided notion that they needed to explain everything to him in simple terms and often with perplexing euphemisms. Occasionally, he did let his frustration show, such as the time a young care assistant had asked him, "Have we performed today, Mr Leonard?" Lord just could not resist answering, "Well, I had a good shit this morning, but I don't know about you." Fortunately, the comment caused amusement rather than offence, but Lord did receive a metaphorical slap on the wrist from the manager.

"I just wondered if you fancied a spot of lunch at the Barge?" asked Terry. The Barge Inn was a local pub that served very reasonable meals, and the pair went fairly frequently for lunch.

"It's a bit sudden. Sounds very attractive, but I'll have to clear it with the camp commandant. They get a bit miffed if you suddenly don't muster for meals."

"Don't worry. I've cleared it with the manager, and she knew you wouldn't mind too much missing spaghetti bolognese. Anyway, it's a sort of celebration. My treat."

"Is it my birthday?"

"Not that I know of."

"Did I die?"

"It would appear not."

"Good, I'm determined to get at least one more crack at the Crompton money."

Terry was a bit perplexed by this last comment, but he was in too much of a hurry to dwell on it. Although it was now quite a warm day, Lord insisted on going for his blazer. And as he returned, Terry was once again impressed by the appearance of his friend whom he took to be in his late eighties but who had the upright bearing of a man 20 years younger and this image was enhanced by the fact that Lord always insisted upon being very smartly dressed.

As his friend got into the car, Terry couldn't resist the temptation to ask, "What's all this about Crompton and his money?"

"Shh!" said Lord. "Wait until we get away from the camp. The bloody warders hear everything."

Lord frequently likened Tranby Manor to a prison camp, but it was an innocent, almost affectionate reference to his home. Despite his age and sometimes feigned eccentricities, Lord had lost none of his mental alertness, and he had conjured up his own version of life in Tranby Manor, largely to amuse himself and his fellow 'inmates'. Whether it was Tranby Gulag or Stalag Tranby, it was now home, and he was generally happy there.

"So what's with Crompton?" insisted Terry as they drove out of the grounds.

Lord chuckled and then explained, "It's a thing we have going at Tranby. The staff have this code that they use, which is supposed to be their little secret way of not upsetting the residents. Mr Crompton used to be the undertaker of choice for Tranby Manor, and if a resident died, they would say something like 'Mr Crompton came to see Mrs Evans' when what they meant was that Mrs Evans had died. Mr Crompton himself went on to require the services of his own company, but his name is still used to discreetly announce the death of a resident."

"So where does Crompton's money come in?" asked a bemused Terry.

"It's our version of a tontine," replied Lord.

"A tontine? So what's that?"

"A true tontine is an agreement between a group of people who each invest a certain amount of money, and the total amount goes to the last surviving member of the group. A bit macabre I suppose, but you have to make your own fun when you get to our age. We devised our own version of the tontine, and a small group of us each put £10 into a kitty. We then put the name of the person we think will be the next to die at the top of a piece of paper and our own name at the bottom. The papers are then put into an envelope, along with the kitty, without showing anyone else, and they are only taken out when the next resident dies. Anyone who correctly forecast the name of the latest person to be visited by Mr Crompton gets to take the kitty, and if two or more get it right, then they share the Crompton cash."

"So what happens if no one had forecast the name of the latest one to die?"

"We have a rollover. It happened last time. Mrs Drury went to meet her maker last month. No one would have guessed it; she was as fit as a fiddle, only 70 and still regularly attending yoga and keep fit classes. She was the life and soul of our music soirees, and after a couple of drinks, she would demonstrate the relative elasticity of her body by adopting a number of yoga positions. I wouldn't have been able to achieve some of those poses even as a young man. Her other party piece was telling jokes, most of which were rather blue. The staff expressed their disapproval, but only after they'd had a good laugh. Good old Mrs Drury: she could spill out double entendres all day long and then feign innocence. Then she just upped and died. When the envelope was opened, it was no surprise that no one had voted for her, although I was a bit alarmed to see that my name appeared on four of the sheets. I'm more determined than ever now to see a few more of them off."

"So what happens if you vote for yourself?"

"Absolutely against the rules, old chap; apart from anything else, I'm sure that one or two of them are dotty enough to top themselves just to get a share of the money."

"Fair point," commented Terry before asking, "But doesn't it run the risk of someone in the group 'engineering' the outcome they might wish for by removing a contestant forcibly?"

"We did think of that; that's why we restricted the stake to £10. It wouldn't do to have too great a temptation."

"No, of course not," added Terry. "And what do the management think of the whole thing?"

"We did try and keep it secret, but some of the old dears are a bit indiscreet. The staff were not pleased, firstly because they thought it a rather tasteless form of gambling, but largely because they realised we had broken the Mr Crompton code. That being said, I bet some of the staff run their own little sweepstake."

CHAPTER FOUR

The Barge Inn looked like countless other small village pubs from the front, not a particularly old building but one that liked to suggest some history. Lord had frequented the place for over 50 years and seen it run by three different breweries in that time. He had also seen off a series of landlords who seemed to come and go with increasing rapidity over the last few years. The interior of the pub had undergone a number of refits since he had first become a regular in the fifties, and successive alterations had resulted in the place now ostensibly being considerably older than the day he first walked in. The ubiquitous fruit machine and the pool table sat uneasily in an interior with tudoresque timber, plaster walls and fake beams, and the old coal fire had been replaced by a gas model that was able to dispense instant heat when the need arose. Lord had preferred the old coal fire, which had displayed a marked reluctance to being lit, but sitting in the chilly bar had been a small price to pay for the entertainment value offered by the sight of a succession of landlords over the years trying to breathe some life into the smoky contents of the grate.

The redeeming feature of the pub was the food. The meals were not particularly adventurous, but they were well prepared and of generous proportions. This suited Terry and his companion, who regularly dropped in for lunch. As usual, they chose to go straight up to the bar rather than going through to the restaurant area. This had been Lord's choice because he always insisted that he liked pub lunches and that meant sitting in a pub, not in a conservatory stuck on the back.

Looking at the menu was largely a formality because the two invariably had the pie of the day, and today was no exception. Having placed their order at the bar and picking up a drink each, they walked over to their regular table. In the moment's silence after they had sat down, Terry reflected on the fact that on the rare occasions when he had taken Lizzie there for a meal, she had chosen the restaurant area and spent what seemed like an eternity selecting her meal.

"So how are things with you and your Lizzie?" asked Lord, almost as if he had been party to Terry's thoughts. "Have you managed to patch things up?"

In their recent meetings, Terry had touched upon his problems, and now he felt he had to make it clear what had been going on. Carefully avoiding any reference to the bridge episode, he gave Lord an account of having lost his job, Lizzie's unreasonable attitude about the surprise holiday he had arranged for her and her subsequent departure from his life.

"So sorry to hear that, Terry," said Lord, demonstrating genuine concern. "The job is no great loss, but you must miss Lizzie. I always thought you were made for each other."

"Yes, so did I, but it just shows you can't rely on people."

"But she really cared for you. It was obvious."

"I thought so too, and I cared for her, but she didn't seem to realise it."

"Did you ever tell her how you felt about her?" asked Lord tentatively.

"Of course. I loved her. I even mentioned marriage on a couple of occasions, but she always changed the subject."

"Yes, but did you actually tell her how much you cared? Did you tell her that you loved her?"

"I adored her, she must have realised. I think she was just frightened of commitment," suggested Terry. "She sees a lot of failed marriages in her work, and I think that put her off."

"Perhaps that's it," replied Lord, in a less-than-convinced sort of way.

"Look, Lord, you were married to Mary for over 50 years. You understand women."

"Rubbish!" interrupted his friend. "Any man who tells you he's been married so long that he understands women is deluding himself, as is any woman who makes a similar claim about men. The bald truth is that no one ever understands entirely what motivates others. Some people like to think they have some mystical understanding of human nature, but it's all just horse feathers. One thing in life is absolutely certain, if anyone tells you they are a good judge of human nature, they most certainly are not. As we get older we might, I stress might, develop some slightly deeper understanding of the behaviour of others, and that's about all."

"OK. But you must have more idea than I have. What do you think went wrong?"

Their conversation was broken by the arrival of their lunches, which gave Lord a welcome moment to think of his response. After taking the opportunity to put salt and pepper on his meal and to make favourable comments about its appearance, the older man continued.

"Are you sure that you made it clear to Lizzie just how you felt about her? I mean, you can be a bit reticent; you've never been a demonstrative sort of person."

"Demonstrative?" queried Terry defensively. "In what way?"

Lord felt the situation was not going well, so he attempted to rephrase his comments somehow.

"Well, you might be seen as a bit on the reserved side, not prone to unnecessary shows of emotion."

"I'm not one of your 'touchy-feely' sort of blokes, I'll give you that, but you don't need to be constantly kissing and cuddling just to show you care, do you?"

"You sound a bit like your grandfather." It had been an uncharacteristically unguarded remark and one that Lord half regretted.

"What do you mean?" asked Terry in an inquisitive rather than confrontational way.

"People are different. I remember that Mary and I were in the kitchen one morning, and I heard a tune on the radio that was one of our favourites, so we started dancing. Your grandfather came round to return a drill he had borrowed and caught us. From the look on his face, you might have thought he had caught us in flagrante delicto. We just laughed and remarked that obviously he and your grandmother must have their romantic moments. He was visibly shocked and said they were long past that sort of thing. They were never to be listed among life's great risk-takers either. Your grandad thought he was being a bit racy if he went out without his pullover on."

"No. I don't think I ever saw them cuddle or even hold hands," commented Terry in an absent-minded way, "I was thinking something similar this morning when I was looking at their photographs, and they never seemed 'close'. But they were happy, weren't they?"

"Perfectly content. It suited them, or they had convinced themselves it did. They settled for what they had; it was a pretty watered-down sort of life, but it seemed to suit them. Their Janice, your mum, was a different kind of person. I often think her rebelliousness was as much against that emotionally under-charged atmosphere at home as anything else. Even as a toddler, she was out to have fun, and as a young girl, she was always keen to enjoy life. She would spend a lot of time with Mary and me playing in our garden more than hers. She had a lively spirit, and we were always pleased to see her."

"It must have spoiled her fun when I came along. No wonder she didn't want me," commented Terry. There was no trace of self-pity or resentment in his remark, just a recognition that his mother had never bonded with him.

"It wasn't as simple as that, Terry. It wasn't a matter of not wanting you; it was the fact that she was frightened of the prospect of bringing up a child. She didn't come from a family where children were openly loved. She was 17 and frightened of the prospect of being forced into the lifestyle of her parents, of losing her identity and just becoming 'Mum', locked into a role that the title implied. She would have seen it as being buried alive, so she chose to escape. True, it was irresponsible and selfish but understandable, she was just a product of her own upbringing."

Terry sat for a while in silence, eating his lunch and mulling over his friend's observations. It seemed to make a lot of sense. He'd never thought about it before, but it was true his grandparents had been two individuals sharing a marriage rather than a loving couple. He'd been brought up in the same environment, so what did that mean for him?

"I can see why my mother might have reacted the way she did, but I was brought up in the same household and I didn't rebel. I have always done things the proper way, so why didn't I go wild like her?"

"Enough psychoanalysis for one day. I shouldn't have brought it up. Let's just enjoy lunch," said Lord in an attempt to get the conversation onto more comfortable ground, but Terry wanted answers.

"I just don't get it. Why am I not like my mother? The more I think about it, the less I seem to remember about her. What was she like back then?"

Lord smiled at the memory as he explained to Terry, "Your mum was a lovely girl. Sure, she was a bit of a rebel, but everyone liked her. She had spirit, but she was never really naughty or disrespectful. Janice wanted to be her own person and was scared of turning out like her parents. I remember her telling me once that she was a rainbow person living in a grey world; she had that way with words that children often have, imaginative and fanciful but alarmingly insightful. I rather think your grandparents hoped that your arrival would somehow make your mother 'face up to her responsibilities' and calm down. Her childhood ended dramatically with the pregnancy; she was expected to change overnight, and when she didn't, it was taken as a sign of weakness that she was just not up to the job of bringing up a child, so your grandmother effectively took over. I'm sure that Janice would have settled down to the job of looking after you if she'd been given a real chance, but it was all or nothing with your grandparents. There was no middle way; Janice might have been prepared to settle down a bit, but she wasn't ready to stagnate. She wanted excitement and romance in her life, but unfortunately she was woefully ill-prepared to cope with the latter. She persisted with that story about the bass guitarist, but she never disclosed who your father was. Still, if it was a mistake, it was surely one of her better ones."

"So why did I turn out so differently?"

"I honestly don't know. Perhaps your grandparents were so disappointed at the way your mum turned out that they were extra careful not to encourage any wild behaviour in you, and let's face it, you were about the most sensible young man that ever drew breath. Come to think of it, you were always treated as a young man, even as a boy. You never stole apples from our tree like your mother had done, and in all conversations with adults, you were inordinately polite. You were a young adult by the time you were 12, quite the precocious little gent."

"So you think I should have been more like my mother?"

"Stop looking for simple answers. If they exist, they are generally valueless. We all have to come to our own conclusions about what we have become. Real answers can only come about if we understand ourselves. I can't give you any answers, I can only make observations, and they are not necessarily any more valid than the next man's. As the Oracle at Delphi proclaims, 'Know thyself'."

"So if I'm a rather boring cold person, I should try to be more demonstrative?"

"I came out for what I was led to believe might be some sort of celebratory lunch, and it turns out to be twenty bloody questions. Shall we order a pudding, as it's your treat?" asked Lord in an emphatic way.

"Yes. Sorry, I have been a bit obsessed with my own misfortunes recently. How about the treacle sponge pudding as usual?"

"Now you're talking."

The pair sat and ate their puddings while Lord regaled Terry with recollections of what the pub used to be like and some of the characters who had once been customers there. When the plates had been taken away, Lord suggested they might take their drinks outside, so they made their way to the benches outside the pub door and sat in the warm afternoon sun.

"This place has certainly changed a bit since I first visited," observed Lord, looking down the street. "But that is hardly surprising since it is over half a century since I came here with Mary just after the war. There were six pubs round here then, and now we are down to two. As I recall, a pint of bitter was nine pence in real money, not your new pence. You could have a good night down at the pub and still have change from five bob."

"Five bob?" queried Terry, "I've told you before, you might as well talk in terms of doubloons or pieces of eight for all the sense it makes to me."

Lord smiled and took a sip of his beer before continuing, "We had thought we might find it difficult to settle in, having come from Lincolnshire. Our parents would regale us with stories of the savage Yorkshire tribes, but we were made very welcome, and we found some of the savages here on the north bank were quite friendly."

"Were my grandparents living round here at the time?" asked Terry, who was becoming increasingly aware of just how little he knew about them.

"I seem to recall that they came here in the late fifties. They hadn't been married long, and I believe your grandfather inherited a tiny cottage in the village from his aunt. They lived there for a couple of years before moving in next door to me. They were good neighbours, but we were never close in terms of meeting socially. Most of our socialising took place if we were out in our respective gardens. They were very much for keeping themselves to themselves. It was some years before your mother arrived on the scene. I rather think it was a bit of a shock to your grandfather; probably unsure as to what caused it. Mary and I were a bit surprised. As I said, they were never what you'd call a close couple, but they obviously had their moments."

"Or moment," added Terry with uncharacteristic nerve.

"They were good neighbours all the same, and Janice was a joy to have around. As you know, we never had any children of our own, so we enjoyed having her visits and watching her grow. It's a horrible thing to say, but I think she much preferred her time with us than at home. We would play silly imaginative games, and your mother would just glow with the vitality of youth; she always seemed to be laughing, so full of life."

"You make her sound like a nice person. Gran never spoke ill of her but always gave the impression that she had been a great disappointment to her parents. 'Flighty' was a word she used a lot to describe my mum on the rare occasion that

I managed to get her to talk about her at all. As you know, I didn't see much of Mum during her 'travels', and I think Gran and Grandad were happy just to exclude her, even to the point of rarely mentioning her name."

Lord smiled at the comment before saying, "The problem was that they were as different as chalk and cheese. Your mum was an exciting free spirit while your grandparents were more prosaic; she wanted to love, live, and be happy, and they wanted to be sensible. There was no animosity, just a complete lack of understanding. The longer they lived together, the further they would have grown apart."

"I wonder where she is now. It's a question I have often asked myself. When I was younger, I used to dream that she would come back to live with us and bring my father back with her, and everything would be perfect. But I soon realised that all that about the famous pop star was just a fabrication," commented Terry.

"It was all part of your mother's craving for excitement and adventure."

"Did you ever have any idea who my father might have been? Did she have a regular boyfriend that you met?"

"Janice had lots of boyfriends in her teens. In fact, she had an extensive following of young men. She was an attractive young woman who was fun to be around, but as far as a particular boyfriend is concerned, I just don't know. She was never encouraged to bring any of her boyfriends home, and she was actively discouraged from having any boyfriends, so we never saw anyone regularly around the house. The pressure was always on your mum to concentrate on her studies at the expense of her social life. She was a bright girl, and the expectation was that she would achieve high marks in her school work and then go on to a respectable white-collar job and earn a big salary. That was all her parents ever expected of her. If Mary and I had ever been blessed with children, then our main hope would be that they would be happy."

"I was never aware of a time that she actually moved out. She just sort of drifted away. I have vague memories of her coming back from time to time, but I've got no idea where she had been or what she had been doing. As I said, she was never discussed, and I think my grandparents were pleased to see her drift from our memories."

"She was a bit of a mystery to us all. She went up north, Newcastle, I think, to take a degree course, and after that she just disappeared. Mary and I had a number of letters from her periodically during the first few years, but then they dried up as well. The last time I saw her was at your grandfather's funeral, and even then she didn't stay over."

"I'm sure that we are completely different," reasoned Terry. "And I don't know if she would ever want to meet me again, but I keep thinking that I'd like to meet her. I started trying to trace her through public records on the internet once. I found quite a list of possible Janice Hendersons in Newcastle, even tried phoning a few, without success, but then I realised that she might not even be still living there or she might have married or changed her name for some other reason. I realised my search was futile and just gave up."

"I'm quite sure that when she came to her father's funeral, she said she had to get away early because she had a flight to catch," added Lord, "but I don't know if that was just an excuse to get away quickly. And, speaking of getting away, I think you'd better deliver me back to Stalag Tranby, or I'll be in solitary for a week."

Terry couldn't help feeling that the conversation about his mother was being brought to a swift conclusion, but he knew it was useless trying to press his old friend for any more information.

CHAPTER FIVE

When Terry let himself into his house, he was a little surprised to see Lizzie there, and for a brief moment he thought she might have come back to him, but his optimism was short-lived when he noticed that she had a businesslike air about her; polite, but not the same old Lizzie.

"Sorry to arrive unannounced so to speak, but I had hoped to catch you so that we could sort out my belongings and get them from under your feet," started Lizzie before looking around and adding, "But I see you have already created quite a bit of space. You've been having a tidy-up."

"Yes," he replied, trying to sound relaxed in what was a very uncomfortable situation for them both. "I just felt it was a good time to sort a few things out, new broom and everything."

His attempts at small talk were doing nothing to ease the obvious tension, so he resorted to offering some hospitality. "Would you like a cup of tea," he suggested, moving towards the kettle.

"I tried that, but I see you don't have any milk in. In fact, you don't appear to have much in at all," she commented, with a sense of irritation in her voice.

For the second time that day, Terry had been caught out by his own over-zealous efforts to literally put his house in order.

"No, bit of a clean-up." he blurted out. "There's a couple of beers in the cupboard."

"No thanks," she replied curtly.

"I could go and get some milk in," offered Terry. "I'll be back in 10 minutes."

"No, really, I can't stay long, I just wanted to sort some things out, but I can come back when it's more convenient if you like?"

"No, now's fine. What did you want to talk about?"

"There isn't much of my stuff here. I suppose that's one advantage of having rented my place out as a furnished flat, but I just wondered about the little table in the lounge you bought me."

"The Georgian tilt top side table?"

"Yes, you did say you had bought it for me."

"Yes, it was a bargain that one, £150 it cost me, and it's worth at least twice that. A birthday present, I think?"

"I don't care about the bloody price," commented Lizzie with an obvious trace of annoyance in her voice. "I'll buy it off you at the full price."

"No. It's yours," replied Terry, a little surprised at the suggestion that he wanted any money for it and the fact that she was so obviously annoyed. "It was a present."

"Then why mention the price? Why does everything have to have a price tag? All you ever talk about is the price you've paid for something. Take that etching on the wall," she said, pointing at a large, framed print. "Why did you buy that?"

"It was £25."

"And? That's your answer?"

"Well yes, it was £25, and it's worth £40 of anyone's money," replied Terry a little defensively.

"But do you like it?" continued the cross-examination.

"Like it? It's OK."

"So you have a picture on your wall that you are confronted with every day, but you don't particularly like it? Can't you see how stupid that is?"

"It was a bargain."

"Oh, Terry! Why does everything have to be measured in its monetary value? Can't you see that things can be valued for just what they are? I love that little Georgian table you bought me, I don't care what it cost. You have a house full of 'bargains' that you might, but probably won't, sell someday, and you surround yourself with them even when you don't particularly like them. Added to that, you have mountains of junk that you insist you will 'restore' at some point and in the meantime they clutter up the whole house."

Terry realised that there was little point in continuing this line of conversation, and he avoided any of the implied questions. After a few moments, it was Lizzie who continued, "I'm sorry, Terry, I didn't come round here to criticise."

After a few minutes' silence, a somewhat calmer Lizzie continued, "You're all dressed up. Have you been to a job interview or something?"

"Oh no. I haven't thought about that yet. As you pointed out, there's more to life than working all hours, and I've got quite a bit of holiday pay due, so I'm having a few days off."

"I never thought I'd hear you say that," interjected Lizzie. "You have changed a bit, dressing up, taking holidays and even tidying the house a bit. So where have you been in your Sunday best?"

"I went for an early morning walk and then took Lord out for lunch." Terry was pleased that she didn't press him about where he had been walking, and to avoid dwelling on that episode, he quickly continued, "Lord's still making life interesting for the staff at Tranby."

"Yes, most of the residents love the comfortable monotony of the place," commented Lizzie. "They're content to shuffle increasingly slowly to the next event in their life; meals, visitors, the odd day out and eventually death, but Lord wants to have greater control. He needs the mental stimulation of gently annoying the staff, and I think that most of them quite like the challenge he poses."

"We went to the Barge for lunch. It's the sort of thing you do on holiday. He seemed very well, but he is showing his age a bit; he's lost none of his mental acuity, but he's no spring chicken. We had a lengthy chat about my mother."

"That's strange. In all the time I've known you, you've never been keen to talk about her at all. I suppose Lord knew the set-up in your home very well?"

"Yes, he knew the family quite well for years. We've never discussed the issue at all, but it occurred to me that when Lord died, I would lose the only connection I have with that phase in my life. When he's gone, I will have no one to ask. I just feel that I want to know more about who I am and why I turned out this way. I can't change, develop, improve or whatever if I don't know why I am like I am." This announcement of his perceived need for introspection was the nearest Terry had come to admitting that he might have contributed in some way to the break-up with Lizzie, but his gesture failed to impress her, and he did nothing to help his cause by continuing, "I got a full refund on the hotel booking so you don't need to worry about it."

"I wasn't worried," she replied forcefully.

Having Lizzie back in the house suggested a superficial normality, but Terry knew things would never be the same. Their previous relationship meant there were obviously still feelings between them, but there was also an emotional chasm. Perhaps it had been the very intensity of their relationship which made the current situation seem so stark. When Lizzie had entered his life, she brought a love that went way beyond any previous feeling he had had of purely being cared for, and it had made him happier than he had ever thought possible. Their love had been like an emotional forest fire hitting his world that had previously been devoid of such passion, but the fire had apparently burnt itself out without leaving the tender shoots of a deeper love to replace it. Terry had been eager to take that love, and to make love, but he was increasingly conscious of a suspicion that he was somehow not able to really show love or to give it. He wanted to explain this to Lizzie, but he felt quite incapable of expressing it. He wanted to tell her how he felt, and he wanted to tell her about the bridge and his will, but he knew it wouldn't come out right, so the couple sat in silence for a while.

"So haven't you given any thought to a job?" asked Lizzie in another attempt to start up a conversation. "Didn't you have an offer of some part-time work as a porter at the auction house?"

"That was a while ago. They're often short of people to hump the furniture about, but it's only a few hours a week. Most of it is more like furniture removal than being involved with antiques."

"Yes, but if it's got part of the job where you can enjoy being near antiques and you have the chance to learn about the business, you might find it has reasonable prospects."

"Perhaps. I'll think about it," said Terry in a non-committal way that reflected the fact that he was more concerned with getting back with Lizzie than getting back into work. He knew it was hopeless, but he couldn't bring himself to give up on her.

"So where are you staying now? Are you planning to move back into your flat?"

"No, there's another five months to run on the lease, and the tenants have been so good I wouldn't mind them staying on beyond that, so I've moved in with Veronica for a while. She's got a three-bedroom place, and we get on quite well. It suits me, and my rent helps pay her mortgage."

"You could always move back in here," suggested Terry before quickly adding, "No rent or anything, but you are welcome."

"I'm sure that would not be for the best, Terry. We need our own space while we sort our lives out. We can still see each other now and again, but I need to be away from here."

Terry was disappointed but hardly surprised, and he tried, without success, to sound matter of fact when he replied, "Yes, I understand. You're right. Perhaps I'll see you down at Lenin's place."

"Yes, perhaps. I haven't seen Lenin for over a week now. We've been taken up with a particularly distressing case in town for a few days now, so I can't just drop in at Lenin's for a break. I suppose he's still hovering somewhere near the bridge."

"Yes, I saw him this morning, actually; he was saying he missed your visits. Still the same old Lenin, muttering on about the rights of the workers, but he does serve the best bacon banjo for miles around."

"You were there this morning? So, does his current site have a good view of the bridge?"

"You can see the towers but not the bridge itself. Why?"

"It's just that a police colleague told me they had a call early this morning to say that a motorist had seen someone loitering on the bridge. Some poor souls have jumped from there in the past, so it needed to be checked in case something could be done to discourage them from going ahead with their plan. We have staff trained in managing such cases, but fortunately, in this case, nothing was found to cause alarm. It might have been someone who was there to simply admire the view. The problem is that, if someone does get into the water, it can be days before a body turns up, so all the relevant agencies have an informal grapevine to keep us all aware."

"Well, I couldn't see anything from Lenin's place," commented Terry, quite truthfully, before continuing, "So is that part of your job? To follow up such incidents?"

"I'm part of the emergency response team covering the region. We can be called out in all sorts of situations. In cases involving mental health problems, the police might ask us to get involved, depends on how things turn out."

Terry was taken by the fact that he knew Lizzie had recently started working in some specialist response team within social services, which caused her to have bizarre working hours, but he never knew anything about what she actually did. He recognised that this was largely due to the fact that she would never discuss any confidential aspect of her work and that she was adamant she was not bringing her work home with her. He had gleaned that she apparently spent a lot of her time dealing with the aftermath of domestic conflict, and to this he attributed her reluctance to commit to marriage. Not for the first time, he wished she had an ordinary job, and then they would have married, and everything would have turned out perfectly. Terry felt he knew a bit about marriage; couples got married and then settled into a comfortable, if predictable, routine. If he'd been married to Lizzie, then this recent minor problem between them would not have split them up. Despite this belief that marriage would have solved all their problems, he could not escape the feeling that the relationship had possibly been flawed. He would have done anything to get her back, apologised, and even gone down on his knees, but he couldn't see what he had done wrong.

Terry's thoughts were interrupted by the ringing of Lizzie's mobile phone.

"I'm sorry about this, Terry," she said, checking the caller's number on the screen, "it's the team. I told them I was off duty, but something must have come up." She put the phone to her ear, and Terry was able to hear her half of the conversation.

"Lizzie here... Yes... I can be there in twenty minutes. Meanwhile, can you just try and keep a lid on it? Bye."

Not for the first time, Lizzie was called away, and Terry hadn't the faintest idea what it was about.

"Sorry, Terry, but I have to sort something out. I'll see you around," blurted out Lizzie before picking up her car keys and moving to the door, where she stopped briefly and, turning to him, said, "Really sorry. Have to go, I'll ring when the dust settles on this one. We have to talk."

In a second she was gone. He listened as her car accelerated quickly away from the house, and then he sat down at the table. The house was quiet as if all the life had been sucked out of it, and he once again experienced that sense of hopeless emptiness that had driven him onto the bridge earlier that day. He knew that he had to get her back; it might be completely hopeless, but he had nothing else to take up his time. Lizzie obviously disliked the clutter in his house. She'd never professed to be a minimalist, but clutter was to be a thing of the past. This would be his first task. He looked around the room and noted some of the 'bargains' he had bought in the past; they would all have to go. This was a new, decisive Terry. How best to dispose of the offending items? A trip to the local tip, or rather three or four trips. He would have to change into some less formal clothing if he was to be loading items into the car. It wouldn't do to mess up his funeral suit.

As he was hanging his suit up in the wardrobe, it occurred to Terry that he might be being a trifle hasty. The items definitely had to go, but why throw them all away? Perhaps he should try and sell them, but how? He knew all the antique shops in the surrounding area, but it could take weeks of traipsing from one to the other, and he would still probably have some items to take to the tip. An auction: that was the answer. Take them to an auction. As Lizzie had pointed out, he had a connection in the auctioneering business. Perhaps he should look into it? That would show Lizzie he had changed.

Being a regular attendee at the local auction house, Terry knew that there was an opportunity the next day to take items for valuation in a forthcoming auction, and he vowed to be there as the doors opened.

CHAPTER SIX

"Hello, Terry," said an elderly man in a brown overall as he opened the dark wooden doors of the auction room, allowing the early morning sunlight to flood in. "By heck, you're eager to get in to view; the sale isn't until Saturday."

"Hello, Colin. I'm not here to buy this time."

"They all say that until they spot a bargain and auction fever grabs them. I've seen it thousands of times over the years. People come in to buy a specific small item and then need a transit van to take their purchases away."

Terry looked around the large auction room that was so familiar to him. Rows of low tables covered in an assortment of items took up much of the space, but the walls were likewise adorned by pictures, clocks and rugs, and even the space underneath the tables was filled with assorted boxes packed with all manner of general junk. Although the staff made every effort to keep the place clean, there was still that musty smell that pervades such places. Terry's expert eye instinctively scanned the room for something special. Much of it was of little value, but there were bound to be the odd hidden gems. He had already picked out a pair of early twentieth-century ceramic spill jars when he remembered his resolution not to buy, so he put them carefully down and just muttered, "Those are quite nice, Colin."

Colin, more generally referred to as 'Old Colin' gave a knowing smile and nodded. He had been a porter at the auction house when the present owner had bought up the business nearly 40 years ago. It was often said that he needed to keep on the move during the sales or risk being taken for an antique himself and sold off. His uniform had never changed over the years; a full-length brown overall that was always buttoned up, white shirt with dark tie and a flat cap. The entire ensemble was set off by a pencil in his top pocket alongside a pipe that no one had ever seen him light. In his more extravagant moments, particularly for those sales exclusively for antiques, he wore a bowler hat, the ceremonial donning of which would elicit a brief round of applause from his regulars.

"No!" said Terry determinedly. "This time, I want to sell a few things, Colin, so how do I go about it? I've spent many happy days in here, but I've never tried to sell anything."

"It's simple enough. You bring the articles in, or we can collect larger items for a small fee, we catalogue them, the punters come in and see the items before the auction, and then we try and sell them. What sort of stuff did you have in mind? You must have a house full, judging by the lots you've picked up here over the years."

"I haven't got that much," replied Terry, a little defensively. "I have sold some of the things on, but a friend pointed out that I do have quite a number of things I ought to consider releasing back onto the market. When would I be able to get them into a sale?"

"We don't generally finish the cataloguing before Thursday night, so if you could get them in by Thursday afternoon, we could add them in. Judging by the masses of items you've bought from us over the years, if you really want to sell on the lot, then it would make sense if we collected them." The old man paused and checked a notebook he had taken from his pocket before continuing, "At eleven thirty on Thursday. We can fix any reserves you want to put on then."

Terry was rather taken aback by the possibility of getting a date so soon and felt slightly pressured, but there was no going back.

"Sounds great, Colin. I'm not putting any reserves on. They all have to go, even if they make pennies. I'm bringing nothing back home with me. Someone will probably get some real bargains."

Having spent a while discussing the fees, Terry strode resolutely out of the showroom into the bright sunshine.

That's the way to do business, no messing, no delays, carpe diem, he thought to himself before adding, *What the hell have I just done?*

Terry spent the next couple of hours at the supermarket, stocking up on his provisions; when Lizzie next came to visit, he could at least offer her a cup of tea. Shopping was not his favourite pastime. Walking up and down the aisles was reminiscent of his time in the stores, and he frequently found himself questioning the logic of the product placements on the shelves. He could have suggested one or two improvements, but he doubted they would listen. This shopping expedition had been particularly frustrating because his travels about the store brought him into frequent contact with a small elderly lady who appeared single-minded in her determination to get in his way at all turns. Her habit of frequently abandoning her trolley across the middle of the aisle was annoying, but not as much as her lack of control of the said implement, which led to her ramming him on two occasions. By the time he got to the checkout, he was not in the best of moods. Usually after a shopping marathon, he would treat himself to an all-day breakfast and a cup of tea in the supermarket's café, but today he was convinced that his grey-haired assassin would be lurking in there, so he opted to go directly to the car park.

As he loaded his car, he became aware that he was hungry. Perhaps it was because his body was expecting its post-shopping treat in the café or, more likely, it was because he had nothing in the house for breakfast before he left home that morning. The solution was an easy one, so he started up the car and went to look for Lenin. His search was not a difficult one because the mobile food van was on the same site as the previous day.

"Good morning, comrade," came the statutory greeting. "You didn't have to rush round to settle your debts so quickly."

"Oh yes, £2.50, wasn't it?" said Terry, sorting out some change. "And while I'm here, I'd like one of your breakfast specials, I'm starving."

"Tea while you're waiting?" queried Lenin as he set about marshalling the ingredients for the meal.

"Thanks, and have one yourself." Terry watched as the proprietor expertly set about cooking the meal while pouring out two mugs of tea. "How's business been then?"

"Could be better. It would help if I had a fixed spot, then my regulars wouldn't have to search me out. It's a well-known fact that if I'd been some multi-international fast-food chain, then the authorities would be falling over themselves to let me put some massive multi-coloured outlet on the site. It's all part of the capitalist conspiracy to put the little man down. In spite of their efforts, my little business is ticking over. On the bright side, I even saw Lizzie yesterday."

"Lizzie?" said Terry with ill-concealed interest. "How was she?"

"She looked terrible, not her usual bouncy self at all. I was just about to shut up for the night when she arrived. She didn't say what she'd been involved with, but it had obviously been a very difficult issue. All I know is that she'd just got back from town, and I don't think she could be bothered to cook at home. I've seen her looking a bit haggard at times when she's been involved in some of her cases, but I've never seen her looking quite so tired."

"Yes. She was at my place yesterday when she was called out to some sort of emergency."

"Oh, so you two are back together then?" asked Lenin. "Congratulations. About time too. You were too much of an item to ever break up."

"I'm afraid nothing's changed. She just came round for a chat about some things she still has at my place. She hasn't moved back in, and frankly she wasn't in a good mood."

"Shame," said Lenin, showing genuine concern. "I thought she didn't look full of the joys, but I just put it down to her work. Even when she was here having a chat, she was asking if I'd seen anyone acting strange near the bridge yesterday morning as there'd been reports of a possible jumper. I told her that the only strange person I'd seen was you, and you're obviously not the sort to chuck yourself off the bridge."

"No, hardly!" added Terry. "Now get a move on with my breakfast, I'm starving."

"Typical of you bourgeoisie, it's all pressure on us workers. Come the revolution, comrade, and you'll have to fry your own bacon."

The breakfast was every bit as good as Terry had hoped, and as he finished it, he felt compelled to show his appreciation. "That meal, Lenin, was as good as you've ever produced. I don't know what's wrong with me these days, I could eat for Britain."

"You can't beat a proper breakfast, comrade. I do serve the odd bowl of muesli to some of my stranger customers, but it's just not natural to eat something that is better suited to filling a horse's nosebag. All these health food junkies, don't they realise that frying kills off half the calories?"

"I wasn't aware of that, Lenin," replied Terry with more than a suggestion of scepticism.

"Oh yes. It's a known fact; ask anyone in the trade."

"By the way," said Terry, trying to sound not too concerned. "Did Lizzie mention me at all last night? I mean, did it sort of crop up in the conversation?"

"Afraid not, pal, but as I said, she was almost dead on her feet and preoccupied with her work issues. Even over her sausage sandwich last night, she was concerned about that poor chap on the bridge. She never talks about her work, but you can see her mind is often somewhere else."

"Yes, she was sometimes like that in the evening after a particularly testing day. She would be sitting there but in body only."

After a few moment's silence as the two sat and took in the view of the towers on the bridge, Terry said, "I've decided to have a bit of a clear-out. I'm sending a lot of my collection to the saleroom for the auction on Saturday. It just had to be done."

"Are you planning to attend the auction, comrade?"

"I hadn't thought of it. Why?"

"If you go, you'll probably come back with more than you went with. You know what you're like at spotting the real bargains."

"No. This is the new Terry, and to prove it I will certainly attend. It will be interesting to see if any of the punters have the good sense to snap up my lots. In the meantime, your favourite capitalist will be rushing off to collect together all the items for the auction."

"Well, before you go to make yourself a fortune, perhaps you'd like to pay for your breakfast?"

"Sorry, Lenin, nearly forgot."

"This is getting to be a bit of a habit with you," joked the café owner as he took the proffered money and put it in the margarine tub that passed for his till before adding, "If Lizzie does drop round, is there any message for her?"

"Yes. You could tell her I miss her. No, just tell her that I was asking after her." Terry wanted her to know that he missed her, but it wasn't right to pass on that message through his friend.

The house was still tidy when Terry arrived home, but he knew that wouldn't be the case for long as he started to draw together his eclectic mix of items for Saturday's sale. Nostalgia has a habit of being very time-consuming; Terry reflected that previous attempts to catalogue some of his old photographs had taken hours as most of the pictures brought back their own set of memories. There had also been the thankless task of trying to identify individuals on some of the images, which wasn't helped by the fact that so many of them had no scribbled names on the back. The items he was selecting for the sale were his life's work, and he knew it would be difficult to gather them ready for collection without experiencing a reawakening of his interest in them and his reasons for their purchase. Terry knew he had to be methodical, objective and ruthless. He decided to collect the easily transportable objects and place them on the kitchen table, and he cleared a space on the floor for some of the more substantial items. This was the start of a plan. Sorting and categorising had been a big part of his working life at the stores, so surely this would be easy.

The first objects for selection were three cast iron doorstops. Terry remembered that day in late November at a car boot sale when he had picked up this particular bargain. The stall holder was keen to get off home, and he and Terry had haggled over a few pounds. In the end, the seller caved in. After standing for six hours in the pouring rain and becoming chilled to the bone, he had almost lost the will to live, let alone to negotiate. Terry looked at them, and his valuation brain clicked surreptitiously into gear. Cast iron doorstops, probably early twentieth century but could be relatively recent, or could even be Victorian. They had been a good buy at ten pounds for the three and should make a reasonable profit even if they were modern. But do people use doorstops these days? It was the sort of question that Lizzie would pose. Terry began to inspect the doorstops more closely to try and date them a little more accurately. Two of them were relatively crisp castings with very little sign of wear, but the other looked as though it had been around for longer. But had some duplicitous individual deliberately scuffed it and then buried it in the garden for a few weeks in an attempt to artificially age it? Terry had got as far as this in his valuation and was about to specify what each might be worth when he realised that he was wasting his time. He was selling the items at whatever price they could get. This was not a financial operation, it was personal; to show Lizzie that he could be decisive and clear the house of his collection. Terry put the three objects together on the table. That was one of his lots established, or was it? Terry realised that he had routinely propped the kitchen door open in the summer and used whichever of the cast iron pieces that came to hand, so he couldn't sell all of them. Which one should he keep? Obviously, the 'older', more expensive one. He didn't particularly like that one, but it was the most expensive of the trio. Terry realised again that he was drifting off-task, so he turned away from the table and set out for his next object. Having taken twenty minutes to sort one lot, Terry realised that he had to be a lot more decisive than this or he would take weeks to gather them together.

The process of collecting his sale items was a lengthy one. For a while he would do well, collecting the objects from the various rooms in the house and stacking them neatly on or near the table, but certain of his possessions caused him to pause and think. There was the pair of Victorian mantlepiece dogs that he had bought for next to nothing. He remembered it well. It had been near the end of a particularly long auction on a day when the saleroom was oppressively hot, so many of the buyers had left. Terry had put in a ridiculously low bid to start the bidding off, but no one else had bid at all. It was days like that that made auctions so rewarding. Terry's mind automatically calculated what the dogs were worth now and how much profit he might make. It was a gratifying thought but a moment of self-satisfaction that he could not afford to relish. The dogs were placed on the table, and Terry resumed his search.

It was late in the evening by the time Terry felt he had finished, and he stood back for a moment to survey his hoard. Before him was the product of over 10 years of buying at car boot sales, jumble sales and auctions. There were even one or two small pieces that he had bought after seeing them advertised on postcards in the post office window. Despite what Lizzie had said, he had sold a number of items, but he had still amassed quite a collection, and they were all to go. Terry was too tired to bother cooking a meal, so he took a pre-cooked meat pie out of the fridge and a bottle of beer and took them through to the lounge. Lizzie wouldn't have been happy about his supper-time diet, but Lizzie wasn't there, sadly.

CHAPTER SEVEN

It was nearly half past nine the following morning when Terry eventually woke and checked his watch. It felt strange being in bed so late in the day, and the bright sunshine illuminating his curtains emphasised the fact that the day was well into its routine, and Terry had missed a sizeable chunk of it. He took a swift shower and dressed quickly before going down to breakfast before realising that the kitchen was unworkable in its present state; it would have to be Lenin's for breakfast.

Breakfast at the café was disappointing, not because of the quality of the food but because there was no news of Lizzie. Terry had realised that there was only the slimmest chance of actually meeting her, but he had hoped to have the comfort of hearing about her, so he was less than cheerful by the time he arrived home. He remembered that there were still a few items he had to sort in the shed, so the next two hours were spent collecting the pieces for the auction. While he was doing so, it dawned on him that Lizzie might have had a point about the folly of some of his purchases as he felt it was probably a bit excessive to have four garden forks and a selection of nine assorted spades, particularly in light of the fact that he rarely did any gardening. He also had to concede that, while he had bought them for a song, it made little sense to have two golf bags crammed with clubs, particularly when he didn't play the game. Terry couldn't resist the temptation to draw one of the clubs out of a bag and wave it about aimlessly. He inspected the head of the club to discover that it was a four-iron. He momentarily wondered what a four-iron was for, but he just had to accept his ignorance of all things golf. He slipped the club back into the bag and noted another four-iron beside it and another and another. Out of curiosity, he inspected the rest of the clubs and found a random selection of makes and sizes, but six of them were four-irons. Terry wouldn't claim to be a golfer, but he had a sneaking suspicion that there were few golfers who would be over-reliant on one club size, particularly as two of them turned out to be designed for left-handed players. The golf bags were set to one side, along with a collection of large pieces of electrical equipment that had been purchased because of their price rather than their functional or decorative value. Terry had justified some of the purchases by reasoning that they might appeal to different groups of collectors; some people collected scientific instruments, and some people collected nautical items, so a piece of ship's navigational apparatus should appeal to both. The reality, as pointed out by Lizzie, was that such items often tended to appeal to neither group. She had argued that many people like football and many are interested in cooking but, whatever the merits of such a book might turn out to be, who would want to buy the Paul Gascoigne cookbook? It took a while, but Terry eventually felt he was ready for the goods to be collected.

Lunch took the form of a sandwich and a cup of tea, which Terry chose to take into the garden. It was a hot afternoon, and he was glad of the shade offered by his patio umbrella as he quickly finished off his meal before sitting and looking around at his garden. Was this what holidays were all about? Terry's life had previously taken the form of a sequence of predictable activities with few gaps in between for leisure, no need to plan anything to fill an hour or two, no time for idle reflection. Much of his time had been taken up by work, and a lot of the rest of his days were filled by his buying, selling and restoration work. Now he had time on his hands, and he was completely at a loss as to what to do with it. Housework? No, the house was the cleanest it had been for years. Gardening? Perhaps he could get some use out of his selection of garden tools before they were consigned to the auction? No, it was just too hot, and the garden had been designed to be low maintenance because he was not a natural gardener.

Despite the almost irresistible urge to do something, Terry just sat and thought. The last time he had spent any appreciable time in the garden had been on one of his mother's later brief visits when she had busied herself doing some weeding in the rockery, largely as a way of avoiding being drawn in to conversation with her mother in the house. He tried to focus on that day; his mother had been polite, even kind, and had tried to chat with him, but there was no natural bond. She didn't know how to converse with a young boy, and he knew so little about the stranger who was his mother. She knew nothing of his collection of old coins, and he knew nothing of some far-away place called Newcastle. Terry was suddenly filled with questions about his background. As a child, he had lived his life with a largely egocentric view of things, and he had been absorbed by his many hobbies. He had never found the time to even begin to think about those around him. He now found himself wanting to know what his mother was like, why she had acted the way she did, and what part he had played in her decision to move out of his life.

For the first time in his life, Terry began to experience a niggling feeling that he might have been somehow responsible for his mother leaving him; it wasn't a feeling that he would have described as guilt, but it was uncomfortable. Lizzie had often talked about people who had undergone times of emotional turmoil wanting to attribute blame to someone even if it meant ultimately accepting most of it themselves.

Terry definitely did not feel guilty, it had not been his fault, but he still wanted to try to establish why things had turned out the way they had. He thought back to his previous aborted attempts to trace his mother; he now had more time on his hands, and for a while he considered having another go at finding her, but he conceded that he didn't know where to start. The only tenuous link with his mother was through Lord, so he would have to talk with him again. It wasn't a plan that offered any great prospect of success, but it was his only chance.

When Terry arrived at Tranby Manor, he was a little surprised to hear that Lord was not in the communal lounge where he used to spend a lot of his free time, so one of the young staff members showed Terry to his friend's flat. Terry knocked on the door and listened carefully for the faint call of, "Come in."

Lord was sitting by the French window in his lounge area, looking out towards the gardens with an open book on his lap. He looked tired but obviously pleased to see his visitor.

"Afternoon, Lord," said Terry. "I thought you would be in the lounge with the others at this time."

"No, I just fancied a bit of peace and quiet, and it was a bit hectic in there. Old Mrs Walker keeps banging on about her nephew 'the barrister' and how he's been involved in some big case in York. The way she rabbits on about him you'd think he was Perry Mason. I remember that the illustrious nephew visited briefly one day; he had all the person skills of a mortician, but old Mrs Walker praises him up to the skies."

Terry was mildly amused that his friend referred to 'old' Mrs Walker even though he was probably a good 10 years her senior. Lord had never been able to stand pretentiousness in people, and his natural modesty meant that he never countered such displays by recounting his own achievements.

"She probably has nothing else in her life," commented Terry before changing the subject by asking, "So what are you reading?"

"Just an old book I found on the shelf," he said dismissively, "I wasn't really reading it. So what brings you here again so soon?"

"I'm on a sort of holiday, so I thought I would just drop in while I have a bit of free time."

"Pleased to see you. Would you like a sherry?" he asked, pointing towards a tray with a decanter and a selection of glasses. "I may even be tempted to join you."

Terry took the hint and poured two small glasses of sherry and took them over to join his friend by the window. The two sat for a while in silence sipping their drinks. Lord continued to stare out onto the immaculately maintained gardens while Terry looked around his friend's room. It was the first time that he had been into Lord's private quarters, and he was struck by the strange mix of a very tastefully decorated modern room within which were displayed some of the items that Terry remembered seeing when Lord had been in his own home. The shelves in the apartment contained some of the many books that Lord had brought with him and of course there were the photographs, some of which Terry had never seen before, and the large mantle clock that had once had pride of place on the fireplace but which now stood somewhat incongruously on a small table.

Lord observed Terry looking at the room and said, "A whole life condensed into a couple of rooms. It wasn't easy deciding what to select. It was easy to pick out the things that had to come with me, but it wasn't enjoyable rejecting some of the things there just wasn't room for. Still, we all have to face changes at some point, and soon I will be going for the ultimate down-size, and I won't even be able to take this lot with me."

"Don't go getting morbid on me, Lord. I came here for a chat, not a discourse on the frailties of man."

"Just facing up to reality. I'm not likely to be claiming a lot more of the Crompton money, more's the pity, but I've had a good life. A bloody good life, but it is important never to overstay one's welcome."

"I haven't seen that picture before," observed Terry in an attempt to change the subject. "Is that you and Mary?"

"Oh, yes," answered Lord, smiling broadly. "That was just before we were married. It was just a snap taken by a friend of ours on a day trip to Skegness. Of all the pictures I have, that little snap is my favourite; years later, we would take it out of the shoe box where we kept our family photographs and laugh at the memories it brought back. After Mary went, I put it in that little frame. When I move on, that's the only little luxury item that I want to take with me. I've left instructions that I want it buried with me. I know it's daft, I'm not going to sit on a cloud with Mary for eternity marvelling at that product of a Kodak Brownie, but that little picture is how I want my life to be remembered."

Terry strolled over and picked up the photograph. It was a small black-and-white picture of a young couple laughing as they messed about on the beach. Terry smiled as he thought that, apart from the slightly dated swimwear and the lack of colour, it was the kind of picture that could have been taken yesterday, and as he returned to his seat by Lord, he commented, "You were a handsome couple."

"I was just a gawky young man, but Mary was an absolute beauty as you can see there. I couldn't believe my luck when she first agreed to go out with me, and I never got over that feeling of being thankful that she had agreed to take me on. The silly thing is that she later told me that she felt she had been the lucky one to 'land' me." He gave a little chuckle before continuing,

"We really enjoyed that day on the beach. I was still in the army and glad to get out of uniform for a while. Mary was just lovely and the weather was perfect. We both knew, even then, that we would get married. We never really discussed it, but it just seemed natural. That's something I just can't understand about you and your Lizzie."

The sudden change of direction in the conversation took Terry a bit by surprise, and all he managed to comment was, "Sadly, she's not my Lizzie. I just seem to have got it all wrong somewhere along the line."

"Don't go looking for blame; perhaps you're just going through a bad patch. It happens in all relationships, every individual has their ups and downs, and so every relationship does."

"Not with you and Mary, though," suggested Terry.

"Oh no?" The older man laughed. "Our life was a bed of roses, thorns and all. We had days on end when we hardly spoke, usually over some issue that was far from earth-shattering, but for the main part you are right, we had a marvellous marriage because we both wanted it to work. It didn't get off to a great start, as Mary's father never really liked me. He couldn't see any long-term prospects for a future son-in-law who was in the army and the war was ending. He came round in the end as he saw my career with the electricity board getting under way, but it was hard to start with."

"At least I didn't have any problems with my father not taking to Lizzie, and I got on quite well with her family. I don't know how Lizzie would have got on with my mother, but that's all academic now as I don't have either," said Terry, feeling quite pleased with himself at the way he had steered the conversation in the direction of his mother. Lord did not take up the proffered topic, but Terry felt it not unreasonable to push it a little further.

"Do you think they would have got on well, Lord?"

"Hard to say, of course," replied the older man after a lengthy pause. "They are both gregarious people with a flair for getting on with others, but one can never tell. If you had ever got married, I'm not sure how Janice would have taken to being a mother-in-law."

"She obviously never took to being a mother," commented Terry. "Or so I believe."

Lord was astute enough to realise that he was being pumped for information. His initial response had been to ignore the comment, but he realised that his young friend was desperate to find out all he could.

"I can't give you a simple two-sentence description of Janice. It might be convenient for you, but people are much more complex than that. She was not perfect, but none of us are. On the other hand, the picture your grandparents painted may not have been entirely accurate. Your mother left you, and that showed a degree of selfishness, but she honestly believed you would be well looked after by your grandparents. There was also the fact that she loved fun, and life at home had been largely devoid of that. When your imminent arrival was announced, your grandparents assumed that Janice would just have to face up to her new responsibilities. Your mother could not stand the prospect of turning out like them. She needed a bit of space."

"Moving up to Newcastle certainly gave her a bit of space," suggested Terry with an uncharacteristic sense of resentment in his voice.

"I don't think she ever planned to abandon you. We had a few letters from her after she had gone, and she always asked how you were doing. I think she just became caught up in her new life, and on her infrequent visits home, she would have noticed that you were completely settled into a life with your grandparents. She had missed the chance to get to know you as a baby, and the older you became, the harder it was to establish a link. The last few times she wrote it was clear that she had considerable regrets about moving out when she did, but she just felt it was too late, and she didn't want to cause you any further distress. She could never have moved back in with her parents, and she probably felt it would be too traumatic to move you out of the place you knew as home."

Terry gazed thoughtfully out of the window for a few moments before commenting, "I wish she'd given me the chance to decide if I could cope."

"I feel she would probably concur with you on that point, but adults have a condescending way of making decisions for children, and life doesn't give us the opportunity to rewind and try another way."

"I just wish I could meet up with her. I don't expect any great emotional reunion, but it would be good to talk to her."

"I'm sorry I can't give you any more help. I remember that some of her later letters came from France, but she might have just been on holiday. She never spoke much about what she had been doing, and the last time we had a long-term address for her was when she was still in Newcastle, but I don't recall what it was. Mary did much of the corresponding, and I threw out our old address books and a lot of old letters when I moved in here."

Terry felt that a last possible chance to find out about his mother had been snatched from him, and he was bitterly disappointed. The couple sat in silence for a few minutes before Lord looked up suddenly and exclaimed, "Wait a minute. We did have a postcard from Janice at one point. It was a picture of a pub, and I remember her saying that she had a nice flat above it. Now, let me think, what was the name of that pub?"

"More importantly, where was it?" asked Terry, hardly daring to think he might have a line to follow.

"Oh, it was certainly in Hull because Mary commented that it would have been nice to go and see her. I think the pub was named after royalty. The King George? No. The Queen Victoria? The Albert? No. Or was it something to do with royalty? The Crown? Sorry, Terry, after a lifetime of visiting hundreds of pubs, the names sort of blend together."

"And I guess there are dozens of pubs in Hull with royal names. I suppose it was just never meant for me to get in contact with my mother."

"The Kingstonian!" exclaimed Lord. "It was the Kingstonian, a big pub somewhere near Cottingham Road, up towards the university."

"The Kingstonian? Are you sure?"

"Yes. I remember now. I once went to the university for a few days to attend a conference on rebuilding Hull after the war. I'm pretty sure it was the Kingstonian we visited on a couple of evenings; a big old pub, I can't remember what the beer was like," replied Lord as he wrestled with his memory.

"So it's somewhere on Cottingham Road?"

"I'm not sure if it was on Cottingham Road itself, but it was definitely in that area and within crawling distance of the university. I remember the landlord looking at us a bit suspiciously when we mentioned we had just come from the university. Evidently he wasn't too keen on having students in."

Terry felt a buzz of excitement. He had a clue to his mother's whereabouts, or at least somewhere she had once lived. He tried to be rational; she may have moved on and in fact probably had, but someone might remember something about her.

"Don't get your hopes up, lad," commented Lord, who had seen the sudden change in Terry. "It was many years ago."

"I know, but I haven't got a lot on at the moment. I may just get along and see if anyone remembers her. It's a slim chance but it's all I've got. I may even pop along there tomorrow afternoon," said Terry, trying to sound casual.

"I could go along for the ride; act as your native scout if you like," offered Lord with ill-concealed pleasure at the thought of a day out.

"Great. I could pick you up just after lunch tomorrow. About one-thirty?"

"Couldn't make it a bit earlier, could you? Then we could have lunch at the Kingstonian. I seem to remember that they served quite good meals."

"I've got Colin from the auction rooms collecting some stuff at eleven thirty, but I can make it here as soon as I can after that."

"Great! It's fish pie for lunch here tomorrow, and it's never been one of my favourites. I'll tell the commandant I will be out."

Terry felt that he had just been expertly manoeuvred into taking Lord out, but he didn't mind; he was just delighted at the prospect of finding out something about his mother.

CHAPTER EIGHT

Colin arrived promptly at half past eleven, and despite his protestations about being far too busy, he was easily persuaded to have a cup of tea. He cast his eyes over the articles on the table and stacked on the floor before commenting, "You've got some reasonable stuff here, Terry. You should see some of the articles we've been asked to auction off in the past. We have to say no because if we could get any price for them at all, it wouldn't be worth our while. I remember one deluded soul who brought in a chest he honestly believed had been made up from planks taken out of HMS Victory during some renovation work. Such provenance can be hard to prove or disprove, but that particular chest had obviously been made of new pine that had been stained. The poor guy had been sold a rather obvious replica that could have been made the previous week."

"I often marvel at what some people try and off-load," commented Terry, "I've thrown better quality articles in the bin."

"This is a fine bit of porcelain, 1820s, I should think," said Colin, handling the delicate statuette with an apparent lack of care that belied his expertise. "Should make about a hundred to a hundred and twenty in a general sale, probably a fair bit more if you sent it up to one of the big auction houses."

"That's about what I thought. I just want to shift the lot, though, or I might have considered sending it down to London," replied Terry, recognising that he would have to press on with loading and not become distracted by a conversation with Colin. Terry had frequently been impressed by Colin's knowledge of antiques. To many people, the old man was merely someone who held up lots during the auction and helped load heavier items into waiting vans afterwards, but over the years he had seen so much go through the salerooms and along the way he had learned a considerable amount, to the point where his views were sought by the auctioneer when it came to estimating the potential sale price of certain articles.

The two men loaded Terry's collection into the transit van. Terry stood for a moment, looking at the articles he had collected over the years before briskly closing the back door of the van, saying goodbye to Colin and returning to the house. The house seemed very different, certainly bigger but somehow more clinical and less home-like. Like a house that had been prepared for letting. Terry hadn't got time to waste standing about, so he grabbed his car keys and went off to pick up Lord.

Lord was standing waiting in the foyer when his friend arrived and obviously eager to get on with his day out.

"Morning, Lord, sorry if I'm a bit late," started Terry, "I had to help Colin load my stuff into the van."

"You're not late at all," replied his friend. "I just wanted to get a swift getaway."

"It may seem a daft question, but you do know the way to this pub, don't you?"

"Yes. Well, sort of."

"How 'sort of' exactly?"

"Well, if you can get me to the university, I am pretty sure I can get us to the pub. It's almost a homing instinct with me. I can remember it as though it were only last week. Well, that's fortunately not true; some of last week's events are a bit cloudy, but things that happened when I was a young man are much clearer. Trust me."

"Not exactly inspiring confidence there, Lord, but we'll give it a shot."

The route to the university involved the pair travelling around the outskirts of Hull, and along the way the older man gave Terry an extensive commentary on how things had changed since the forties. Eventually they arrived at the university, and it took Terry quite a while to find somewhere to park before they walked back to the main entrance. Lord stood for a while, looking around the area and getting his bearings.

"It's changed a bit. But then it is over half a century ago that I was last here."

"You mean you've got no idea?"

"The pub is that way," said Lord in a determined fashion as he set off along the road.

"You're quite sure of this?" asked a less-than-convinced Terry.

"We used to come this way frequently. I remember we had Snubby Ackroyd with us. We had to show him the way every time we went to the pub or he would never have got there. Good old Snubby, he was in the Pathfinder Squadron during the war; he could navigate a plane to a target half way across Europe, but ask him to find a pub three streets away and he was useless. We'd have died of thirst if we had relied on him to guide us. Come on, it's this way."

The pair walked on for about a quarter of an hour before Lord stopped and looked around him.

"I don't remember it being so far, but then I was a lot younger then," explained Lord, before having some obvious inspiration and again declaring enthusiastically, "Come on, it's this way."

After a further five minutes walking, Lord stopped again and declared, "I could have sworn it was about here."

They had stopped at a crossroads, and Terry looked up and down all four roads. There was no sign of the elusive Kingstonian, but there was an elderly man delivering circulars, and as he approached, Terry asked, "Excuse me, you don't happen to know where the Kingstonian is, do you?"

The stranger looked at the two intrepid pub-hunters, paused for a moment and then replied, "If you are going for lunch, you're a bit late, mate."

"Why? Have they stopped serving lunch now?" asked Terry, instinctively checking his watch.

"You might say that," replied the old man, absent-mindedly sorting some of his bag of leaflets before adding, "The old Kingstonian was pulled down years ago. It was just 50 yards down there. Just behind that ornate brick wall." The stranger pointed in the direction of the absent pub.

"I knew it was down here," exclaimed Lord triumphantly before pausing and adding, "But that doesn't help you much, does it, Terry? Sorry."

Terry stood for a moment. He had been stupid enough to allow himself to be optimistic about finding a link with his mother, and he felt the sudden emptiness as his dream was cruelly snatched from him again.

"Never mind, we tried, Lord," he said, trying to conceal his disappointment. "We'll just have to find somewhere else for lunch."

The couple retraced their steps towards the car.

"Hull was an interesting place just after the war," commented Lord in an attempt to lift the feeling of disappointment. "It was full of large informal car parks, courtesy of the Luftwaffe, but hardly anyone owned a car. If you were fortunate enough to have a car as we did then, you could park within yards of the city centre, and the car parks were never full."

"I guess not," replied the younger man, with little sign of interest.

"The bombing patterns often seemed incomprehensible. There was a lot of damage around here, but it was nothing to do with there being anything of strategic importance. It was just the luck of the draw. I had an uncle who lived about two hundred yards over there, and half his street was demolished in 1941. He was doubly annoyed because his allotment was nearby, and he lost most of his early potato crop as well."

"I thought they just bombed the docks and the railways."

"That may have been their intention, but it's not like shooting fish in a barrel. Added to that, there were a number of aircraft returning to Germany after bombing targets further inland who would just jettison unused bombs on any 'target of opportunity'. Hull was easy to find as bombers just followed the Humber, so it took more than its fair share of bombs. Consequently, there was a hell of a lot of work to do to rebuild the city after the war."

"I remember my grandad saying that you were part of the team which redesigned the city after the war."

"Very flattering," said Lord, and he gave a short laugh. "I was working with the electricity company, and we had to help sort out the power supply. I certainly didn't single-handedly redesign the city. I just played my very small part. There was certainly plenty to do. It was a strange time. I remember Snubby Ackroyd commenting that he spent the war trying to flatten cities and the time afterwards helping to rebuild them. Over three-quarters of the housing stock in Hull was either completely destroyed or damaged in some way. What a bloody waste, and it was replicated, to a greater or lesser degree, throughout towns all over Europe."

Lord was quiet for most of the rest of the walk back to the car, and now it was Terry's turn to try and lighten the mood.

"Come on, let's find ourselves a nice pub and grab some lunch. I am still on holiday; perhaps if we head out of town a bit?"

"Yes. Good idea, young man," concurred Lord. "I remember that there were a number of pubs Mary and I used to call at out in the Wolds; they can't all have closed."

It was late afternoon by the time Terry dropped his friend off at Tranby Manor. They had made the most of their half day out and were pleased with the late lunch they enjoyed, but Terry could not dispel the feeling of disappointment at not having been able to find his mother's old flat. It wasn't just the fact that he had not been able to speak to anyone at the Kingstonian; it was that it had been knocked down and the site redeveloped. It was so final. His route back to his past came up against a brick wall, metaphorically and literally. As Terry drove home, he toyed with the idea of going to look for Lenin's place. It was just possible that on such a lovely evening Lizzie would be down there by the river. He quickly discounted this possibility; with his luck that day, he knew he would have no chance of seeing her, so he drove straight home.

Terry sat in the garden with a bottle of beer. It should have been a pretty idyllic time; warm summer evening at the end of a day out, no work tomorrow and a bottle of beer. What could be better? But Terry was unable to count these blessings. Lizzie had left him, and he couldn't understand why. He knew couples do often break up, but there was usually a reason. He could have understood it if he and Lizzie had had a blazing row or if she had left him for someone else. A chilling thought came into his head; had Lizzie found someone else? It was only a fleeting question; he knew that if Lizzie had found someone, then she would have discussed it openly in her usual reasonable, case-conference way. He couldn't escape the feeling that perhaps he had contributed in some small way to the split, but all the self-examination and reflection was a new experience for him and it was proving harder than he had expected. Lord's comments about Terry's family had been interesting rather than illuminating, and Terry was frustrated that he couldn't find out more, and quickly. His thinking style was methodical rather than intuitive, so he just had to revisit the facts. Lizzie, for whatever reason, had left him. She had commented on his cluttered lifestyle, and he was doing something about that, but the trigger had been the holiday he had planned for them. He tried to remember the phrase Lord had used to describe him; not very 'demonstrative'? Terry had tried to examine his upbringing to establish why he had turned out as he had and why he had been unable to hold on to Lizzie when he had assumed everything was perfect between them.

As he sat in the garden, he recalled how, when he was about 10, his school friend Sheila used to walk back from school with him. He remembered that she would try to hold his hand along the way, and he would recoil slightly and try to pretend it hadn't happened. At the back gate to the house, she would linger for a while and stand very close to him, obviously waiting for him to do something. Terry's response had invariably been to make his excuses and rush into the house to his grandparents. It wasn't that Sheila was unattractive; on the contrary, she was the prettiest girl in his class. He loved standing beside her in the dinner queue at school, feeling the gentle softness of her as they were jostled by the rowdier children and smelling that soft indefinable scent of girl as she brushed past him. It had always struck him that it was a sweet smell somewhere between dolly mixtures and baby powder. He wouldn't have minded her kissing him at the garden gate. It seemed an innocent and almost natural thing to do, but his grandparents had always stressed that he shouldn't have anything to do with girls as there would be 'plenty of time for that sort of thing later'. They had given him the same advice all through his secondary school as well, so he began to wonder exactly when it would be appropriate to display the interest in girls which he experienced increasingly. He remembered his grandfather's claim to Lord about being 'past all that sort of thing'. Presumably, there had to be a window of opportunity at some stage in life when 'that sort of thing' was to be permitted if not actively encouraged? As he sat and sipped his beer, he wondered what Sheila was doing now. He used to see her around the village, but she had gone to a different secondary school and he had lost touch. She had developed into a very attractive young woman and probably had a young family by now.

Once Terry started to think about his grandparents' attitude to his love life, he realised that they had consistently discouraged any interest he might have shown in girls. They had never tried to suggest that the topic was in any way dirty or wrong, only that he ought to be concentrating on other things at that particular stage in his life. When he had first tried to make sense of his grandparents' attitude, he had assumed that it was simply the fact that they were very old-fashioned, but he came to recognise that they were merely acting in a misguided way to ensure that Terry didn't make the same sort of mistake they felt his mother had.

Largely as a result of his grandparents' influence, Terry had been a bit of a late starter in the romance stakes and it had not been easy. He craved love, and he was a hopeless romantic, so, as a complete novice, he displayed an over-enthusiastic approach to romance. Not surprisingly, some of his initial attempts to cultivate girlfriends had put some of them off; he was looking for the love of his life immediately, while they initially just wanted to have an enjoyable evening out. It took a while and some particularly forthright advice from one girl before Terry realised that he needed to slow down a bit. By the time he had started going out with Lizzie, he had learned to be more restrained in his displays of emotion, less passionate and obviously less demonstrative.

The very thought of Lizzie reminded him of how much he missed her. He sat and sipped his beer and remembered the long summer evenings they had spent together in that very garden, engrossed in conversation. To be more precise, the conversations were largely a time for Terry to outline his business plans to Lizzie because they couldn't discuss her confidential work. Lizzie was a very good listener, another skill that he ascribed to her professional training, but he realised that she spoke very little about herself. It hadn't been a problem because Terry had so many interests that he could easily keep up more than his fair share of the conversation; perhaps he had bored her? They had spent so many happy times together, and she had shown no signs of discontent, at least that he had noticed, until the holiday incident. Why had she suddenly become so irrational? Perhaps it was a hormonal thing? Terry was no expert on women, but even he realised that this was just a convenient non-solution. Certainly Lizzie had exhibited the odd mood swing, but then Terry accepted that even he had his off days. On reflection, he conceded that she had probably been the more easy-going of the two of them despite the obvious pressures of her work. The more he thought about it, the more he realised that his relative ignorance of Lizzie extended beyond just not knowing about her work. He knew that she had been a thoughtful, loving person, and he missed her more than he would have imagined possible, but he didn't feel he knew what she was really like or what she wanted from their relationship. How could he hope to win her back if he didn't know what she wanted? Terry felt his thoughts had come full circle and got him nowhere. He had been so engrossed that he had hardly made an impression on his beer, and now he had no taste for it, so leaving the half-full bottle on the table, he went inside and prepared for bed.

CHAPTER NINE

The auction room already had a few potential buyers at the preview when Terry turned up. He tried to look disinterested as he wandered round the room, which was even more packed than usual with a variety of lots ranging from antiques through collectables to outright junk. He noted that his items had largely been shown to good advantage, but he was a little concerned to see that some of his more esoteric electrical and radio items had been lumped together in what were often called 'lucky dip' lots. Terry couldn't help looking at the guide prices in the catalogue and felt that the valuers had got it broadly right on the main items. He knew that no price could be forecast with complete accuracy; it all depended on who turned up at the auction and how much they wanted a particular lot.

"Morning Terry," said a smartly dressed man in his late fifties. "So what's all this I hear about you becoming a seller rather than a punter? I could hardly believe it when Colin told me."

Terry turned to see John Spivey, the auctioneer and owner of the saleroom. He had always got on well with John over the years they had been dealing with each other and generally enjoyed their sessions trying to out-compete each other in forecasting what a particular item would fetch at auction.

"Hello, John. Yes, I've decided to have a bit of a clear-out."

"Bit of a clear-out? I bet there's nothing left in your place now."

"It looks different, I'll give you that, but it had to be done," said Terry, taking a closer look at an ornate Victorian wall cupboard before adding, "That should make more than your thirty-to-forty-pound estimate, John."

"True, it should," commented the auctioneer, "but the market for such items is not strong. Are you going to have a go for it then?"

"No. Definitely not! I am here strictly as a vendor. If I look like bidding tomorrow, then ignore me."

"Can't promise that, son, it's in my nature, and my interests, to build up a bit of a buying frenzy. If I don't, then my commission goes west, and Mrs Spivey has to go without her new frocks. It's a terrible thing living on the breadline like this."

"You seem to get by," observed Terry, looking his friend up and down. "Or are the charity shops getting a better class of clothing in these days?"

"Merely the apparel of my trade; I have to look respectable. We may not have food to put on the table, but I need to look smart for work."

"You certainly succeed on that front, but then the extensive gold jewellery and expensive wristwatch do help you out a bit."

The auctioneer smiled; he had long made it a habit to proclaim his poverty and his regular customers made it clear that they felt he was doing pretty well for himself. The truth was that he was not a millionaire, but largely due to his wife's income, he lived in some comfort.

"Colin tells me that you've parted company with Enderby's. I'm surprised, Jim Enderby always seemed to value your efforts."

"It appears that the stores have to be computerised so my old job can now be carried out by anyone who can type in a code. It was probably time for me to move on anyway."

"As I've said before, we can always do with a bit of help here. I won't kid you; there's not a great wage to start with, but you could go on to become an auctioneer. You need to learn the ropes, but you already have a pretty fair idea of some of the valuation side. You just have to immerse yourself in the work and your knowledge will grow."

"Thanks, John, I appreciate it, but I couldn't see myself ever standing up there doing your work."

"That's the easy bit," commented John. "That's me in ring master mode. A bit of showmanship, a few tricks of the trade, and the items almost sell themselves. No, it's the bloody paperwork, calculating commission for buyers and sellers, tax to pay, cataloguing to get done on time. It's a nightmare, Terry. I've got a programme on the computer that's supposed to do all the financial calculations for me, but I'm still here late at least four nights a week, as Mrs Spivey is quick to point out."

"I guess I could learn to do some of that routine stuff if you want to try me out for a few weeks. If it doesn't work out, then it's no big deal. To be honest, I'm bored rigid with this holiday of mine, and it would be good to have something to do."

"Good. We'll sort out an hourly rate and see how it goes. Old Colin will be pleased. He is a first-rate employee, but at his age he really doesn't want to be working all the hours he does, and I'm sure he'd be more than willing to give you the benefit of his experience in exchange for lightening his workload a bit. I'll let him know now."

The auctioneer walked off to pass on the good news, and Terry saw a wide smile spread across Colin's face as he was told about the new arrangement. He came over to see his new workmate.

"Welcome aboard, Terry," announced the porter. "It will be good to have someone to help do all the work round here; the boss is about as much use as an ashtray on a motorbike." The latter remark was made in clear earshot of the proprietor, who was obviously used to taking such mild abuse from Colin.

"I'm quite looking forward to it. To be honest, I have trouble finding things to occupy me during the day; I need something to give me a bit of purpose in life."

"Well, there's plenty to do here, particularly as we run up to an auction like Saturday's. I'll see about fitting you out with a brown dust coat like mine, but you'll have to find yourself your own bowler if you want to dress up for the formal auctions. I bought mine in an auction here years ago, it adds a bit of class. When were you thinking of starting, by the way?"

"I don't know. I need to discuss terms with John."

"Well, you'd better grab him now while he's on site. He has a lot of flitting about to do, and we need all hands on deck as soon as possible. Would this afternoon be convenient?"

"Well, I'm not sure," replied Terry, who was a little taken aback by the rate at which things were progressing. "I'll see if I can sort something out with John and perhaps start tomorrow."

Colin quickly ushered Terry in the direction of the office, where John was sitting behind a desk that was covered in sheets of papers and small business ledgers. It was quite obvious that he was eager to secure Terry's services as soon as possible. After some preliminary discussion about wages and hours of employment, it was agreed that Terry should start at eight o'clock the following morning.

Terry felt pleased with the offer of some gainful activity, and his social calendar was not so full that he couldn't have started his new post there and then, but he felt inclined to take this opportunity of going to see Lenin just in case there was any news of Lizzie.

Apart from a rather good bacon sandwich and a mug of tea, the visit to the café was not a success; Lizzie seemed to have disappeared off the face of the earth, and once again he couldn't shake off the idea that she was deliberately avoiding him.

"Not a sign of her, sorry, mate," said Lenin. "But as I pointed out last time we spoke, she seemed to have a lot on her mind last time she dropped in. Not her usual bubbly self at all."

"Never mind," said a dejected Terry, "I just wanted to see if you'd heard anything, and I'm going to be a bit busy myself for a while; I'm doing a bit of work for John at the auction rooms."

"Good for you, lad. It should suit you down to the ground. I'm very pleased for you. When do you start?"

"Tomorrow morning at eight. It's just a sort of trial period to see how we get on, but they are rather busy, and they say it will give me a chance to learn the ropes a bit."

"With your organisational skills and knowledge of the auction scene, you should walk it. Shame though, it probably means I won't see as much of one of my favourite customers."

"To be quite honest, Lenin, much as I love our chats and your cooking, I'm becoming rather bored with being a man of leisure. I just don't seem able to fill my days. Anyway, the new job will show Lizzie that I have changed. She always said I ought to be more 'proactive', and I guess this shows I have been. I'm going to clear out a lot of the clutter I have in my life, starting with the items in the next sale."

"Clear it all out, brother; property is theft!" proclaimed Lenin as Terry wandered back to his car.

Terry rose early the next day; a mixture of excitement and the dawn sun on his window meant that he was up and ready for work by six o'clock. After breakfast, he made himself a second pot of tea and took it out to the garden. The day had a glorious freshness about it, and Terry felt ready to take on any challenge. As he sat in the warming sun, he was reminded again of the last awkward chat that he had with his mother some years previously. He tried to convince himself that she had made an effort to promote some sort of reconciliation and that she had shown some sign, however slight, of wanting to get to know him. However much he tried to recall and reinterpret the meeting, he still knew that the truth was that there was just nothing between them. It somehow didn't feel right, but they were just like strangers, polite but strangers none the less. There was nothing he could do about it now, so he resolved to get on with his life; work was calling, and he was ready for it.

It was still only half past seven when Terry arrived at the auction house, and it was a further 15 minutes before Colin turned up with Julie, who made up the rest of the full-time staff. Julie Redknap was one of those individuals who seemed to have been unfairly blessed with a range of positive qualities. She was an extremely intelligent young woman in her mid-twenties, with phenomenal organisational skills, and as such she was the ideal person to act as the auctioneer's personal assistant. She also possessed the invaluable facility of being able to get on with people, which made her good to have around if there was a misunderstanding with any of the customers. On top of all of this, she was endowed with film star good looks. Terry suspected that she could probably speak a dozen foreign languages, play an assortment of musical instruments and open the batting for England as well; she just seemed the kind of person who could take on anything, and yet she was completely unaffected and this added to her charm.

"You're keen, young Terry. Have you slept out here all night?" asked Colin as he began the laborious process of making his way through the not inconsiderable number of locks that needed to be negotiated to gain access to the building.

"I just wanted some time to get used to the idea of being on the other side of the counter, so to speak," replied Terry before asking, "So what do I do first?"

"Put the kettle on, of course, and then you can help me get the shutters down. The boss will be here soon, and he needs his cup of coffee or he's a right tartar."

"I heard that," came a voice from the doorway as Mr Spivey made his entrance. "And I can't say I disagree with you. Make us all a drink, would you please, Terry, and then I will run through all the basics with you. There are few rules, but they are important."

While the kettle boiled, Colin and Terry took down the shutters, and then the three men sat down to a cup of coffee while Julie took her cup and went through to get on with some of the administrative work.

"As I said, there are very few rules, but they are important," started the auctioneer. "The main thing to remember is that this business is based on trust. This company must be beyond reproach, and that's not just some old-fashioned idea. The customers need to be completely assured that they are being treated honestly or they will stop coming, and an auction without a good crowd will not realise the prices we need to make a reasonable profit. Some auctioneers might resort to taking bids from imaginary punters just to force the price up, but it just isn't worth it. Such a short-term illegal ploy might make a few pounds extra, but the risk of losing customers means it just isn't worth it. Likewise, if you notice a customer is in fact bidding against themselves then you must tell them, perhaps make a joke of it, but don't allow them to pay more just because of their over-eagerness. We have a regular couple who turn up, Jack and Sally White, who often bid against each other, despite the fact that they are supposedly acting together. In such an event, I make a point of telling them that they are, in fact, working against their own interests and perhaps only one of them should be bidding on any one lot. We may lose a pound or so in commission, but we gain immeasurably in terms of our reputation. You've been to enough auctions to realise that item descriptions must be completely accurate in the catalogue and in the auction itself. What you may not know is that we reputable auctioneers adhere to a strict code of practice, but all you need to remember is that if an activity seems to offer quick cash returns but it seems even slightly shady, then steer clear. We make a steady return on this business that is enough to support your wages and to keep Mrs Spivey in frocks, so it is just not worth taking any risks with dodgy procedures."

"Sounds reasonable to me," replied Terry, putting down his coffee cup. "So where do you want me to start?"

"When the clients start to arrive, Julie and I will sell any catalogues that are needed and issue the bidders with their individual numbers. We have one or two casual staff we employ just on auction days for when things are particularly hectic, and they will do most of the heavy work, like moving large items around. That leaves you and Colin to keep a general eye on the room, and then when we start the auction, you can take it in turns to hold up or point out the lots. During the bidding, if you think I have missed a bid then point it out to me. You'll soon get used to the routine. We've got a lot of items today, so I will try and get a bit of a crack on."

As the first clients arrived and started selecting their seats or regular positions to stand, Terry was pleased to see that there had been a good turn out, and by the time the auctioneer took his seat behind his desk, the room was quite full.

"Good morning, ladies and gentlemen, and welcome to Spivey's auction rooms. Regular bidders will note that we have a new porter today; Master Terry."

There was a muted cheer from some of Terry's friends, which caused him to take a slight bow. The auction was quickly underway, and Terry was amazed at the amount of work that was necessary to ensure that each lot was described and pointed out to the crowd. He had hoped to keep some sort of running tally to show how his own items did in the sale, but he found he was just too busy. He did note that some items appeared to do well while others were attracting little attention at all, but he could only gather the vaguest impression as to how things were going. The auction continued at a frenetic pace. Towards the end of the sale, the room emptied slightly as the buyers went outside for a bit of fresh air while waiting to collect their lots, and for a short while the pace was less demanding, but then came the scramble to pay for and collect their goods. By the time the last of the clients had gone, Terry realised he was exhausted. The room still contained a number of lots which were to be collected within the next few days, and the auctioneer and Julie were taking numerous phone calls from vendors who were enquiring as to the prices their lots had realised.

It was a further two hours before a very tired Terry sat down with his new colleagues to a well-deserved cup of tea and some sandwiches that John had brought in. This was apparently a regular perk for the staff who had little time during the day to grab even a drink.

"Looks like it's been a very good day," exclaimed John, with obvious satisfaction at how the auction had gone. "Even some of your more esoteric items found new owners, Terry, although I didn't think we were going to get any takers for that pile of plumber's tools."

"I couldn't really follow how the auction was going, I was too busy," commented Terry. "But I was pleased to see the French mantel clock did so well."

"Yes, a fair price in today's market," observed the auctioneer before continuing, "Pity about the silver-plated teddy bear figure. I was beginning to think we wouldn't find a buyer at all, and we ended up almost giving it away."

"Yes, you might have thought it would appeal to collectors of teddy bears and collectors of silver plate, but neither seemed interested. It's what Lizzie would call one of my regular Paul Gascoigne cookbook lots. It seemed a good purchase at the time, but I obviously overestimated its attraction to the customers."

The rest of the workforce briefly glanced at each other at the mention of the fictitious book, but none of them bothered to seek an explanation; it had been a long day, and they were ready to go home.

"Do you want us to work out your profit from the sale of your lots now?" queried the auctioneer, "or leave it until Monday morning?"

"I'm not in any great rush. Monday is fine by me. What time do you want me in?"

"Eight-thirty is plenty early enough, and then we can start sorting out the uncollected and unsold lots from today's sale, and it would be a good idea for you to have a look at that computer programme that's supposed to make my paperwork so much easier to handle. Even the multi-talented Julie can't make head nor tail of it."

"I'll be pleased to," said Terry, surprised to hear that at least with computers, the incomparable Miss Redknap was not infallible. "In the meantime, I feel as if I've been put through a mincer. I'm shattered."

"Don't worry, it gets a lot easier when you get the hang of it and know the routines," said Colin, by way of encouragement., "After 30 years, it's almost bearable."

When Terry got home, he collapsed into his armchair. It had been a heavy day, but he had enjoyed it in some bizarre way. He didn't know exactly how much his lots had made, but he was sure that even after the auction room charges had been deducted, he had made a few hundred pounds from his items. The small bronze figure alone had realised nearly two hundred pounds, and he remembered having bought it for only twenty pounds at the car boot sale. It was true that other items had not done as well as he might have hoped but, as far as he had been able to notice, none of them had made more than a few pounds' loss. Terry became aware of a growing curiosity to find what he had made, but he would have to wait. He stared around the room. He still hadn't got used to how empty it looked, but at least he could now show Lizzie that he was sorting his life out. But what of the immediate future? Tomorrow was Sunday, a day he regularly attended a local car boot sale, but was that now a thing of the past? He enjoyed his Sunday saunter around the assorted stalls, meeting old friends and bartering with them, but should all that have to come to an end? Lenin had not been far off the mark when he had called Terry the King of the Car boot sale; it didn't make sense to just give it all up, but he would have to be more businesslike. Terry began to draw up a plan; he would still attend car boot sales, but he would only buy items that he had observed were selling well in the auctions and he would not have them hanging around the house. As soon as items were ready, after any minor renovation that might be necessary, they would be straight down to the next sale. This seemed a very good plan, but for the moment he was more focused on the need to make something to eat. After the sandwiches at work, he was far from hungry but knew he would need to have something to keep him going. The fridge offered a rather good piece of Wensleydale, which Terry carried out into the garden with the end crust of a loaf he had covered in butter. He sat his supper down on the patio table and then remembered the bottle of red wine that was in the kitchen cupboard. Within a few minutes, the bottle of wine and a glass were sitting alongside the bread and cheese while Terry took up his place on the sun lounger. What would his grandparents have thought if they could see him sprawled out in the warmth of the late evening, drinking wine in what had been their garden? He felt that his mother would have applauded his decadence.

CHAPTER TEN

The exterior light over the back door had switched itself on at dusk, and it was this that had attracted the flying insects that were systematically being picked off by the bats. It took Terry a moment or two to make sense of what was going on as he gradually awoke. It was dark and appreciably cooler. In the dim light coming from above the door, Terry could see the remains of his supper on the table, and closer examination revealed that he had drunk less than half the bottle of wine, so his present situation was not the result of some bacchanalian revelry; he must have been more tired than he had realised.

As he sat and gathered his thoughts, he remembered the dream he had just had. It had followed a familiar theme; he was back in the stores at Enderby's looking for something among what seemed to be endless corridors. As he went, he came across an odd assortment of fellow staff, none of whom were able to help or even appreciate how important it was to find whatever it was he appeared to be looking for. In that odd way that dreams can conjure up their own logic from bizarre happenings, it had not seemed strange that his fellow workers in the stores included his grandfather and Lord Leonard. His latest dream had a new twist in that he eventually came across Julie, who was sitting at a computer, and she explained that the problem could be easily solved by typing in the search criteria. This had been of no use because, in his dream, Terry was just not sure what he was looking for. He had experienced this theme in his dreams for many months, and it had not taken him long to figure out that it was related to his need to find something out about his family. At first, he had assumed that it reflected a basic need to know who his father was, but he became aware that it was more about needing to know his mother, and no one seemed to be able to help him.

From his position on the sun lounger, Terry looked up at the clear sky. Perhaps he ought to just spend the night there under the stars? No, he had to go in and brush his teeth, so it made sense to go to bed. Terry's romantic streak had almost emerged, but his sensible side soon reasserted itself.

As he stood and brushed his teeth, he checked his watch. It was just after two; he would have to set his alarm to be sure of being up at six to get to the car boot sale before the bargains had been picked through by the dealers.

The following day as Terry set off, he noticed the last remnants of a slight dew in the garden which the early sunlight was efficiently drying up, and he silently congratulated himself on his decision not to stay out overnight. By the time he arrived at the large field that housed the weekly sale, the sun was quite warm, and Terry enjoyed his stroll around the site and bought himself a burger for his breakfast. He met a number of his usual contacts and did some half-hearted haggling over one or two items, but he failed to find anything which he felt sure to make a profit on so he bought nothing. The old Terry would have bought something, if only to justify having spent the few pence on the entrance fees, but this Terry was determined only to buy items that he could be pretty sure of making money on. It was still only ten o'clock as he left the sale site and sat in his car, wondering what to do with the rest of the day. Eventually, he opted for a cup of tea and the prospect of a bit of news at Lenin's café.

The tea was fine, but it would have been much more enjoyable if there had been news of Lizzie.

"Sorry, comrade, still no sign of her," announced the proprietor in answer to Terry's eager questioning. "But then it was often quite long intervals between her visits. Perhaps she'll turn up this afternoon as its Sunday."

This comment offered little consolation to Terry, who was getting the impression that she was deliberately avoiding him. He realised that there was no going back to their previous relationship, but he would have welcomed the chance just to have a chat with her. He had tried to fabricate some excuse for going round to see her, but he had never got on very well with Lizzie's friend Veronica with whom she was staying, and he knew that she would be less than welcoming.

"The problem with Lizzie's work is that she doesn't have regular weekends off and never knows when she is going to be called out," explained Terry. "That's why she enjoys her holidays so much; the feeling of suddenly being completely free from the possibility of being contacted and not being at everyone's beck and call. I tried on numerous occasions to persuade her to switch off her phone when she was at home, but she wouldn't do it. I once even resorted to hiding it before we went up to bed, but she wouldn't rest until she had managed to get me to hand it back. With her blessed phone by the side of the bed, I often felt that I was on call as well, and I admit that I often resented her being called away."

Terry thought for a moment; he'd never considered how much Lizzie's work took over her life. Of course, he'd often been annoyed in those times when their plans had been ruined by Lizzie being called out at a moment's notice, but perhaps he had underestimated the pressure it put on her. The visit to Lenin's place had done nothing to lighten Terry's mood, and he sat for a while contemplating his mug of tea in complete silence as Lenin catered for the steady stream of Sunday visitors. Eventually, Terry tired of inventing stories as to the occupations and relationships between the other customers. It was a game he used to play with Lizzie when they went on one of their mystery trips to discover some new pub. Lizzie had always been so much better at the game than Terry, possibly because he was not generally strong on imagination. Lizzie could see a rather ordinary couple and recount that the elderly lady was in fact a pole dancer who took up the job because her former career as an exotic dancer had been brought to a premature end when she had developed an allergy towards ostrich feathers. Her partner was obviously a former contract killer who now ran a sanctuary for retired pit ponies near Wakefield. Lizzie could then effortlessly recount exactly what the couple were doing in the pub and even give details of their imaginary extended family. All this was done without apparently having to pause for thought. Terry's attempts, then and now, were more prosaic and thus today's game was never going to last long. Eventually, he gave up and just idly watched the traffic going by; he had never been strong on self-occupation, so he decided to go and visit Lord at the Stalag.

Terry was pleased to see that Lord had opted to spend some time in the lounge at Tranby Manor, but when he arrived, his old friend was sitting by himself gazing out over the garden.

"Hello, Terry," greeted Lord, smiling broadly. "It's good to see you. I could do with a bit of stimulating conversation. I got fed up trying to make out if old Mrs Swindell over there was still breathing. She's my bet in the Compton stakes, so I like to keep an eye on my investment."

"You'll get yourself thrown out if they hear you talking like that," replied Terry in a vain attempt to curb his friend's macabre interests.

"They don't care. It's all just a joke. The staff might seem disapproving, but I suspect that they have the odd wager on who will be the next of us to fall off our perch. Anyway,

I'm glad you turned up; I wanted to speak to you about my regular lift to my army reunion."

"It must be about now," interjected Terry before adding, "Oh hell, I haven't missed it, have I?"

"No, not at all. It's set for next week, but I just wanted to tell you that I've decided to give it a miss this year."

"You're not going? But you look forward to it. You certainly haven't missed one for the last few years I've been taking you." The truth was that Terry always enjoyed taking his friend to the regimental reunion, and he particularly enjoyed picking him up afterwards. At the end of such evenings, Lord had been appreciably mellowed by slightly more whisky than was good for him and would slump contentedly in the back of Terry's car, sometimes giving a creaky rendition of some tune that Terry half recognised.

"Yes, I enjoyed meeting my old comrades, but the truth is that most of the fellows my age have died. All the other officers I served with have gone, so now it's just me and the 'other ranks'. Don't get me wrong, they are a fine bunch of chaps, and many of them went through a great deal with me during the war, but we don't have the same sort of shared experiences as I did with the officers so this year I thought I would miss a meeting."

Terry was aware of a sudden feeling of concern for his friend. Lord had always enjoyed meeting with the other men, and their obvious respect for him meant that the reunions had always been a success, even with the dwindling numbers that are an unavoidable aspect of such annual events. Terry knew that Lord was not just deciding to miss one meeting, which would be like a professional footballer deciding to hang up his boots for just one season; Lord had decided that he had attended his last reunion. It was a sort of resignation. Terry looked at his old friend and was once again aware of the frailty within that apparently upright frame. It was a quality in the older man that he had glimpsed from time to time recently, and it concerned him more than a little.

"Why don't you just go along for an hour or so?" suggested Terry. "I don't mind getting you down there and just waiting around for a while."

"That's very kind of you, Terry, but I think it's better if I pass up on the whole thing. Perhaps we can just slip off down to the Barge that evening and have a quiet drink?"

"OK. If you're sure, but my offer still stands for the reunion if you change your mind."

The two men sat in silence for a while, looking out of the French window as the gardener patrolled up and down the extensive lawn with an ageing petrol mower. Terry was reminded of the way his grandfather used to mow the small lawn at his house. It had always been his grandfather's job, even after he had replaced their old push mower with a small electric model that could have been easily managed by his wife. Mowing the lawn took on an almost religious significance for the old man; the lawn was ritually cut on a Sunday afternoon during the growing season, and the finished product was a picture of precisely defined stripes, which were a great source of satisfaction to him. If, heaven forbid, the weather was not conducive to grass cutting on the said day, it had the effect of throwing the whole week's timetable off kilter. For Terry, the smell of grass being cut always took him back to those warm Sunday afternoons, which invariably ended with a plated ham salad for tea with hard-boiled eggs and salad cream. Terry's reminiscences were disturbed by his friend's question.

"Any news of Lizzie yet?"

"No. I keep dropping in to see Lenin in case she has been down there, but there's no news at all. I really think she is avoiding seeing me, and that surprises me a little. It's just not like her. She's always been one for facing up to situations, dealing with things and then moving on, but this time she seems reluctant to meet to try and sort it out."

"Perhaps she's been even more tied up in her work than usual," suggested Lord. "Remember the time she was drafted in with a team of colleagues to offer counselling support after the stabbing incident in that school; she was gone for days, and she was straight into another case when she got back. She often didn't have any time to relax between cases."

"Yes, I know. Last time I saw her she was rushing off to a case that appeared to be going pear-shaped, but she said she'd get back to me, and that was a week ago. Since then, I haven't had any contact with her. She always kept me informed about her whereabouts even when she couldn't discuss what was going on."

"I'm sure she will be in contact soon. Have you thought about phoning her?"

"That's not easy. Her mobile phone is one for work, and I don't have her number, and I don't have a number for Veronica – the girl she is staying with."

"Why don't you just pop round to her new digs on the off chance of seeing her?" suggested Lord.

"Veronica and I don't get on that well, so I don't want to risk going round if she's there. I think I'll give Lizzie a bit more time before I do anything else."

"You know what's best for you," commented the old man, "but don't leave it too long."

The couple sat for a while longer, watching the gardener as he continued his purposeful marching back and forth across the lawn. The day had assumed a warm, still quality, just like summer days are supposed to be, and Terry found himself thinking what it must have been like in Tranby Lodge when the original family who owned it had been there. There were still a number of old framed photographs in the reception hall showing the house as it was in Edwardian days. The pictures were full of smartly dressed people standing in formal groups, having their opulence recorded for others to see and envy. There were even photographs of the staff, no doubt to show how wealthy the owners were rather than to act as personal mementoes for the servants. Horses seemed to figure frequently in the photographs with proud men sitting on them while a groom held the reins and a couple of dogs sat obediently beside them on the wide expanse of drive in front of the house. The modern equivalent would have shown some proud individual standing beside their new luxury car; plus ca change!

"There is something you could do for me, Terry," said the older man, abruptly breaking into Terry's day dreaming, "It's Mary's birthday next week, and I wondered if you could drive me over to Barton Saint Martin to visit the grave?"

"Of course. What day is it?"

"Wednesday. It doesn't matter what time of day; you can fit it in after work. If it proves difficult, then someone from Tranby will be able to take me. They are very helpful, but they tend to be bloody miserable on such occasions, and I think they expect me to stand about weeping. One of them offered to say a prayer last year, and they talked to the grave as though Mary was down there listening. I don't mind people having their religious views; it's a great comfort to some people to think their loved one is waiting somewhere so they can be reunited and live happily ever after. Mary is dead. I know she's dead, and by now she's no doubt worked out that she's dead in that she's not hanging around for me somewhere. She had her faith, and it helped her when she was alive. She enjoyed meeting up with her friends from church, and she was adamant that she wanted to be buried back in her home village in a grave that would later accommodate both of us. That's what she wanted, and it didn't put me out to carry out her request. They can plant me in a church yard if that's what Mary wanted, but I don't harbour any illusions about her being down there waiting for me. I don't expect any grand day of resurrection when Mary and I will pop up and walk off hand in hand. It's an attractive proposition, and if it gives comfort to people, then good luck to them, but it's not going to happen."

"Wednesday after work is fine by me," said Terry, in an attempt to move the conversation quickly away from what he thought was showing signs of Lord's obsession with mortality. "I can pick you up at about 5.30, and afterwards we can stop off somewhere for a bit of something to eat and a pint?"

"That's very kind, Terry; we might as well make it a bit of a trip out. I'll look forward to it."

For a while, the two men looked out on to the lawn as the gardener finished off the last few stripes of the lawn before chugging off to park up the mower. Terry became aware of a niggling feeling that young men of his age shouldn't spend time staring silently out on to the garden. That was a pastime for older men, but he didn't care. He liked spending time with Lord, so the two of them just sat and shared their lazy afternoon.

"Your grandparents never expressed any wish to be planted together, did they, Terry?" asked Lord.

"No," replied Terry, who was a little surprised to hear that his friend's thoughts were still on the subject. "Grandad never gave any specific instructions, so when he died his ashes were scattered in the gardens of the crematorium, and Gran never expressed any wishes to the contrary, so we just put her ashes in the same place. They were never a close couple, but I guess they are now."

"Your grandparents were never one's to be carried away by romantic notions of spending eternity together; they were both far more occupied with getting their earthly affairs in order. They were intent upon ensuring that you were the sole beneficiary in their wills, and so they concentrated on that rather than what was to happen to their own mortal remains."

"They always said that I would inherit, despite my arguments with them about my mother's position. I always felt that the bulk should go to her, but Grandad was adamant; he was very scathing about the way he felt my mother had run away from her responsibilities and had thus forfeited any right to inheriting 'family money'. After he died, I had hoped that Gran would have been persuaded to consider making provision in her will for her daughter, but she was not to be swayed."

"Bless her, your grandmother was never one for thinking for herself. She was only ever going to carry out your grandfather's wishes," observed Lord before continuing, "But I'm sure that Janice would not have been concerned about her lost inheritance."

The mention of his mother caused Terry's thoughts to return to what might have happened to her; she had put in a fleeting visit to her father's funeral, but there had been no sign of her at her mother's.

Perhaps Janice was no longer alive? No, he still received Christmas cards, so someone was sending them. Terry tried to calculate when his mother had last been in touch but could remember few contacts after his grandfather's funeral.

"I don't think I've heard from my mother more than a couple of times since Grandad's funeral, apart from the usual Christmas cards and vouchers, and she never gives a return address. When was the last time you had any communication from her, Lord?"

"It wasn't long after your grandfather died. We had a couple of postcards from France. Basically, the first one was to say how glad she'd been to see us at the funeral, and later she wrote to say we must keep in touch! It's amazing how many people vow to keep in touch with each other; they do so in good faith, but then the years slip by and people forget."

"So was she on holiday in France?"

"There was little by way of information on the card, but I'm pretty sure that it wasn't the usual 'wish you were here' sort of message. I got the impression she might have been living over there."

"And do you remember where in France the cards were from?"

"No, sorry, Terry, and as I said before, when I moved here I threw out all my old correspondence. I seem to recall that the cards had pictures of a town by the sea because I remember Mary saying how blue the water was. That's not exactly a lot of help, is it?"

Terry smiled weakly before replying, "Never mind. So my mother might or might not have spent time living by the sea in France, and even if she did, she might have moved on. I guess I've just got to accept the fact that I have no idea where she is."

CHAPTER ELEVEN

Terry was at the auction house promptly at half past eight on Monday morning. His plan to stop on the way to have a bacon sandwich for his breakfast had been thwarted by the fact that Lenin's mobile diner had been mobile to the point of disappearing completely from the first two of the regular sites that Terry had tried. By this time, he decided that he had better just forget it and get to work, so he was most grateful when Colin made them both a cup of coffee and opened a packet of digestive biscuits. As Terry sat with this welcome sustenance, his older workmate outlined the day's agenda.

"Apart from the usual calculating of Saturday's proceedings and sending out account details, the boss has asked if you could have a look at that blessed computer programme that's going to make all our lives so much easier," concluded the old man with more than a suggestion of sarcasm in his voice.

"I'll have a look at it. Most of these things are easy when you get the hang of them, but it can take hours to read through even the simplest of instruction manuals. So what do you want me to start on first?"

Colin was about to get down to the essentials when Julie arrived. She looked as good as ever, smartly dressed, not a hair out of place, as if she had just finished a photo shoot for some glossy magazine.

"Sorry I'm late, guys, I had to stop off at the post office for some stamps. I'd love a coffee if there's one going," she said before adding, "I got caught up in traffic. I feel quite flustered."

Terry could only marvel at the relative serenity of her 'flustered' state. He had convinced himself that Julie was never anything less than perfectly poised, the sort of person who could get up in the middle of the night to visit the bathroom and see themselves in the mirror without being shocked by their dishevelled image.

Terry spent most of the morning trying to make sense of the thick user's manual that had come with the computer programme, and by the time Julie turned up to ask if he wanted a coffee, he felt he was just about starting to figure out how it worked. By way of a test run, he asked her to enter some of the information about recent sales, knowing that her typing skills would enable her to do so much more efficiently than he could. Terry then methodically entered information about the current rate of VAT and the premiums paid by buyers and sellers before triumphantly announcing, "Voila!"

"So how does it work?" asked Julie, leaning over to get a better view of the computer screen.

"Having entered the information in particular fields, it is simply a matter of asking the computer to give you the combination of bits of data you want back. For example, each seller has their code number, and the computer can pick out all the items sold on behalf of that client and calculate the total amount of money they need to receive after all relevant deductions. It can also calculate the tax to pay.

It can work the same with buyers. In computer terms, it is very simple."

"I see," said Julie. "So let's suppose I wanted to find out how Stan Green had got on with his items in the last sale, how would I do that?"

"Type in his seller's code. What was it, by the way?"

"10 dash 667," replied Julie, reading the code from her sales sheets.

"10 dash 667," repeated Terry as he laboriously typed in the code. "And then we press thus, and there's your answer."

"Impressive!" exclaimed Julie. "But there is one small point; according to your screen display, Stan sold three items for a total of just over four hundred pounds and ended up having to pay over a thousand pounds in commission. I can't see him being too pleased about that."

"You're right," agreed Terry. "Stan is the sort to spot a little error like that, now let me see, yes! Some idiot, and you're looking at him now, has only gone and entered the decimal point in the wrong place for calculating our commission. Now, if I rectify that little glitch and run another calculation, we find that Stan should have received that much," explained Terry, pointing to the screen.

"Seems about right," commented Julie. "It does look quite simple when you get the hang of it."

"Yes, and if you correctly enter all the data about the sales, you can get all sorts of information out of the system, and if the rate of commission or tax ever change, you can simply change the percentage at the press of a button," added Terry who had even impressed himself with the efficiency of the programme.

Their conversation was interrupted by the arrival of Colin, who announced, "I've just had the boss on the phone, and he wants the pair of you to go and visit a Mr Bolton in Swanland. It appears the gentleman is acting on behalf of himself and his brother who have just inherited their aunt's house, and they want to look into the possibility of putting the contents up for auction. The boss would normally do such interviews himself, but it appears that Mrs Spivey has decided that his day would be better spent taking her shopping in York."

Terry knew that Julie had accompanied Mr Spivey on such visits in the past but still felt sufficiently unsure of the situation, so he suggested, "Wouldn't it be better to leave it until John gets back? After all, I haven't dealt with this sort of thing before."

"The boss has assured Mr Bolton that someone would be there at 12.30 today and anyway it's not difficult, just give him an outline as to how the sales work and answer any general questions about the valuation of any items you feel confident to comment on. The address is here," added Colin as he handed Terry a piece of notepaper.

"It will be easy," reassured Julie. "It's not as if you are expected to give an exact valuation on every item in the house; it's more a case of establishing if it's worth us putting them through our auction."

Terry was not absolutely convinced, but he knew that with Julie he would have a very competent partner, so they collected the appropriate paperwork and set out in Terry's car for the address in Swanland.

The property in Swanland was an impressive, detached building, which Terry estimated to have been built sometime between the wars, and both he and Julie commented on the fact that there were likely to be some good quality items inside. When Mr Bolton answered the door, his appearance seemed strangely at odds with such a property; it wasn't that he was scruffily dressed or unclean, but the man and the house did not match up.

"Good afternoon, I'm Terry Henderson, and this is my colleague, Miss Redknap. We represent Spivey's Auctioneers, and we've come to do the valuation you requested."

"Hello, I'm Jim Bolton, the part owner of this house. Come in, I'm sure you are keen to see the quality stuff in here. We can start in the hall. Pretty impressive, eh? Our aunt used to like surrounding herself with good stuff. You can see that all around you."

Terry cast his eye around the hallway, but before he could start to make any sort of tentative valuation, Mr Bolton had ushered the party into the lounge.

"Look at the three-piece suite, so comfortable and not a mark on it. Auntie never had pets or children so she could keep her things looking nice. The television is absolutely top quality and just look at the fine table lamps. Auntie must have spent thousands on this room alone, and the whole house is like this, three bedrooms, all done out with the same top-end products. Auntie was the one in the family who made a success of life, and she lived in style. Look at those pictures on the wall there; they must have cost her thousands with those fancy frames. Look at the coffee table, no scuff marks on that, she really looked after her things. That grandfather clock has been in the family for years; I can remember when it used to chime, probably needs tweaking, but it still keeps quite good time, and the wall clock there is a gem, perfect time-keeper and that chimes on the hour. Yes, auntie had some quality stuff, but we can't let ourselves be sentimental; it all has to go."

Terry glanced at Julie. It was obvious that both of them were reeling as a consequence of this verbal onslaught about the obvious value of the contents as viewed by Mr Bolton.

"It's a fine house," ventured Terry when he had a chance to get a word in, "and it's obvious that your aunt had good taste."

"And good taste always demands good prices," asserted Mr Bolton. "Auntie must have spent over ten thousand pounds fitting out the lounge alone. And money well spent! Bless her, she never indulged in expensive holidays, just put all her money in to the house, and it shows."

Terry was becoming increasingly concerned that Mr Bolton expected to get a lot more from the contents of the house than was realistic, so he was relieved when Julie commented, "I can see she spent a lot of time and money on creating a beautiful home, and it seems cruel that some of the items would not now sell at a price that reflected their original cost."

"But they're quality; you get what you pay for," objected the owner. "She would never buy tat."

"I can see that," commented Terry as he took up Julie's theme. "But even quality items don't necessarily hold their price."

"Quality is quality," asserted Mr Bolton with more than a suggestion of irritation in his voice. "Take the old grandfather clock there; I've seen clocks like that in antique shops where they are asking six thousand pounds and for clocks that don't look as good as ours, so I should expect to make at least six thousand for that one. How much do you think you would make in auction on it for us?"

Terry had been afraid that he might be put on the spot in this way, so he was careful about his answer.

"I'm not a clock expert, and even if I were, I could only give you a general idea of what the clock might make in auction. In an auction, an item makes as much as the customers are prepared to bid for it. If you have any doubts about the suggested auction value, then we would strongly recommend that you contact a specialist clock seller and negotiate a private sale."

"So what would you offer me on that clock?" asked the owner.

"We don't offer a price in that way," explained Terry. "We can carry out an extensive audit of the items you wish to sell and, if you wish, we can arrange for you to have our estimate as to what each item is likely to make in auction. I must stress that the price guidelines we suggest are based on our experience as to what similar items have realised in the past, but the price achieved in auction is entirely dependent on how many people at the auction want the item and how much they are prepared to pay."

"So you can't tell me how much I'd get for…" Mr Bolton paused as his eyes scanned the room before settling on a small side table. "For that antique table there."

Terry walked over, briefly looked at the object in question and then suggested, "Between sixty and eighty pounds."

"What? As little as sixty pounds? I know for a fact that table came from my grandmother's house. It's at least two hundred years old. If you bought a new table like that, you wouldn't get change from two hundred quid," asserted the indignant owner.

"You're absolutely right," interjected Julie. "And a modern table with that degree of workmanship would probably cost far more, but we have to base our estimate on how such items have sold in the recent past, and the fact is that we sell tables like that at every auction, and they tend to make between sixty and eighty. If you're lucky and two people really like the table for some reason, you might make as much as a hundred or even a hundred and twenty, but if nobody wants it on the day, then you might be lucky to make twenty, if it sells at all."

Jim Bolton was quiet for a while as he took in the facts. He gazed round the room and then after a while concluded, "So you can't actually tell me what we'll make on all this?"

"We can give you an estimate based on our extensive experience of recent sales," suggested Terry. "But you might want to get specialist advice on the clock, for example. It is only fair to point out that you are extremely unlikely to get back anything like the prices your aunt paid for some of these pieces. Quality as they obviously are, you have to remember that they are now second hand."

"But she bought such lovely stuff," protested Mr Bolton. "It's not fair to sell all this and to make such a loss."

"I think you are absolutely right," agreed Julie. "But I'm afraid that the only way you would get the benefit of all these lovely items would be for you and or your brother to just move in and live here."

"There's no way we could live under one roof, and neither of us could afford to buy the other out, so I guess we have to sell up the contents; just get shut of the lot."

"If that is your decision and you want us to handle the clearance, then we would be pleased to carry out the work for you," offered Julie. "We can arrange for a detailed audit of all the items you want to sell and arrange any reserve prices you want to put on specific lots."

"I don't want to keep anything, sell the lot."

"Very well. I'll draw up an agreement and get it to you, and we'll try and sort the whole thing out as quickly as possible for you," said Julie as she moved into efficiency mode.

As they were getting into the car, Terry couldn't resist a last look back at the house, an impressive building that had been a very well-appointed home.

"It seemed such a shame to disillusion him," started Terry. "Such a lovely home, but he won't get a fraction of the money that was spent in creating it, and he had some pretty inflated notions about the price of some of the so-called antiques. I have no doubt that he puts a high value on the items, but it doesn't reflect their financial value."

"I know what you mean, but the truth had to be pointed out, and it's better to have it made clear now than having to deal with him as an irate client after the sale when the lots don't make the tens of thousands that he expects. Anyway, we all have to learn to take life's disappointments."

"Too true, Julie, too true."

Terry had planned to drive straight back to the auction room offices, but on the way he had one of his rare impetuous moments. They were driving past the Barge Inn when he suddenly indicated and turned into the car park.

"What the hell, Julie! We haven't had any lunch. Why don't we pop in here and grab a sandwich and a coffee?"

"Good idea," replied his friend. "I must admit it's not like you to suddenly have these wild moments, but after the potential business we've arranged this morning, I'm sure Mr Spivey won't object to us eating here rather than grabbing a quick sandwich and eating it back at the office."

CHAPTER TWELVE

The pub was rather busier than Terry had expected, but most of the customers appeared to have chosen to sit out in the dining area. Terry perused the menu with Julie, and having ordered their sandwiches and coffees, he guided her to what was the regular spot he habitually shared with Lord.

"I haven't been in here for years," commented Julie as she stared around the room, "but it doesn't seem to have changed at all. I used to come in here with Brian – my partner – but he's now dead keen on saving up for us to get married, so we don't go out as often. Are you still with Lizzie?"

The sudden mention of Lizzie took him a bit by surprise, and he asked, "How did you know about her?"

"We went to school together, and I've often seen you out with her. Well, when I say I went to school with her, what I ought to say is that we went to the same school. She was a couple of years older than me, so in the general run of things, we didn't mix much. It wasn't cool to socialise with girls who weren't in your year group, particularly younger ones, but Lizzie was always very kind. She was always a caring sort of person. I assume that's why she went into social work."

"I suppose so," offered Terry. "But to get back to your original question, I'm not with Lizzie anymore."

"Surely not? You always seemed so good together, a natural couple. People don't need to wear matching anoraks for it to be obvious that they just suit each other."

"A lot of people seemed surprised when she left me, not least of all me, but obviously we were all wrong."

"I'm so sorry to hear that," commiserated Julie with obvious sincerity.

Terry was waiting for her to delve more deeply into his loss, but Julie knew better than to stir up more pain for him and carefully attempted to change the direction of the conversation.

"So why did you decide to come into the auction lark? Obviously, I've seen you as a punter at a number of sales, but I never expected to see you on our side of the counter."

"My former employer decided to release me, and Mr Spivey had offered me some part-time work in the past, so when he asked me this time, I decided to take the opportunity. I've always half hoped to go into the business, but I guess I needed the extra nudge that unemployment offered."

As he said this, a slight smile spread over his face, prompting Julie to ask, "What's so funny?"

"It's just that when I told Lizzie about leaving my last job, she tried to console me by saying it was an opportunity to try something new, and I'm beginning to think she may have been right."

Terry enjoyed their brief lunch break; Julie was good company, the sandwiches were more than welcome, and all this was happening in his local pub, where some of the locals were obviously making up their own minds about his relationship with such an attractive young woman.

Back at the auction rooms, Terry settled down to learning the routines of his job. After years in a job where he knew everything there was to be known about his work, he found it quite taxing in such a novel environment. He no longer had the familiarity of routine and had to think everything through.

By the time he arrived home that evening, he was very tired, but he had convinced himself that this was to be expected when starting a new job; it had to get easier. He toyed with the idea of going out to see if he could find Lenin, with just a slim chance of hearing about Lizzie, but he just could not be bothered, so he made himself a sandwich, opened a bottle of beer and took his dinner out to the garden.

Sitting on the patio, he soon finished off his sandwich and sat quietly with his bottle of beer. It had been a very full day, but his mind kept returning to his late lunch with Julie. He had enjoyed himself, Julie was good company, and he kept coming back to the almost guilty feeling of pleasure he had experienced in being seen with her by the locals. No doubt there would be rumours among them, completely unfounded, but that wasn't going to get in the way of a good rumour. Terry knew that the next time he went into the pub with Lord, there would be references made to the visit with Julie. No doubt by then the reported story would have developed to the point where Terry had been ostentatiously flirting, almost to the point of indecency, with a mysterious blond. Terry smiled at the thought, finished the last of his beer and went into the house to avoid the attentions of a small flight of midges.

The next day at work was hectic, but the staff worked well together and generally had a lot of fun. The boss seemed pleased with Terry and Julie's report of their visit to Mr Bolton in Swanland, and it was with a sense of satisfaction that Terry set off to drive home that evening, so he decided to celebrate his day by eating out at Lenin's. Terry's feeling of well-being increased when he found the café on one of Lenin's better sites with a fine view out over the river.

"Evening, comrade," came the routine greeting. "And where were you last night?"

Terry was a little taken back by the sudden questioning but managed to reply, "At home, with a cold beer and a sandwich, why?"

"All these times you've been asking after Lizzie, pestering me for information, and then she turns up when you're not here."

"She was here last night?" asked Terry with more than a hint of disappointment in his voice.

"Yes, comrade, her and that Veronica woman she hangs around with."

"So how is she? Did she ask about me?"

"She didn't say much at all, but Veronica more than made up for it, and you were her sole subject of conversation."

"Me? Why was she so interested in me? It's no secret that we've never got on."

"That was more than obvious from what she had to say about what you'd been up to."

"What the hell are you on about, Lenin? I hardly know Veronica; I didn't have to know her that well to realise that I didn't like her, but I've never knowingly done anything to upset her. What's she been saying about me?"

"She spent most of the time here talking about having seen you and a woman cavorting in the Barge yesterday lunchtime."

"Cavorting? Me? A person less inclined to cavort never drew breath. I was having a quick sandwich with a colleague, and she's not renowned for being a cavorter either."

"Veronica took great delight in telling me all about it. She had obviously already told Lizzie, and she was taking the meeting with me as an opportunity to repeat the story in front of her. She's a nasty piece of work that Veronica, making lots of digs about the way you were hiding in the bar with your new woman."

"Hiding? I was in my usual seat in the bar where Lord and I always eat when we go in there. I suppose Veronica was in the dining room at the back. It's strange I never saw her, or at least heard her cackle. I bet she's embellished the story more than a little by now."

A sudden thought struck Terry, which prompted him to ask, "And how did Lizzie seem to respond to the news of my lunchtime liaison?"

"She was fine, a bit on the quiet side, but she wasn't showing any of the vitriol that Veronica was trying to promote," answered Lenin as he poured a cup of tea before continuing, "But if you will go off to these posh places for lunch."

"We were rushing back to work and happened to pass the Barge; if we'd decided to dine chez Lenin, it could have been late evening before we even found you."

"Good point, comrade, you're forgiven."

Terry resisted the temptation to respond, but after a while he tried once again to get some information from the café owner.

"Didn't Lizzie mention me at all? No asking after how I'd been or anything?"

"She was lucky to get a word in edgewise, the way Veronica was dishing out the venom. She really has it in for you, squire. Come the revolution, and her sort will have to go. Lizzie did ask if you'd been round to sample the delights of my emporium. She didn't appear to have changed much at all, though she didn't seem to be quite her usual perky self. Even so, she was still the same sweet Lizzie. She did ask if I'd seen you and how you had been keeping, but every time she made an attempt to make polite enquiries, her evil-tongued friend piped up with some spiteful comment. Lizzie was getting quite annoyed at one point, and I thought she was going to tell Veronica where to get off, but her friend would always back off a bit when she knew she'd over-stepped the mark."

"It must be complicated when you are staying with a friend; if you want to say something that might cause a row, you have to remember that you are living under their roof."

"I saw little sign of domestic harmony in that couple," observed Lenin. "And I can't see the relationship working for long. What does she see in the malicious cow? They are just so unlike each other."

"They have known each other for years, but I never saw the attraction in Veronica. She's the kind of woman you can justifiably take an instant disliking to, if only because it saves time. I've never knowingly done anything to upset her. Perhaps she's jealous that Lizzie chose to spend time with me?"

Terry sat for a while, sipping his mug of tea and trying to remember if he had done anything to annoy Veronica in the past. He had a vague recollection that she had once shown some interest in going out with him while he was at school, but he had shown no interest in her. This was largely due to the fact that his grandfather had insisted that it was the wrong time for the young Terry to be involved in 'that sort of thing', but the other factor was that he had never really liked her. Perhaps she had felt spurned and intent upon getting her own back later? While Terry was deep in thought, Lenin was busily serving a couple who had turned up at the mobile café. Other people were visiting the café this evening, but there was no Lizzie. It reflected his current run of bad luck in that on one of the rare days he didn't visit the café he had missed Lizzie. He felt a little reassured to hear that she was still in the area, and he knew that he would have a chance of meeting her at some time, but he also realised that visiting her at Veronica's place was not going to work if Veronica was around.

It was a beautiful evening; the intense heat of the day had been mollified by a cooling breeze. Sitting there and enjoying the view out over the river and to Lincolnshire beyond would have been quite idyllic, with the right company. He had to arrange a way of meeting Lizzie, but he couldn't think how he would be able to do it. He couldn't predict where she would be at any particular time, so it wouldn't be easy to 'accidentally' meet her, and even such a meeting might be fruitless if Veronica was around.

Lenin was busily cooking up some bacon to make one of his famous sandwiches for a recent arrival at the café.

The smell would usually have been enough to persuade Terry to order one for himself, but this evening he had little appetite, so he finished his tea, waved farewell to Lenin and went home to his lonely house.

CHAPTER THIRTEEN

The following day at the auction house offered little time to dwell on his situation, so Terry got stuck into his work and tried to forget how much he missed Lizzie. He consoled himself with the fact that he and Lord were going out for a pub meal somewhere that evening after visiting Mary's grave in Barton Saint Martin.

While he was going over the new computerised sales system with Julie, he couldn't resist the temptation to remark, "According to the local gossip, we evidently shared a quiet romantic lunchtime liaison at the pub yesterday."

Julie laughed before replying, "I suppose it was to be expected. Some people can't resist the temptation to embellish their accounts of things they've seen; it's symptomatic of the small-town mentality. So who did you get the news from?"

"It appears that Lizzie's evil-mouthed friend Veronica saw us, and she has taken the greatest delight in portraying me in the dimmest possible light. I was at the mobile café down by the bridge last night, and Lenin told me that Veronica and Lizzie had been there the previous evening when Veronica had recounted her version of what had happened at the pub."

"But surely Lizzie knows you well enough to realise that it was an innocent pub lunch?" asked Julie before adding, "She certainly never struck me as the sort to be swayed by such stories."

"Of course Lizzie wouldn't suspect anything, but then we are sort of separated. Perhaps she thought I was setting myself up in a new relationship, and Veronica is a vindictive little piece of work, and I'm sure her persistent snide comments could sow some seeds of doubt."

Terry derived some small comfort from Julie's reassurances, but he still felt he could have done without Veronica's input. He knew he had a difficult task trying to patch things up with Lizzie, and anything that complicated matters was most unwelcome. Nevertheless, Julie's attitude went some way to improving Terry's mood, and by the time he left work that evening he was feeling a bit more positive. For a while, he even toyed with the thought that it might be a good idea if Lizzie was a little bit jealous. Perhaps that would make her realise just what she was missing? It was a consideration that did not occupy his mind for long; Lizzie was not the sort to be swayed by a moment's capricious jealousy. She and Terry had enjoyed a good relationship, so she must have thought long and hard before she had chosen to end it, and if he was to stand any chance of getting back together with her, he had to figure out why she had acted in such a way. These thoughts were still preoccupying Terry as he drove up to Tranby Manor, where he found Lord sitting on a garden bench outside the front door.

"Good evening, young man, right on time as usual," greeted Lord as he picked up a small bunch of flowers from beside him on the bench and moved towards the car, adding, "Let's get away quickly before the camp commandant realises I've liberated some of the flowers from the garden."

"Nice flowers," observed Terry. "And I'm sure they wouldn't begrudge you a few roses, given the fees you pay there."

"They were one of Mary's favourites. I always grew roses in the garden so she could have a few in the house. She had that special skill of taking a random bunch of flowers and greenery and producing an arrangement that made any room look lovely. I just thought it would be nice to take her a few this evening."

Terry drove off, but after a while he couldn't resist asking, "I don't want to pry, but, well, you've always made it perfectly clear that you understand Mary is dead. I mean dead, not just 'passed over' but dead. You say your Mary is not there, but you're visiting her and taking flowers. She's not going to know you're there, and she won't appreciate the roses, so why do you want to do it?"

A smile spread across the old man's face, and he paused for a while before replying, "You're absolutely right, old boy. Mary is in no state to appreciate my visit or the flowers, but she would have wanted me to go, and she would have wanted the roses. So you see, by honouring her wishes, I keep the memories of her alive. No one is dead as long as they live in the memories of others, and I will never forget her."

The couple drove on, over the Humber Bridge and into Lincolnshire. Terry had been over a few times, but he knew little of the small villages in the area; he usually used the bridge on his way down to Lincoln or some of the antique fairs and auctions. He knew where Barton Saint Martin was as he had frequently seen road signs for the place as he sped through on his way south, but he couldn't remember ever having been there. He had heard of it from Lord, who had pointed out the general location one evening when Lenin's café had occupied a prime spot near the river bank.

"You will have to give me directions as we get closer," prompted Terry as he took the minor road that was signposted towards the village.

"Just carry straight on until you come to the Fickle Fox, and then turn sharp right along the narrow road immediately beyond the pub. It looks as though it only goes to the pub car park, but carry on straight past the pub for about a hundred yards, and you come to the church car park."

Terry was rather disappointed to find that Barton Saint Martin was not a typical rustic village with a well-defined centre but more of a sprawling hamlet. Most of the houses were pan-tiled red brick terraces of what were presumably the former homes of farm workers. Here and there the odd modern bungalow had been constructed, and they stood there somewhat incongruously with their large plate glass windows, wide driveways and manicured lawns. Eventually, Terry spotted the sign outside the pub, and he slowed down. The Fickle Fox was the end building of a small terrace of cottages, and as he approached he indicated his intention to turn right. Lord's directions had been accurate, and Terry drove past the pub and its car park onto what was little more than a track which he had travelled down for some 50 yards before he rounded a slight bend and caught sight of the church for the first time.

"I'd never have thought there was a church down here," commented Terry. "You can't see anything of it until you get here."

"No, it's a well-kept secret, not exactly an architectural gem but quiet, just like a village church should be."

The track widened out and terminated just before the church in a small space that offered barely enough room for a couple of cars to park. Terry tucked the car away in a corner and switched off the engine. The relative quiet of the countryside invaded the car, and for a moment the two men sat in silence.

"It's a lovely spot," observed Terry before asking, "I assume the car will be OK here?"

"Fine; we seem to have missed the crowds," added Lord dryly.

The two men got out of the car, and Terry resisted the temptation to lock it. There was no elaborate carved lychgate, and the car park was separated from the church only by a simple wire fence in which was set a basic wooden gate. The men followed the path that led up to the church, and then

Lord gestured that they should walk around to the north of the building. The graveyard was bigger than Terry had expected for such a small village, and he stood for a moment looking at the scene and sharing its tranquillity. Lord had set off down one of the small paths that ran between the rows of graves, and about 50 yards from the church, he stopped by one plot. The old man smiled as Terry re-joined him and pointed at Mary's grave.

"That's it," said Lord. "My Mary's little bit of the village."

The two stood for a moment in natural reverence, and Terry read the inscription to himself. Apart from the usual details offering her dates of birth and death was a simple line that Terry could not help but read out aloud, "Ever yours, Lord."

He looked up at his friend, who smiled mischievously and then commented, "Few people will understand the ambiguity of that statement, but it is exactly what she wanted."

"I'm sure it was; one way or the other!" observed Terry before suggesting, "I'll leave you here for a moment while I have a browse around."

Terry walked back towards the church and noticed that the graves nearer the building appeared to be generally older. One small gravestone grabbed Terry's attention, and he carefully brushed away some of the moss so he could read the inscription.

Here rests Michael Lampeter Hodge
1889-1919
Also his loving wife Mary Victoria Hodge
1888-1917
And their son George Lampeter Hodge
1915-1917
Together at last in the arms of the Lord

Terry instantly recognised the name as that of the individual he had met on the bridge, and it occurred to him that this grave must have been where the visitor had got the names he wove into his elaborate story. Obviously, the guy must have been a local to have found the grave tucked away in this remote graveyard. Terry chuckled to himself at the audacity of someone stealing someone else's grave details to concoct a story, but his levity did not last when he calculated that the young couple sharing the grave would only have been about his age when they died.

He read some of the other inscriptions that he could make out and was mildly surprised to see how many of the graves contained children and many, like young George Lampeter, had been buried with relatives and their names tagged on the bottom of the gravestone like some pathetic footnote. Being conscious of the need to leave Lord for a while, Terry wandered around the graveyard until he came to a wooden bench. He was about to sit down when he read the inscription on the back: *Suffer the little children.* As he took his seat and looked in front of him, he saw the significance of the biblical reference. He didn't need to read the inscriptions to know that the graves were those of children and babies. A small number of the graves were adorned by a collection of soft toys, which had presumably been the soother or inseparable friend of some child that had been taken at an indecently young age. Most of the toys showed signs of having spent some time at the mercy of the elements; their faded, bedraggled forms contrasted sharply with the assortment of brightly coloured animals on other graves. The area had a quiet serenity to it, but Terry found the thought of all those little graves rather upsetting.

Rising slowly, like someone discreetly and reverently leaving their pew halfway through a church service, Terry walked off to explore some other area of the graveyard. It struck him that

Lizzie had sometimes had to deal with the aftermath of infant mortality in her work. She rarely spoke of it, but he knew that it was one of those areas of her job that caused her particular distress. Poor Lizzie often had to deal with the less attractive consequences of the personal tragedies that entered the lives of others. When Terry had worked in the stores at Enderby's, at the end of every shift, he left all thoughts of his work with his overall in the depot. Lizzie was always trying hard to make sure she didn't bring her work home, but it is easier to declare this as a goal than to achieve it. The very nature of Lizzie's role meant that she could be called out at just about any time, so 'switching off' was doubly difficult. His mind returned to the conversation with Lenin about her longing to get a break from work. Terry was conscious of the feeling that perhaps he ought to have shown more understanding of Lizzie's feelings before the break-up. He came to the conclusion that it was something to do with the nature of graveyards that promoted such reflection.

Terry looked back over the graves where he could still see Lord. His old friend was showing no signs of wanting to leave, so Terry sauntered off to explore another area of the graveyard. As he walked, he idly picked out some of the names on the graves. Certain surnames appeared regularly, indicating that some of the families had been living and dying in the village for over three hundred years. It was difficult to ignore one of the family graves that was surmounted by an ostentatious statue of a winged angel looking down at a marble plaque upon which was emblazoned what was presumably a family coat of arms. Out of curiosity, Terry read the names of some of those recorded on the monument. It appeared that the family name was Pearson, and many of their individual names were followed by strange concoctions of letters that presumably indicated titles they had held. Terry didn't recognise the family name and knew even less about the rank or status inferred in the letters after their names; all he did know was that they were dead. The evidence of the gravestones indicated the occupants may have had very different lives, but beneath the ground the incumbents shared the ultimate equality, and Terry found himself reciting the words of a poem that he had learned at school.

Sceptre and crown
Must tumble down
And in the dust be equal made
With the poor crooked scythe and spade.

When he had finished, he sheepishly looked around to see if anyone might have overheard him, but fortunately there was no one near. Terry followed the path round by the side of the church and wandered into the porch, where he found a board festooned with notices. He stood for a while looking at this array of information, most of which, fastened up with rusting pins, appeared to have been there for some years and gave information about service times, the name and address of the vicar and sexton and all such details that an inquisitive parishioner might need. Among these antiquities stood out a brightly coloured and laminated sheet offering details of the mothers and toddlers group that was evidently held at the church and another professionally produced poster seeking donations to support a child in some African village. Out of curiosity, Terry tried turning the large cast iron ring on the door, and to his surprise, it opened easily and he tentatively stepped inside. He had expected it to be dark and gloomy, but the sunlight streamed in through the windows, and the pale stone walls appeared to bounce the light back into the building. Behind the back pew were several hymn books waiting patiently in a row to be doled out at the next service. Terry wondered when the books would be needed next; the general air of the building suggested that the church was no longer in regular use, but a selection of flowers in a brass vase by the pulpit and a subtle scent of furniture polish indicated that someone still cared for it. Along the side walls were a few brass plaques that had also been recently polished, and Terry idly wandered over to read what was on them. Once again, there were references to the Pearson family, some of whom had apparently donated various sums of money in the past for the upkeep of their church, while others, as high-ranking officers, had fought and died in the service of their country in a variety of wars and other skirmishes.

It didn't take long for Terry to wander down to the business end of the church, where he looked up at the hymn numbers displayed on faded cards slotted into a simple wooden frame and the large brass eagle that adorned the lectern. Standing behind the lectern, Terry looked at the large bible on it, which was open at the book of Corinthians. He read a few lines but resisted the temptation to address the empty pews, and then he turned to the altar and the stained-glass window above it. He was no expert in stained glass, but he estimated that it would make a lot of money at auction because it 'had some age to it', as they say in the trade, and it had been well executed. For a brief moment, Terry was tempted to make a closer inspection of the window but something stopped him from going up the single step to the altar to get a better view; he wasn't a religious person by any means but it just did not seem right. Turning to the main body of the church, Terry made his way to the back where he had come in. He walked in a leisurely but somehow dignified way as if in procession, and for a brief moment he wondered what it would be like to make this journey as a newly married man with his new wife. At the back of the church, he turned again and looked at the altar with all its implied theatricality. Was this what he would have wanted with Lizzie? He had never thought of the practicality of the wedding arrangements, nor had he ever harboured any romantic fantasy about the day. All he had wanted was to marry her, but somehow he had got it wrong. Feeling somewhat despondent, Terry turned to the door and it was at this point that he saw a large oak collection box adorned by an impressive old padlock. Instinctively, he checked his pockets but found he only had a few pence in loose change, which he methodically fed in one at a time through the slot on top of the box. He felt that he would like to be a bit more generous, but all he had on him now were a number of five pound notes, and donating even one of those would have been more generous than he wished to be, so he vowed that next time he would bring some more appropriate contribution.

Outside the church it was appreciably warmer, and the young man experienced a feeling of general contentment. It was a lovely evening, and he was about to go out for a meal somewhere with his old friend Lord. It was the sight of a few pieces of faded confetti caught in the grass at the side of the path which caused him to revisit his thoughts about what his wedding to Lizzie might have been like. His air of contentment left him, and he started once again to try and figure out why she had behaved so strangely. He ran through the events surrounding her departure, but it still made no sense; everyone said they were an obvious couple, but now they weren't.

Terry was conscious of the fact that he was becoming reflective to the point of becoming morbid, so he wandered over to the fence around the graveyard and, turning his back on the churchyard, he looked out at the landscape beyond. He could see the towers of the bridge in the early evening light. Terry loved this time of year with the long hours of daylight, and he felt content to just stand and gaze out at nothing in particular. This part of the world seemed to have more than its fair share of sky, an impression created by the relative flatness of the land, and this evening the sky was a particularly impressive one without a single cloud and only the benign graffiti of a plane's vapour trail to break it up.

Terry felt that he had probably left Lord for an appropriate length of time, so he wandered back to find him. He approached his friend slowly as he didn't want to interrupt his 'chat' with Mary. On seeing Terry, the older man smiled and then, resting his hand on the top of the gravestone, said, "Bye, old thing," and set off towards the car park.

"I've been very lucky," observed Lord. "Despite spending years fighting a stupid war, I still had the good fortune to have the time to meet up with Mary and have a marvellous marriage." The old man paused, and turning to Terry, he added, "I do hope you manage to settle down and share many years with someone you love."

The pair walked on for a while and Lord continued, "It's not hard to see the attraction of religion at a time like this, Terry. It must be a great comfort to die 'secure in the knowledge' of meeting one's loved ones. I've watched a lot of them at Tranby Manor who become firm believers as their time draws near. Hedging their bets, I suppose. The vicar comes round from time to time and chats with some of the old folk, and I can't get the image out of my head that they are cramming for their finals, but if it makes them feel better, then good luck to them. I know my plot's booked, and not too long from now I will be put in with Mary. After a while the coffin will decay, and our bones will probably intermingle in some macabre embrace, but neither of us will be aware of it."

Terry found his friend's observations mildly disturbing and was pleased when they got back to the car and he could take the opportunity to change the subject.

"I've just seen a grave for a Michael Lampeter Hodge and his family. It's so sad to see a group together like that, and the young couple would only have been my age."

"Young Michael and his family are almost part of the local folklore," recounted Lord. "Parents would recount the story of the young mother drowning with her child as she tried to rescue him from the Humber as a warning to their children to stay away from the river bank. Poor Michael died of grief shortly afterwards, according to the story."

Terry smiled to himself as he thought of the audacity of someone to plagiarise such a tragic story as his mysterious bridge visitor had done.

"So where shall we go for a spot of dinner?" he asked, in a tone that sounded even more upbeat than he had intended, "Does the Fickle Fox do food?"

"They used to, but it's years since I've been in. We could give it a try."

CHAPTER FOURTEEN

The Fickle Fox was one of those rarities, a pub with genuine age to it. Terry couldn't help feeling that it was a bit like walking off the street into someone's small front room. The walls displayed an eclectic mix of prints and yellowing advertising signs for products that Terry doubted even existed anymore. The paintwork on the walls had the genuine patina born of years of cigarette smoke, and the general atmosphere was one of a strangely welcoming threadbare drabness. The couple walked across the carpet square and up to the small bar. The air in the room bore the faint smell of something savoury cooking somewhere, and this smell was reinforced as an elderly woman opened the door from what was obviously the kitchen, allowing even more of the enticing smell to enter the bar.

"And how can I help you, my loves?" asked the old woman with a genuinely welcoming smile.

"Two pints of bitter, please," responded Terry before asking, "That smells good. Are you doing meals tonight?"

"I certainly am, love. I'm doing steak and kidney pie tonight, but it will be another quarter of an hour before it's cooked," she replied as she carefully pulled their pints through the creaking beer pump.

"What do you think, Lord?" asked Terry, turning to his friend.

"That smells like proper steak and kidney, so I think dinner here would suit fine," replied the older man.

"Oh yes," interjected the landlady. "Proper steak and kidney with real pastry done in a proper oven. I don't serve those little golden packets of fat heated up in a microbe oven."

"Great!" said Terry. "Two plates of steak and kidney it is then, please."

The old lady left the men with their pints and dutifully went off to check her kitchen. Terry carried the pints over to a seat in the corner by the window and put them down on the small table.

"Mary and I spent many happy hours in here when we were courting," said Lord with a smile. "The place doesn't seem to have changed a bit."

Terry sipped his beer and looked around the room before commenting, "It's strange to think that I've never been over to this village before. With the bridge, it's not far from home, but by the time you've paid the toll on the bridge, it's hardly worth popping over for a quick pint in the evening."

"True. I spent all those happy times here, but it must be some years ago, 30 at least," said Lord hesitantly before continuing, "No, it must be 40, no, nearer 50. It's strange to think that I can recall things so easily from half a century ago. The village hasn't changed that much and hasn't become too gentrified, although I do think some of those modern bungalows look a bit out of place, but that's just me."

The landlady appeared from the kitchen with an assortment of cutlery and condiments on a tray and set them out on the table in front of the two men. She paused for a moment, looking at Lord before asking, "Aren't you the fella that married Jack Riby's daughter Mary?"

"Indeed I am, but how do you remember me?" asked the older man, who was obviously surprised to be recognised in this way. "I would have thought I'd have changed a bit since then."

"Sorry to disappoint you, you have changed, but we don't see many people called Lord in here, and you look about the right age, so it was a reasonable guess."

"I'm afraid I can't quite place you," added Lord, with a smile. "But I guess you were just a young girl when I left."

The old woman laughed and said, "You flattering old devil. I seem to recall that we were about the same age. I was Jessie Waterford in those days, and I've lived in this village nearly all my life."

"You're not related to Jack Waterford by any chance?"

"He was my dad. Mind you, he fathered a lot of other children in the area, and I'm not sure he owned up to some of them. I had to be so careful about not marrying a half-brother that I ended up marrying a man from Ulceby." The village was emphasised as if it were a continent away rather than just a few miles.

"So who was this Jack Waterford?" asked Terry in an attempt to get himself into the conversation.

"Old Jack Waterford," explained Lord, "was the chap who came round to the pub to dispatch the pigs that the landlord kept in the back garden here. He was a general farm hand who was particularly adept at slaughtering and butchering the odd pig. It wasn't uncommon in those days for people to keep pigs, and then someone like Jack would come round and kill them."

"It was one of my dad's many little sidelines," explained the landlady before adding, "Along with fathering children all over the village. You couldn't slaughter pigs like that anymore. If you wanted to kill animals these days, you'd need enough hygiene certificates to fill a small suitcase and a slaughterhouse at least as clean as an operating theatre. No one ever had any problems with food poisoning, though, and the landlord here at the time was famous for his hams. Many pubs kept a few chickens and grew the odd lot of vegetables round the back; it was the only way to get a living out of some small village pubs." The old woman paused for a moment and then added,

"Well, I can't stop here chatting. I've got a pie to check." With this, she went off to the kitchen, leaving Terry and Lord to take in the rustic calm of the old pub. Terry looked at the assortment of cutlery and condiments that the old lady had set out in front of them. And couldn't help but notice that none of the items appeared to have been made to go together, unlike in most modern corporate eating chains where you can eat with identical cutlery off identical plates no matter where you are in the world.

Both men looked out of the small window onto the street outside. Nothing was happening, and it seemed like their part of the village was asleep, but neither man was bored.

"Have you seen Lizzie yet?" enquired Lord.

"No. Evidently she was at Lenin's place the other night, but I missed her; one of the few nights I hadn't dropped in."

"Shame."

The conversation petered out, but there was no awkward silence, just a general atmosphere of quiet contentment and after a while, Terry asked, "So how are things at Tranby?"

"Much the same, comfortable rather than exciting; nobody has died recently. Things looked like getting interesting on the Crompton stakes front when it seemed that Mrs Swindell was on her way out, but it was a false alarm and there was no payout."

Their domestic meditation was interrupted by the arrival of a third customer, an elderly gentleman in a thick woven tweed jacket wearing a non-matching flat cap, cord trousers and stout working boots. The new arrival seemed surprised to see fellow guests and nodded acknowledgement before shuffling over behind the bar, where he carefully pulled himself a pint and then took it to one of the other tables in the room and sat down.

The three customers sat in comfortable silence, which was only broken by the arrival of the landlady carrying two large plates with more than generous servings of a delicious-smelling meat pie.

"Good afternoon, Jessie," said the most recent arrival with an almost unnatural degree of formality.

"Good afternoon, Herbert," replied the landlady with matching solemnity before setting the plates down on the table in front of Lord and Terry and declaring, "There you are, sirs, proper steak and kidney dinners."

The landlady wandered back to the kitchen, leaving the two diners to admire the culinary delight in front of them. Each plate had a generous segment of pie accompanied by a mound of mashed potato and an assortment of vegetables, all covered in a thick gravy.

"Proper food," observed Lord. "Not like those tiny pieces of decorative art they serve in the Carpenter's Arms; you get an acre of white plate with a cube of meat pie, three slices of carrot, a smear of mashed potato and a drizzle of gravy with the consistency of gnat's piss but without the depth of flavour."

The two men shared a loathing for nouvelle cuisine, which they took as an excuse to serve tiny portions of food to maximise profits.

"Lizzie persuaded me to go to the Carpenter's for her staff Christmas party once. There was nothing wrong with the food, but you felt you needed to stop off for fish and chips on the way home to calm the hunger pangs. And the prices! I could have had a weekend in Bridlington for the price of our meal, and I was still starving! Needless to say, we never went there again."

The two men went on to say little as they sat and enjoyed their meals. Terry was surprised to notice that, for once, Lord had not completely cleared his plate but put it down to the fact that they had been very generous portions, so he refrained from commenting.

"Mary and I used to spend a lot of time in here when we were courting," said Lord with a smile. "The place hasn't changed much over the years, and it even looks like the same cutlery. To think that Jessie is still around! I suppose I should have tried to get back more often, particularly since the bridge was opened, but life has a habit of filling up your spare time. It's not that you don't want to see old friends, you don't want to cut people out of your life, but the present seems to take over. It would appear that in our quest for progress and what tomorrow might bring, we lose sight of how important the past can be."

"I think I see what you mean, Lord," said Terry hesitantly. "I guess my mother didn't consciously want to ignore me, but her new life got in the way."

"Your mum was a good woman, despite any impression you might have got from your grandparents, and I'm sure she would like to get to know you, but you've got to be prepared to start from scratch if you ever meet up."

"But do you really think we will ever meet? I mean, I haven't seen her for years."

"It must be 50 years since I saw Jessie, but we met up. I'm sure your mum will return someday, perhaps not for good, but she will come back. A lot of people may be reluctant to admit it, but they like to return to their roots. Take my Mary, for example. All that time we were away in the wilds of Yorkshire, but she still wanted to be buried in Saint Martin's, so now she's home."

Lord's philosophising was interrupted by the entry of the landlady carrying another plate of meat pie, which she dutifully placed in front of the mysterious Herbert, along with the obligatory non-matching cutlery. No words were exchanged, and the landlady came over to where her new guests were seated.

"Can I get you anything else, loves? Apple pie? Cheesecake? Another drink?" the old lady proffered.

"No, thank you. That was wonderful, but I couldn't manage anything more," replied Terry. Lord signalled his agreement, and the landlady shuffled back to her kitchen.

"Mary and I used to sit in this corner when we came here all those years ago," reminisced the older man. "The last time we came here was shortly after we were married. It was raining, and we had managed to get wet through as we walked over here, but we didn't care. There was a blazing fire in the grate there, and we stood and tried to dry ourselves in front of it, then we sat down over here, still wet, and enjoyed a couple of drinks. There were more people in here then, all of whom are long since dead. Mary and I were the young married couple of the village, and all the others seemed incredibly old to us then." Lord's eyes gazed slowly around the room as if remembering the locals who had been in the pub that night.

"This was a thriving little pub in those days," continued Lord, determined to sound a little more cheerful. "A lot of the agricultural workers dropped in on their way home, and there was a fair amount of bartering went on with assorted produce exchanging hands. All sorts of items were swapped in their respective seasons, jars of home-made pickles or jams, small parcels of fruit or vegetables, ducks or geese that had met their ends while flying over the reed beds, eels from the river and, of course, the occasional bit of game that had mysteriously died at the feet of one of the local countrymen. Jack Waterford had a reputation for being a bit of a poacher, but it was his wife who was the more adept at coming across the odd pheasant. The local constable, Morgan Drinkwater, never seemed to catch the poachers, but he didn't try too hard. If ever there was a man who couldn't live up to his name, it was Big Morgan; I don't think he ever drank water in his life. He was a regular in here, and he knew full well what kind of items were changing hands, but he was a past master at turning a blind eye to anything that he didn't want to know about, and he didn't want to find himself unwelcome in his regular pub by being over-zealous in his police duties. Mind you, it was easy to turn a blind eye when he had been mellowed by a few pints. Morgan would ask for a bottle of stout at the start of the evening, which he would use to mix with his beers throughout his session. He was never drunk, mind, except once after the harvest festival when he was persuaded to try some of Mrs Hawthorne's elderflower champagne. Poor old Morgan had already had a few pints and couldn't see any harm in having a couple of glasses of the 'cordial'. We knew that something had happened when we suddenly found we had a laughing policeman on our hands, and we later calculated that he had consumed nearly a bottle and a half of Mrs Hawthorne's seasonal special. Morgan would always refer to it later as 'firewater', and I don't think he ever tried it again."

"Sounds quite a character," commented Terry.

"Oh, the place was full of characters. Everyone met in the pub or the church. Gamekeeper, poacher, police officer, assorted petty villains and even the local magistrate all seemed to spend some of their time together in either the Fickle Fox or St Martin's, and at Christmas, the regulars at the pub attended the service at the church. That was quite an event with the regular choir members 'assisted' by enthusiastic rather than talented villagers. They were good times, Terry."

Terry was surprised to hear his friend talking about the past in this way because he was generally a man concerned more with the present, but presumably the setting had triggered this flow of memories. He looked at Lord, who was obviously enjoying recalling snippets from the past, and once again he was aware that his friend was not looking as robust as he usually did.

"This is quite a warm spell we're having," observed Terry in an attempt to lift the conversation a bit.

"Yes," replied Lord. "Most unlike this area. It makes a change to be able to plan outings a couple of days in advance without having to make alternative plans in case it rains. I've particularly enjoyed having breakfast out in the garden at Tranby. Got to make the most of it; you never know how long it's going to last. But then, at my age, you have to get the most out of life for the same reason." The last statement was delivered with a little chuckle. There was no trace of melancholy in the old man, no sign of sadness, just a blunt acceptance of the fact that he wasn't going to live forever. The couple chatted on for a while as they finished off their drinks, but their conversation was interrupted by the departure of their fellow customer, Herbert. The latter rose abruptly, bid Terry and Lord a good afternoon and left without making any attempt to pay for his meal or the drink he had helped himself to.

Terry and Lord exchanged looks of confusion, but before they could comment the landlady returned from the kitchen and started to polish some glasses as she stood behind the bar, apparently unaware that one of her customers had gone.

"Excuse me," said Terry, "but I think that man just left without paying."

"Oh, he does that every day," replied the landlady in a matter-of-fact sort of way. "But I don't mind."

Terry couldn't conceal his surprise at this unusual business practice, but before he could comment, the old lady explained, "That's my husband. In all the time I've been running this place, he's refused to be associated with the pub; says it's his Methodist upbringing. He likes to give people the impression that he's just a customer who happens to have popped into the pub. He's quite daft but harmless enough. He lives next door, but I've noticed that his Methodist background doesn't stop him from coming in for dinner and a pint every night. I tell you, they're queer folk in Ulceby."

Terry and Lord sat for a while, with the latter obviously enjoying reminiscing about the way life used to be in the village over half a century back. After a while, the old man looked at his watch before remarking, "Good grief! It's nearly half past nine. It's so easy to lose track of time on these long summer evenings, but I'd better get back to Tranby before they release the guard dogs into the grounds."

CHAPTER FIFTEEN

It was very busy at work the next day, but Terry felt that he was getting into the routines of the auction house. The updated computer system appeared to be working, but Colin still refused to get involved with it. In this way, informal job descriptions were established, with Julie gradually transferring more and more administrative tasks to the computer while Colin and Terry moved the mountains of goods around and helped the boss to put tentative valuations on new lots.

After work, Terry went to try and find where Lenin had parked his mobile café. This was more in the hope of getting news of Lizzie than actually buying a meal, but the nomadic communist was not to be found on the first few sites. Before he went home, Terry decided that he would drop in to see Lord in the hope of getting a few more scraps of information about Janice's past.

As he strolled into Tranby Manor, he was met by a new receptionist, and he politely stated that he had come to visit Lord. There was an embarrassed silence before the young girl behind the counter replied, "Mr Leonard?"

"Yes," said Terry as he looked around the desk for the visitors' book to sign in while the receptionist made a call on the phone. This was not the usual procedure as Terry was such a regular visitor, and he usually just signed in and wandered through to the residents' lounge.

The young girl looked up from making her call and informed Terry that the manager wished to speak to him. Terry panicked a bit and wondered what aspect of Lord's subversive behaviour had led to this summons to the office. Had he been trying to encourage Mrs Swindell to ignore her medication in the hope that Mr Crompton would visit?

Terry was shown into the office. He had never been in here before, but he was met by the friendly face of the manager, who quickly pointed out, "I'm afraid Lord is no longer with us."

For a brief moment, Terry thought his old friend must have been thrown out, but he soon realised that this was the manager's professional, if somewhat ambiguous method of saying that Lord had died. Terry was naturally shocked, and the manager directed him to a seat. He sat for a moment, recalling how he had seen signs lately that his old friend had not been looking too good. The death shouldn't have been such a shock, but even when one is expecting it, the finality of death has a certain incomprehensible impact.

Terry sat in a daze while the manager explained that they had been trying to contact him with the news throughout the day, but the phone had gone unanswered. He muttered something about being at work all day before asking about how Lord had died.

"When he didn't come in to breakfast this morning, Milly went to his room to check on him," answered the manager in a calm, soothing manner.

"Lord was sitting in his chair holding a small photograph, and at first Milly thought he had just fallen asleep. The bed hadn't been slept in. It seems that he was just sitting there looking out over the garden, and he must have passed away peacefully."

The manager left a moment for the news to sink in, and Terry, accepting a tissue which had been discreetly offered him, dabbed at the few tears that had started to roll down his face. He inwardly chastised himself for being so emotional but then realised that, while Lord was not a relative, he was the only link with his childhood. Terry never shed a tear at his grandparents' funerals, but this was different because this was losing someone who had really loved him, and he suddenly felt very alone.

When the manager saw that the emotional tide of the bad news had receded slightly, she moved into a more rational mode to explain some of the administrative procedures that needed to be carried out. She opened a dossier on her desk and began to talk through some of the contents.

"Mr Leonard had no listed next of kin, but he left a list of people to be contacted when he passed, including his old regiment, the British Legion and you as his executor."

Terry half-remembered the position of executor being mentioned, but he had just assumed that it was just some administrative necessity when Lord had gone into the residential home.

"The immediate arrangements have been made," continued the manager. "Mr Leonard has been removed to the chapel of rest, and the undertakers have been instructed to arrange for the internment in accordance with the deceased's wishes. Unfortunately, the company have been extremely busy during the recent very hot weather so the funeral won't be possible until late next week. In the meantime, I have been asked to pass on this letter to you with a request that you would sort out the items in Mr Leonard's room for him."

Taking the proffered envelope, Terry was escorted into his old friend's room. He sat for a moment in the chair he had occupied the previous weekend before opening the letter.

Hello Terry,

I have taken the liberty of asking you to sort out my personal belongings. Do what you like with them as I will have no further use for them. The funeral has been arranged and paid for, and there is an envelope addressed to you in the Tranby Manor safe with cash to cover incidentals. Please inform all those you feel ought to know about my death. Thank you for your friendship. As you will know, I have no family left now, and I don't have any fond ideas about going up to meet them and many of my old friends on some cloud or other. It's a beguiling notion that death is just another door we pass through to meet up with old acquaintances. It would be very nice to meet up with some old friends and Mary of course but it's not going to happen.

I hope you will remember Mary and me. I am sure she would have joined me in saying that we both loved you like the son we never had, just as we loved your mum. I'm sorry, but I told you a little lie about my will. What money I have left is to go to you as you are the nearest thing I have to a relative, and it's what Mary wanted as well. Now I've gone you can't try and convince me that you don't deserve it.

Goodbye old chap,
Lord

Terry sat for a while and smiled at the thought of how his old friend would have been jubilant at having been able to leave his money to Terry knowing that it was a fait accompli, so he couldn't argue about it.

Terry looked around the room. Some might suggest that it was not a lot to show for a life, but he knew that Lord's life had been full and meaningful, and the lack of domestic trappings did not reflect what he had achieved nor how much he had contributed to the lives of others. Terry felt reluctant to change anything in the room if only to hold on to his old friend for a little longer, but he knew he had to sort the contents out quickly as the room would be needed for future occupation. With some reluctance, Terry started to sort through Lord's belongings. It felt as though he was prying into his old friend's personal life, but he knew Lord wouldn't have minded. In one drawer, there was the expected assortment of old photographs and an ornate certificate from the Hull Corporation in recognition of his contribution to the rebuilding of the city after the war. Like the contents of most people's assorted albums and loose photographs, there was no obvious chronological order to the images and very little by way of explanation on the backs to suggest who was depicted on them. One couple did appear in a number of pictures, and Terry calculated that it was Lord's parents. The father figure was in regimental dress uniform and appeared regularly with a lady in a long Edwardian dress. The faded nature of the sepia image led Terry to assume it was taken some time in the early 20th century, and he couldn't help trying to work out just how old Lord would be now. He had little time for such speculation, so he tipped out a few more photographs. Among the assorted images, he searched for the one of Lord and his young wife in Skegness, but it wasn't there. He looked around the room for the missing image and found it next to Lord's chair. It was the logical place for it to be, not tucked in among the other lesser images but on the small side table next to the old man's favourite chair. Someone must have taken it from his hands and put it down on the nearest surface. Terry carefully picked it up and gazed for a moment at the happy young couple enjoying that beach holiday together so long ago. It was just a small, slightly faded, black-and-white snap taken on a cheap camera and placed in a plastic frame, but Terry knew that, to Lord, it had been the most valuable thing he possessed. Terry felt the frame was somehow inappropriate, so he removed the photograph and slipped it reverently into the envelope with the letter from Lord.

The late evening sun lit up the room, and Terry found himself staring out onto the manicured lawn. He realised that he wasn't going to be able to make much of an impression on the job of clearing Lord's room, and after making arrangements with the staff to return at a later date, he set off home.

As he walked out, Terry was thinking how normal everything was; the world was just as it was when he had gone to visit his friend, he passed the same shrubs along the drive, exited through the same ornate gates onto the same path that he knew would lead him home. Everything seemed just too normal. He had lost the central figure in his life, but the world went on. For the second time that day, he felt his eyes watering and a tear rolled down his cheek. He stopped for a moment and stood silently watching a blackbird attempting to dislodge a worm from the dry grass at the roadside, and he wiped the tear from his face. The bird was going about its foraging as if nothing had happened, but Terry knew that something very important had occurred that day, and he wandered off home.

As he approached his house, Terry stopped for a while to look at the neighbouring property, which had once been the home of Lord and Mary. It hadn't changed much, and the sight of it, rather than bringing back all the happy memories of his childhood, only reminded him of his latest loss.

By the time he arrived at the auction house next day, the staff already knew about Lord's death. In the small local community, such news was quickly shared. The staff had all known Lord after his years in the village and knew what a friend he had been to Terry. On hearing about the young man's need to sort out a lot of issues following the death of Lord, Mr Spivey insisted that Terry should have a couple of days off. At first Terry had protested, but he soon acknowledged that he had a lot of business to sort out with Lord's estate.

Fortunately, the Tranby Manor staff had a well-rehearsed set of procedures they followed in such eventualities, so the plans for the funeral and the relevant paperwork were all sorted out efficiently. As requested by Lord, his old regiment had been informed, as had the local branch of the Royal British Legion. The hall where Lord's regimental reunions had been held was booked for the wake. At the suggestion of the manager at Tranby Manor, Terry arranged for an announcement to be inserted in the local paper. Lord had already reserved his place with his late wife in St Martin's churchyard, and Tranby Manor staff confirmed the details with the vicar. Terry was surprised that the ceremony would take place in the church, given Lord's declared atheism, but apparently he had agreed to it to comply with Mary's wishes.

Clearing Lord's room took a while. At first Terry tried to sort the contents into several different categories but soon realised that, apart from a few mementoes he would like to keep, the rest was either to be thrown away or put in the auction. A quick call to John Spivey sorted the problem as his firm were very experienced in clearing such properties, and he promptly arranged for the room to be cleared. Among the old man's possessions, Terry found a small box containing a collection of medals that he recognised as those Lord had put on each year for his regimental reunions, and which his old friend had frequently declared he would leave to him. These were not going to find their way into a tray of assorted ephemera at any auction, so Terry carefully set them aside.

As he sat in his kitchen the following Sunday, Terry felt that he had most of the immediate issues concerning the funeral more or less sorted. He was surprised to look up from his breakfast to see Lizzie standing in the open doorway. Instinctively, he rushed over and hugged her. She did not appear to object, but Terry knew that his old Lizzie had not returned.

"I was so sorry to hear about Lord. I only heard the news late yesterday. The team have been a bit tied up over the last few days," she explained. Terry had heard this sort of explanation many times before but, while in the past he had usually resented how her commitments had kept her away from him, this time he felt some appreciation of the stress she must frequently experience in her job. He couldn't help but notice that her usual sparkle was not there. He had seen her looking tired many times when she had finished a spell on duty, but this time she displayed a worrying air of weariness. His immediate compulsion was to hug her again, but he felt that would not be welcomed; instead, he offered her a cup of tea and made a weak joke about actually having milk in the house this time. The levity was not appreciated, but Lizzie accepted the offer.

The couple sat together in a rather awkward silence, drinking their cups of tea before Terry declared, "I've missed you these last weeks." He paused, waiting for her to give some sort of supportive comment, but she said nothing. After a few moments of painful silence, he asked, "I hope you can make it to the funeral? It's set for next Friday afternoon over in Barton Saint Martin church."

"Yes, so I heard. I've already told the office that I won't be available that day. I always got on so well with Lord. He was a good friend and lovely neighbour." This reference to the fact that she had shared a home with Terry next door to Lord for two years was something she didn't want to dwell on, and the awkward silence returned.

"So what have you been doing of late?" he asked in an attempt to further the conversation. "Lenin told me you had been to the café with Veronica."

Lizzie went on to describe her recent activities, but Terry found it hard to concentrate. All he could think about was the fact that this woman sitting opposite him had been such an integral part of his life, sharing his home and his bed, and now she was recounting such mundane accounts of what she had been doing recently, but he was just pleased to have her sitting there. There was no suggestion of intimacy, but at least she was there. After half an hour, Lizzie declared that she had to go and implied that there were some important matters she had to deal with. He saw her to the back gate and ventured a kiss on the cheek. She did not object, but he felt no sign of any emotional response. As she walked off, he felt that the woman who had visited had been strangely cold and was not the Lizzie he loved and missed. For days, he had looked forward to meeting up with her, but the visit had been a crushing disappointment.

CHAPTER SIXTEEN

When Terry arrived at the auction house the next morning to finalise the collection of Lord's belongings, John Spivey could hardly wait to impart some news. He was holding a copy of the *Times*, and he greeted Terry with, "Guess who's made it to the paper?" and before the younger man could respond, John answered his own question, "Lord Leonard of all people."

Before Terry could formulate any coherent response, his boss opened the paper and began to comment on what was on one of the inner pages.

"Here among the obituaries. It's a tribute to Lord Balaclava Leonard. I had no idea that he had achieved so much."

He gave the paper to Terry, who read through the article. It gave a full account of Lord's military career, including the medal which recognised his gallantry. Terry knew that his old friend had been in the army and that he had got some medals, but Lord had never given any indication that he had been awarded a medal for bravery. The account of how Lord had faced great personal danger to assist two of his comrades during a particularly heavy bombardment was all news to Terry. His old friend had displayed the modesty of many heroes and never made the briefest reference to his wartime experience. There was also some coverage of the part he played in the rebuilding of Hull after the war, and this amounted to more than putting in a few electricity cables as Lord had implied. Terry remembered how his old friend would only wear his medals on his reunion nights and how reluctant he had been to be seen with them on even while he was being transported to and from the meeting. He knew from his auction days that there were different types of medals, but he was far from being a military historian. For all he knew, the medals he saw briefly once a year were the type that everyone was awarded just for having behaved themselves for the duration, but Lord's medals and the letters after his name indicated that he had done something special. This fact was emphasised when, the next day, the local evening paper ran an article emblazoned with the title *Local War Hero Dies*. It was followed by extensive coverage of Lord's achievements. No doubt Lizzie would have seen the article, and Terry would have loved to have chatted about it with her, but on his regular visits to the Red Star Café, he failed to meet up with her, and Lenin could offer no comforting news as to her whereabouts. The lack of news convinced Terry that she was deliberately avoiding him. He recognised that they'd fallen out, perhaps even broken up, but her absence seemed deliberately cruel and quite out of character. Surely the case she had been on recently couldn't have dragged on for so long? Once again, he was tempted to go round to Veronica's place to see if she had any news, but he soon convinced himself that would be a waste of time, and anyway he was beginning to feel that Lizzie wouldn't want to have anything to do with him. He did find some consolation in the fact that he would see her at the funeral on Friday, but he knew that would hardly be a suitable venue to have any meaningful conversation, and he was certain that at some point he would have to have such a discussion.

The undertakers and Lord's former military contacts appeared to have the funeral in hand, so Terry didn't have that pressure on him, but he could not relax; Lizzie's behaviour was often on his mind, and it worried him. There was still one thing that Terry knew he had to do for Lord, so on Wednesday morning he made his way to the chapel of rest where his old friend had been placed. The staff at the undertakers were very supportive of Terry, who had never been in such a place. They showed him through to the chapel of rest and left him to have a few moments on his own. He had never been in such a place before, and he approached the open casket with some sense of apprehension; he had never seen a dead body. He need not have worried. The mortician had done a good job, and Lord did indeed look as if he were asleep. He was wearing the suit he always wore for his reunion meetings, and his shoes had that impeccable shine befitting an ex-soldier. Terry stood for a few moments and then took something out of his pocket. He looked at the small photograph of the young couple on the beach and smiled. It was absurd. Lord had known he was not going to really need the photograph, and he wouldn't be admiring it with Mary for eternity, but he wanted to have it with him, and Terry knew he had to honour the old man's wishes. Terry hesitated for a minute and then gently placed the photograph in the inside pocket of Lord's jacket. As he left the room, he felt the need to repeat the last line from Lord's letter.

"Goodbye, old chap."

On the day of the funeral, Terry woke early. This had become a regular routine with him over the last few weeks. Dawn came early at that time of year, and the bright sunshine the area had enjoyed recently illuminated his bedroom. He glanced over at Lizzie's side of the bed and realised that he still slept on 'his' side. Perhaps it was because he felt she would return some day to claim her place? He was reminded of the happy mornings when neither of them had needed to get up early, but now there seemed no reason to stay in bed once he was awake. He put on his dressing gown and wandered downstairs. Breakfast this morning was a cup of tea and a piece of toast in the garden. He wasn't hungry, but he knew he had a big day ahead of him and had to eat something. Although the morning sun continued to shine brightly there was still a slight chill in the air. Terry looked at his watch and was mildly surprised to see that it was still only half past five. He sat for a while thinking about the day ahead, but as he thought of how much he would miss his old friend, his mind kept returning to how Lizzie would behave at the funeral. He felt guilty about allowing thoughts of his own relationship to intrude on his memories of Lord, so he decided to get on with the practicalities of the day.

He laid his clothes on his bed ready for the funeral. The suit was the one he wore at his grandmother's funeral and for his cancelled dive from the bridge. He remained thankful to Michael Lampeter Hodge, whoever he had been, for his intervention on that day, although Terry had tried to convince himself that he would never have dared to execute his plan, he could never be entirely sure. He had no doubt that many of those who had taken the tragic decision to end their lives had what they saw as valid reasons, however misguided, for doing so and he wondered how many of them might have turned back from that awful step if they had been blessed with someone they felt they could talk to.

Terry decided that he had to be at the church early just to check everything was in order. In his dark suit with obligatory black tie, he got into his car to make the short journey across the bridge towards Lincolnshire and Barton Saint Martin. He had wanted to contact Lizzie to see if she wanted a lift to the church but once again found it impossible to get in touch. As he drove over the bridge, he found himself looking to see if the mysterious Michel Lampeter Hodge was on patrol, but he failed to appear.

On the approach to Barton Saint Martin, he was waved down by a young boy in army cadet uniform who, having confirmed that Terry was on the way to the funeral, directed him through a gate into a field. He learned that this was to be a temporary car park for guests and remembered the very limited parking near the church. The military machine had moved in with admirable efficiency. There were cones to restrict parking near the Fickle Fox, and there was another young cadet standing by the entrance of the narrow lane that led to the church, presumably to discourage anyone from attempting to drive up to the churchyard.

Resisting the temptation to have a cool drink in the pub, Terry strolled down to the church. Saint Martin's normally exuded that feeling of timeless tranquillity, the kind of scene that Victorian painters would rush to depict as part of some rural idyll, but today the scene was not one of pastoral calm. The car park was devoid of cars, but there were groups of people obviously engrossed in their joint plan to ensure Lord had a good funeral. Others were in the graveyard apparently acquainting themselves with 'the lie of the land', and one young man, dressed in some kind of officer's uniform, was addressing a group of soldiers and at least trying to give the impression that he was in charge of the whole event.

Terry realised that he was superfluous to requirements, so he walked into the empty church and took a seat at the back. He looked around the place and was struck by the fact that there were quite a lot of flowers throughout the church; someone had obviously made an effort. He caught sight of the large wooden offertory box and dutifully went over to place a donation in. This time he had come prepared with more than the few meagre coins that he had contributed on his last visit only a few days earlier. Having paid his 'entry fee', he went back and sat down. He amused himself by looking up at the stained-glass windows and trying to determine which biblical event they portrayed, but his mind kept returning to the topic of Lizzie and whether she would turn up. Some months earlier, he would have felt sure that she wouldn't miss Lord's funeral, but her recent behaviour caused him to have some doubts. After a while, he became aware of activity outside, and he went to the door to peer out into the bright sunlight in time to see the hearse creeping towards the car park. What had previously appeared to be a random group of people milling about aimlessly suddenly turned into a synchronised funeral parade. Six soldiers moved forward to carry the coffin towards the church, preceded by what Terry took to be an army chaplain while the young officer brought up the rear. At either side of the path approaching the door were two lines of elderly gentlemen in smart blazers with regimental insignia on their breast pockets and wearing regimental berets. Each of them stood proudly displaying rows of medals on their chests, and they stiffly saluted as the remains of their former brother-in-arms were taken into the church. Behind this there was a large crowd of mourners who politely followed in after the coffin.

A member of staff from Tranby Manor escorted Terry to the front pew, having apparently taken him to be the nearest thing to next of kin. As he sat with a number of dignitaries he tried to look discreetly around the packed church to see if Lizzie had turned up, but pretty soon the chaplain began his address, and Terry felt obliged to look towards the alter, vowing to get out as quickly as he could afterwards to look for her.

The eulogy was enlightening as the chaplain gave an account of Lord's achievements. He had apparently been a brave soldier, and as an officer he had been respected and even loved by his men. There were details of his post-war involvement in the rebuilding of Hull and a passing reference to his long marriage to Mary. It struck Terry as odd that so much emphasis was put on Lord's military and business life, but his marriage seemed to be a footnote. Lord never spoke of his military life or his subsequent civil duties, but he would speak fondly and proudly of his long marriage to the woman he loved. At least his old friend had got his own way in the end. He didn't want to take his medals with him, and the certificate from Hull Corporation had been discarded, but the little picture of him and Mary on Skegness Beach was the one thing he had to have with him to the end. Terry felt pleased to have been able to secrete the photograph in his old friend's jacket pocket. Terry knew that, in some small way, he had helped Lord make his final gesture to show what had been really valuable in his life.

CHAPTER SEVENTEEN

Eventually the congregation followed the coffin out to the grave. The chaplain said a few words as the coffin was lowered, and the crowd began to move away. The chaplain went over to see Terry, and in an almost conspiratorial way, he whispered, "It is general knowledge that your friend was not a religious man, but he deserves to be in heaven – whether he believes in it or not." With a smile and a little wink, the chaplain went off to chat to other mourners.

Terry looked around the diminishing crowd and was delighted to see that Lizzie had made it. He almost ran to see her, and it was only as he got near her that he saw she was chatting to another woman, and when she turned towards him, he slowly recognised it was his mother. Obviously, Janice had changed, but it was definitely her. He was understandably confused and at a loss as to what to say and to whom. In the end, he opted to just declare, "It's nice to see you both." It was not the most eloquent or imaginative of greetings, but it was undoubtedly sincere. He went over to Lizzie and kissed her gently on the cheek, but how should he approach Janice? He needn't have worried as she gave him a warm hug.

As she stepped back, she announced, "I'm sorry to shock you like this, but I only heard about the funeral yesterday, so I just got on a plane and here I am."

Terry wanted to ask a thousand questions of Janice, and he still needed to speak to Lizzie, but he wanted somewhere more appropriate, perhaps over a drink, to find out more about the two women in his life.

"You are going to the wake, aren't you?" Before they had time to answer, he suggested, "Can I give you a lift?"

Lizzie explained that she had her car and had to get away because she was due at a review meeting in Hull later that day. Once again, Terry had an unpleasant feeling that this was just an excuse, but he knew not to press her on the subject and just said. "We really do need to talk, darling." The term of endearment was not planned, but its genuine spontaneity appeared to get through to her.

"Yes, you're right. I will be in touch soon, honestly." With that, she said goodbye to them and hurried off to her car. For the first time in weeks, Terry felt that he had seen a glimpse of the Lizzie he knew; it wasn't much, but he experienced a tiny bit of hope. Still feeling slightly elated, he turned to Janice.

"Can I give you a lift to the wake? I think we have a lot of catching up to do."

"That's kind of you, but I have a taxi waiting for me down in the field."

"Pay him off and then come with me," said Terry with uncharacteristic decisiveness, "I can be your transport while you are here. How long were you planning to stay? Have you got accommodation fixed up, or do you want to stay in my place?"

Terry was aware that he was bombarding her with questions, so he stopped to let her have the opportunity to answer some of them.

"I had no firm plans. As I said, I just got on the first available flight. I grabbed a weekend bag and intended to just find accommodation when I got here. It seems rather cheeky to stay at your place. I haven't seen you for years and then drop in to take advantage of your hospitality."

"Don't be silly. After all, you are family. Which brings me to the issue of what I should call you."

"Well, I don't think 'Mum' is appropriate given the complete dog's breakfast I've made of that role, so perhaps you could call me by my name? Just call me Janice, and I'll promise not to call you 'son'."

Terry felt the faint beginnings of a developing bond with this strange relative he had become reacquainted with, and after settling the fare with the taxi driver, the couple set off across the bridge towards the north bank.

"This is one of my favourite views," she exclaimed as they drove on. "I've travelled quite a bit in my lifetime, but the view of the Humber from this majestic piece of engineering always impresses me. I may be prejudiced, perhaps because it reminds me of coming home, but it almost takes my breath away every time I see it."

Terry resisted the temptation to take his eyes off the road and enjoy the view, and he took the opportunity to find out more about his passenger.

"I gather you've travelled a lot since you left home?"

It seemed strange to talk about his mother's 'home', but he realised that she had lived the first 18 years of her life in what was now his home.

"I guess I have been a bit of a gypsy, rarely settling down anywhere at first. When I left here, I spent some time in Newcastle and managed to get a degree at the university there. I followed that up by doing my MA at Hull, where I worked in a pub as a barmaid to finance my studies. Fortunately, that was in the days before student loans were introduced, but living on a grant was not easy."

"At the Kingstonian," interjected Terry.

"Why yes, but how did you know that?"

"Something Lord told me. You sent a postcard from there to Mary and him."

"Yes, I always tried to keep in touch with them. It was my only way of finding out how you were getting on. You will gather that I did not get on with my parents, but Lord and Mary were always supportive. They were more like my real mum and dad."

"Yes, and I guess my arrival must have caused a rift between you and your parents."

Janice cut him short and with an almost aggressive tone, declared, "Don't you ever suggest that you were the cause of my leaving. For a while, you were the only bright spot in my life. I don't pretend that it was planned, but I wasn't devastated to find I was pregnant. In a way, I saw it as an opportunity to break away and set up in a life of my own. I had that unshakable naivety of youth, but the reality was different. You didn't turn out to be my ticket to freedom but rather another way that my parents would try to control me.

"I was in my late teens, and they wanted to press me into some mould of conformity. I was supposed to be the good little mother. Sacrificing my real identity to the new role, and I just wasn't ready for it. I didn't mean to run out on you permanently, but after a while I realised that you were better off in the stable home they offered. The longer I was away, the easier it was to convince myself that you were better off where you were. They did love you, and you seemed so settled, and I still have regrets that I might have got it wrong, but it was never your fault."

Terry drove on for a while in silence, partly because he wanted time for all this to settle in. Here was a woman he had hardly met who was disclosing so much of her personal feelings. He was not used to people having the courage to be so open. A life with his grandparents had taught him to be polite rather than emotionally honest. To try and break the mood a bit, he continued with his gentle interrogation of his mother.

"So why did you leave Hull? Lord seems to remember postcards from France."

"I applied for a job that was advertised through the university for a three-year contract in Nantes. It was just an opportunity to travel a bit, but in the end I enjoyed it so much that I sort of put down roots. My decision was largely influenced by the fact that I met Greg there. He is English but has spent most of his adult life in Nantes. He's a few years older than me, but he's just great fun, and his fluent French made it easier for me to settle in. We've been together about eight years now, and I'm loving it. He would have loved to come over with me, but he is in the middle of some project with the university."

"That's a shame," said Terry, "perhaps he would like to come over with you for a short break sometime?"

This comment was uttered almost as a result of automatic politeness on his part, but he knew he actually meant it; he was keen to connect with any part of his mother's life after being excluded from it for so long.

"That would be very nice," she responded, with a sense of natural sincerity in her voice, "and I know it must sound insensitive, but it is far easier to visit now that Mum and Dad have gone. They meant well, but they just wanted me to turn out like some genetic carbon copy of themselves, and I couldn't accept that. I must confess that I was so sorry to miss Mum's funeral, but I didn't hear about it until months later. She didn't make it to the national papers as Lord did. I can't pretend that I was heartbroken, but she meant well. No one produces a reliable handbook on how to be a good parent and, believe me, I should know."

"So you heard about Lord's death from the paper?" he asked in an attempt to steer the conversation away from the subject of failed parenting.

"Yes. Greg has the *Times* delivered each day over in France. He says that he likes to keep in touch with the old country.

But I suspect he just enjoys taking his copy of the *Times* into the senior common room at the university and leaving it among the copies of *Le Monde* and *Le Figaro* as if he's doing a bit of cultural missionary work. It was still little short of a miracle that he spotted the article on Lord. It was the reference to Hull that prompted him to point it out to me in case I might know anything about the subject of the article. I'm so glad he saw it. I would have hated to miss Lord's funeral. He and Mary were more like parents to me than my mum and dad."

"I know how you feel. Gran and Grandad provided a comfortable home for me, and they were generally very supportive, but they always seemed a bit distant, as if emotion was an unnecessary ingredient in any relationship. I used to put it down to the fact that I was their grandson rather than their son, but in some of my conversations with Lord, I gathered that they had the same sort of restricted emotional empathy with you."

"They certainly did. It's as if they had some form of emotional constipation; they daren't let their emotions out in the open. Of course they meant well, but their attempts to force me down a path I wasn't suited to had the effect of trapping me in a cage, and that's why I had to escape. I know that I was young and hot-headed, but I genuinely feel that, given the choice, I would do it all again. My one regret is leaving you. I honestly thought I was doing the best for you by leaving you in familiar surroundings rather than carting you off to share an uncertain future traipsing around the country, but I realise from the limited correspondence I had with Lord that I had escaped the cage only to leave you in it. Sorry, love."

Terry was momentarily stunned, not by his mother's confession about her early life, but by the fact that she called him 'love' and with such obvious affection.

CHAPTER EIGHTEEN

The wake was not the sombre affair that Terry had expected. Many of Lord's former military colleagues were keen to speak about his old friend, and once again it was obvious that Lord had been a very popular officer. Much as he enjoyed learning about Lord's achievements, Terry was keen to find time on his own with Janice, and as soon as he felt it was polite to do so, they made their apologies and left the hall. As they did so, Terry looked back at the room full of people who represented the various stages of Lord's life. The atmosphere had become markedly livelier as the guests steadily mellowed under the influence of numerous toasts to Lord's memory. Terry smiled and reflected on the fact that his old friend would have appreciated the levity.

On the drive back to his house, Terry felt that he was probably being rather too persistent in his questioning of his mum's past, and he was aware that the conversation was one of stops and starts; for periods of time, one or other would speak at length about some aspect of their respective pasts, but then there would be long and rather awkward silences. It was during one of these uncomfortable, quiet moments that they arrived back at Terry's house.

Janice got out of the car and collected her overnight bag from the back seat. For a while, rather than move towards the house, she just stood and stared at what had been Lord and Mary's home.

"It seems strange that they aren't there anymore," she remarked before adding, "I'll miss them. I know I haven't been around for some time, but they always represented home to me because they always had time for me." After allowing herself a moment of quiet reminiscing, she followed Terry into his house. Terry would have found it difficult to consider it *his* home as he still felt it should have passed down to his mother, but he remembered how adamant his grandparents had been that he should get the house. Janice seemed to appreciate his unspoken discomfort and breezily commented, "It seems a bit strange to be here," before adding, "I like the way you've done it up."

Terry busied himself putting the kettle on to make a cup of tea for them both before he picked up Janice's bag and stated, "I'll take this up for you. I'll put it in my old room."

"Yes, I think I can remember where it is," she said with a little laugh.

The couple later sat down to share a pot of tea and exchange pleasantries about the way the funeral had gone well, the fact that Lord had obviously had a full life and the problems Janice had experienced in barely managing to get a plane in time to get back to England. Terry was conscious that he was eager to know everything about his mum's past, but he didn't want her to feel she was being cross-examined so he casually said, "I gather we both got on very well with Lord and Mary."

"Yes," replied Janice as she began to smile, "I think we both seemed to see them as parent figures. My mum and dad meant well, but they appeared to see parenting as a chore. They worked hard, provided a comfortable home and all material needs were catered for."

"But they never displayed any signs of love," interrupted Terry.

"That's being a bit harsh on them. It's true that they had great difficulty in expressing their feelings. They meant well and probably thought they were acting in both our best interests; they just didn't see the need to show it. They often displayed their disapproval of my relationship with Lord and Mary. Dad, in particular, thought they were far too frivolous, but it's just that they weren't afraid to have fun, while Dad couldn't seem to be able to stand the implied guilt of doing anything that might be enjoyable. I had great times with Lord and Mary, but my parents took everything so seriously, as if they couldn't understand a child's need to have fun. I often wonder why they ever had a child. Perhaps I was just a happy accident, just as you were. I remember that Lord and I would often go for a walk along the river bank and have endless fun mud splodging."

"Mud splodging?"

"Yes. At low tide when there are those vast areas of glistening mud exposed, we would throw large stones out and marvel at the small craters created as the stones splodged into the pristine mud. You had to be careful, though, as the stones at the edge of the mud were covered in a light coating of weed and incredibly slimy. I remember that one day, as I stretched to pick up one of the stones for ammunition, I fell forward flat on my face into the mud. Once we established that I wasn't hurt, we laughed at my mud-covered appearance. Mum and Dad didn't see the funny side when I got home, and Lord was almost treated like a naughty child for letting me get into such a state. To be fair, it did take a lot of effort to clean my clothes and in particular to get rid of the smell."

"Yes, I would look forward to my time with Lord. He and Mary weren't afraid of acting the fool at times, while Gran and Grandad seemed to make a virtue of boredom. I think they had both grown up too soon and expected me to do the same. They rarely smiled, let alone laughed. It's not that they were constantly miserable, but they were content to go through life in a comfortable state of bland tedium."

As the afternoon wore on, Terry became conscious of the fact that he was hungry. He didn't feel like cooking and thus wasting valuable chatting time with his mum, so he suggested that they might have bread and cheese and Janice agreed that it was a good idea. The truth was that he had gone to the trouble of getting in a selection of cheeses just in case he had been able to persuade Lizzie to come back after the funeral. Janice agreed to his suggestion that they might eat outside, so he gathered together the food, appropriate plates and cutlery on a tray, and the couple made their way to the garden.

"Would you like wine with your supper?" he asked.

"That would be lovely."

"Red or white?"

"White, please," she replied, barely suppressing a laugh.

"What's so funny?"

"What would my parents have made of this? Janice Henderson sitting in their garden drinking wine! Their little girl having a preference for a particular wine and drinking when it's not even Christmas."

Terry went in to the house and returned with a bottle of wine and two glasses, and the couple sat down to enjoy their meal. After a while, Janice read the label on the wine bottle and commented, "This wine is from the Loire region and isn't far from our place in France. It's rather nice."

Once again, Terry was struck by his mother's cosmopolitan lifestyle. He had only bought the wine because it had a rather impressive label and it had been part of a special promotion in the supermarket. He sat quietly listening as Janice recounted some of her past experiences. Even her early experiences at home seemed more exciting than his.

"It was not like this when I was young," she observed. "Cheese and wine in the garden would have been seen as somehow decadent. I remember our usual Sunday afternoons in those far-off summers. Dad would spend time cutting the grass. Every bloody Sunday if the weather permitted. Then we would have a salad for tea. Salads were more of an artistic arrangement of items on a plate with lettuce, spring onion, tomato and cucumber. That display was augmented by a hard-boiled egg and a slice of ham, and the ensemble was adorned by a splash of salad cream. Dad would have been unable to recognise what we eat now as being salad, bless him."

"That description of Sunday sounds very familiar to me," commented Terry, "but latterly we did recklessly take to having mayonnaise. Garlic never made the menu, though."

Janice looked around the garden and sat for a moment in silence. Obviously deep in thought. Terry was reluctant to disturb her, but after a while she came out of her contemplative state and began to recount some of her early childhood experiences in the garden.

"That was my bedroom up there, and you can see the route I would clamber down on summer nights when Mum and Dad had gone to bed, and they assumed that I was asleep. As a young child, I didn't go anywhere, just sat in the garden. It was a big adventure. I would just sit and listen to the music coming from Lord and Mary's garden. Sometimes, I would creep over to the fence and watch them sitting on their patio or even enjoying a slow dance together, and they drank wine! It all seemed so exotic, so romantic. As I grew up, I often used my escape route from my room and strayed beyond the garden. Mum and Dad never suspected a thing. I guess that, as they had no sense of adventure themselves, they just assumed I would be content to fester in my room all the time. I used to meet up with a group of friends, and we would just chat for hours, and then I would head off home and clamber back into my cell. As a group of kids, we didn't go around causing trouble; we just wanted to meet up. Naturally, there were some romantic relationships that blossomed and faded, but it was all quite innocent for the main part."

Terry resisted the temptation to press her for any information about her relationship with his father. He wanted to know about his mysterious father, but he felt no compulsion to seek the details as to how Lizzie had become pregnant. Terry chose to leave that delicate area for a while, and he opted to tell her about some aspects of his early years.

"As Lord pointed out to me recently, I was never a child to seek adventure or to rebel in any way as you did. I was a bit of a goody two shoes, just conforming to my grandparents' model of how a child should behave. I think they were possibly too keen to ensure that I didn't step out of line, as they felt you had."

"Fair point! I suspect there wasn't any danger of you getting pregnant halfway through you're A levels as I did, but Mum and Dad weren't going to take any chances of you damaging your life prospects."

"They certainly weren't. In particular, they constantly dissuaded me from getting involved with girls. They never implied that there was anything wrong with being with girls, just that it was never the right time in my life to risk such entanglements. As things transpired, I found that I was strongly attracted to some girls. I'm not sure if it was the lack of any overt signs of affection from Gran and Grandad, but I found I would seek it from girls. I had been on an emotional diet all my life, and I wanted to get as much affection as I could. I was lucky in a way that my early girlfriends were not as keen as I was to enter into major relationships. In truth, my over-eagerness put a lot of girls off. If it hadn't, you might have been a grandmother by now."

"Heaven forbid," exclaimed Janice. "I've hardly got used to the idea of being a mother."

The conversation went on for a while as they exchanged information about aspects of their lives. The evening was proving very enjoyable for Terry. He was sitting with someone who had been a relative stranger and whom he was getting to know as a friend. It was a warm evening and the wine was chilled; Terry felt a degree of contentment for the first time in weeks. The wine gradually had the effect of emboldening Terry, and he felt able to press his mother for more information about what he still regarded as her exotic lifestyle.

"So do you have a job in France that you need to rush back to?" he asked, in the hope of persuading her to stay longer with him.

"I work for the local museum service, everything from elementary painting restoration to conservation work. Most of my time is filled with rather monotonous and largely unskilled work, but I enjoy it, and the flexible hours it offers suit me. I have recently been working on some painted wooden panels, and there is no rigid deadline as to when they must be completed, but I really ought to try and get back by Wednesday. I will ring the airport tomorrow and find a suitable flight."

Terry was delighted at the prospect of having a few days with his mother, and he poured each of them another glass of wine before settling back in his chair with an undisguised sense of satisfaction.

"And what about you, Terry; you don't appear to be married?"

"I nearly was. I was living with someone for over two years, but she left me recently. You met her at the funeral. You were chatting to her when I met you. She's called Lizzie."

"Oh yes! She seemed like a bright girl, but she didn't mention you. She did say that she was a friend of Lord's and had been a neighbour, but I didn't make the connection. Yes, a very nice girl. I liked her."

Terry felt pleased that his mum had liked Lizzie. It was a bit like the feeling of pride that a young child might experience when taking home a picture from school and being praised by their mum.

"So, is there any chance of you two getting back together?"

"If it were up to me, I would have her back tomorrow. My life feels empty without her, but she seems adamant that it's all over between us."

"She didn't look very happy about life, and I didn't put it just down to the fact that it was a friend's funeral. She had such a pretty face, but she looked very tired."

"The fact is that she has a job that is very demanding at the best of times, and recently she has been under a lot of pressure. I wasn't aware of it at the time, but I realise that I could, no should, have done more to help her. The fact is that I was bloody insensitive, and because of that I failed to hold on to the most precious thing in my life."

Terry realised that he was becoming more than a little candid about his feelings for Lizzie. He was aware that this was not unrelated to the fact that he and Janice had gone through the better part of two bottles of wine between them, and he had consumed more than his fair share. His usual inhibitions, particularly about his feelings, were fast disappearing. The wine had helped significantly to break down the initial awkward feelings they had shared just a few hours previously. He began to think to himself that the old adage *'in vino veritas'* was germane and that too much vino had, as is often the case, led to too much veritas. He sat in silence for a while, determined to stop his outflowing of emotion which was so alien to his usual approach to life.

Janice broke the silence after a while by asking, "So are you still working at Enderby's?"

"No. I moved on from there and now work in the auction house for John Spivey. It's a sort of trial period."

"So John is still running the business?"

Terry had forgotten that his mother had lived in the village for much of her younger life but soon found that they were discussing what constituted their shared experiences of the village and in particular its older inhabitants. It was Janice who brought an end to their reminiscing by saying, "So, what plans do you have for the future?"

Before Terry could respond, she announced, "God, I sound like a mother!" and started to laugh. He had never seen his mother really laugh before, and he found himself joining in. It had been a wonderful evening, and he didn't want it to end, but he was conscious that he was in danger of entering into that state which is euphemistically referred to as being 'tired and emotional', so he pointed out that it was getting late and perhaps time to get some sleep.

CHAPTER NINETEEN

The domestic arrangements the following morning were in the same informal vein as their supper the previous evening. Terry admitted to feeling slightly under the weather, and Janice was pleased to prepare breakfast. There were predictable difficulties as Terry had relocated many of the domestic utensils, and so, though Janice was working in what used to be a familiar setting, she had to keep asking him which cupboard or drawer she must look in for the components of the breakfast she intended to make. Terry's experience in the store rooms at Enderby's led him to have his own logical location for items in the house. Thus he kept all the cups in a separate cupboard to the other crockery, while most people might have been tempted to keep matching cups and crockery in the same place. He worked on the assumption that function was more important than decoration. The sight of his mother searching for things in the house reminded him of the countless minor disagreements he had gone through with Lizzie in the past about such domestic trivialities, and that's all they had been. They never had a real row about anything, so why had she suddenly left him? He thought back to the previous evening and his statement about being insensitive. He knew that he had disclosed his feelings while influenced by a generous amount of Muscadet, but he recognised that his comments were based on sincerity rather than alcohol. He was certain that if Lizzie knew how he felt, then she would surely want them to get back together, but it's impossible to convince someone of your feelings when you never get a chance to talk and Lizzie seemed disinclined to discuss the issue at all. He couldn't escape a nagging awareness that just because he needed her did not necessarily mean that she would wish for them to get back together. He began to question their whole relationship. Had it been as good for Lizzie as it had seemed to be for him? He had been so content to be with her, but how did she feel? It all seemed to be going so well until the incident of the Oxford holiday. He tried to work out why everything had gone so wrong so quickly. It was true that Lizzie had been rather tetchy for a few weeks, probably unrelated to the fact that she had been under a lot of pressure at work, and he was starting to realise how much she had needed that holiday and why an overnight stay in Oxford was never going to be sufficient.

After they had finished their breakfasts, Terry poured each of them a second cup of tea, and they took them out into the garden. Janice took a sip from her cup and announced, "Tea is the one thing I miss in France. We never went along with the British obsession with baked beans, but we always had a few boxes of teabags in the house. On the whole, though, I have to admit that I like the lifestyle over in France and with two incomes we enjoy a comfortable life over there."

"And does Greg know about me?"

"Of course he knows about you; in fact he has frequently suggested that it would be nice to come over and meet up. He never had any children before we met up, and I guess he just wanted to share a bit of my past in a way."

"So, did you ever have any more children?" ventured Terry, half hoping that he might have siblings somewhere."

"No. We did think of having children but we kept putting it off. The selfish truth is that we were enjoying life, and later, when we'd had our fair share of la dolce vita and thought we were in the right financial state to consider a family, I was a bit long in the tooth. I think Greg was more disappointed than I was that we'd missed the boat. I'd had my shot at parenthood, and I concede that I didn't do too well at it, but Greg never got the chance to become a father. Did you ever want to have children?"

This sudden question took Terry by surprise, and he hesitated before answering.

"I've never given any detailed thought to it in terms of planning the right time, but on one occasion when Lizzie was particularly late with her period, we did wonder how we would react to a little surprise addition to our home. I got the impression that she would miss her career, but I must confess that I was rather pleased at the prospect. I didn't feel tempted to rush around like the archetypical new father handing out cigars to everyone, but I was rather looking forward to a positive result so that I could share the news. When Lizzie took a test and it proved negative, I tried not to look too despondent for her sake, but it was a bit of a let-down, and we've never discussed it since."

"My greatest regret in life is that I never made a success of parenting. It may be that I was too young, but then lots of girls have babies when they are young and it works out. I think I was just not ready; my childhood had been boring, and as a family unit we basically co-existed. I didn't consciously set out to get pregnant, but somewhere I had a romantic fairy tale dream that I would have a baby that would be mine and love me. In the end, I never went on to experience that idyllic life, and the oppressive reality of home took control of me. I had stupidly thought that you would be my way out. I now know that I should have followed my feelings and insisted upon bringing you up my way. In my admittedly poor defence, I have to remember that I was just 18 and had been thrust into the role of mother. I was confused, had no money of my own and an uncertain future. With my parents, you had a comfortable home, were financially well provided for, and they did love you in their way. When I gradually withdrew from your life, I convinced myself that I was doing it for your sake and in a way that's true, but I can't deny that I was also running away from my stultifying home life and my responsibilities."

"Hang on! You had a go at me the other day for blaming myself for the domestic chaos after I was born, and now you are in danger of indulging in a bit of a guilt fest yourself. It would be easy to say that we were both victims of Gran and Grandad's style of parenting, but that's unfair as well. They did what they thought was best, and we can't rerun our lives to change anything."

"You're right, but it doesn't make it any easier."

Terry thought for a while before commenting, "I suspect if I had been in your kind of position, having to choose between giving my child a financially secure future and having to part from them, I would probably have made the same choice that you did. It is only recently that I have become painfully aware that money isn't everything. There are some things that you can't put a price on."

"Oscar Wilde summed it up succinctly with his line about a cynic knowing the price of everything and the value of nothing," added Janice, "but, while it may be easier to quantify the price of something straight away, we often don't value something until we haven't got it. Prices may vary but value persists."

Terry was quietly impressed by how he and Janice were able to have long discussions during which they felt able to openly talk about their feelings. This was a new experience for Terry, who had never had any heartfelt discussions with his grandparents, and even with Lizzie he rarely opened up about how he felt about her. Surely his attentiveness and the way he had shared his home with her would have been enough to show her that he loved her? Perhaps he shouldn't have been surprised at how he interacted with Janice, after all she was his mother, but she had been out of his life so long that he had never dared to think they might get on. Their shared disclosure about their similar childhoods unified them. Terry had found the estranged mother he had wanted to find out about, and he discovered that he actually liked her. Janice had reconnected with her son, whom she had often regretted deserting, and found that they were becoming friends. It would never be a conventional mother-son relationship, but it had already shown the early signs of becoming a loving one.

The rest of the day was spent just enjoying doing very little. They toyed with the idea of going out for a meal somewhere, but they both preferred to just laze around at home and share reminiscences. They had a lot of family time to make up for. They shared the responsibility of making snacks and an evening meal and the opportunity to get to know each other more.

After their simple evening meal and only one bottle of wine, Terry announced, "On a more mundane domestic level, I have to go to work tomorrow. I've already had a few days off with Lord's funeral, so I can't impose on John again. I should be home by just after five, and we could go somewhere for dinner. I could run you somewhere in the morning if you like. Do you have any plans?"

"These last few days have been a bit of a whirl. As I said, I just wanted to get to the funeral. I had nothing firmer planned, but I must own up to a strange ambition; I would love to walk over the bridge. I've travelled over it a few times but never walked it. We have the Pont de Saint-Nazaire over the Loire, which is very impressive but pedestrian access is not so easy at times, and anyway, the Humber Bridge will always be special to me. I saw the initial building when I was still at school, and I watched it progress on my rather infrequent trips back home. It just seemed to grow out of the banks of the river. At times it looked as if it was defying gravity and was bound to collapse."

"And then of course part of it nearly did," added Terry. "It was a great source of excitement in school round here, and we all wanted to go and see what had happened, but the emergency services wouldn't let us get near. Even from a distance, those two heavy sections of roadway hanging from what remained of the cables that had given way were pretty impressive. Naturally, Gran and Grandad were furious that I had been so foolhardy as to go and check out the area, but there was never any risk. I sometimes think that if they'd wrapped me in any more cotton wool, I'd have suffocated on it. There's quite a view from the middle. I've walked out to the centre, and it's an impressive viewing point," he added, trying to block out the memory of his last walk over it that could have become exactly that.

"I can drive you down in the morning. We might be able to find where the Red Star mobile café is, and you could drop in there sometime during the day for lunch if you wanted to."

"Sounds like a good plan. We'll just play it by ear."

CHAPTER TWENTY

As Terry awoke the next morning, he was aware of the alluring smell of bacon. He had long since recognised it as better than any alarm clock for getting him out of bed in the morning. He briefly remembered those all-too-rare Sundays when Lizzie had not been working and she had produced a marvellous 'full English'. She had enjoyed the opportunity to indulge in such domesticity, and they both enjoyed eating the resulting meal. By the time Terry arrived downstairs, he was greeted by Janice declaring, "I took the liberty of making a big breakfast. We rarely have such delights at home; we usually grab what you would describe as a continental breakfast, but we always have tea rather than coffee. Anyway, I thought it would keep us going throughout the day as we don't have particular plans for lunch."

Terry was momentarily aware of how this scene would be recognised by many as normal, a mother making breakfast for her son, but it had a delightful novelty value for him, and he enjoyed it. Even doing the washing up together later didn't seem such a chore as they chatted throughout. It was an inconsequential discourse about little of any importance, but it was a chance to continue the steady progress in getting to know each other.

The Red Star Café was rather elusive that morning, and Terry was conscious of the fact that he was running a bit late for getting to work. He did consider just dropping off Janice close to a point where she could access the path onto the bridge, but he felt it better to show her where Lenin was that morning so she would be able to find it for lunch if she so chose. As they eventually approached the café, Terry indicated its position and had intended to drive on to drop Janice nearer the access point to the bridge.

"No, just drop me off here. I've got all day to saunter along to the bridge, and anyway I'd like the chance to get myself a cup of tea from the mysterious Lenin that you've spoken of so often."

"No problem. I should be finishing about five o'clock so give me a ring there if you want picking up from anywhere," he said, proffering one of the auction house business cards. "Perhaps we could head to the Barge Inn for dinner?"

"Sounds a good idea. Now you'd better get going as you're holding up the traffic."

The auction house was relatively quiet, so John had arranged for Terry to go out in the morning and collect one or two items for future sales. It was the usual selection of small pieces of furniture and assorted pieces of ceramics. Terry couldn't help making a mental calculation of the prices the lots were likely to make. He hadn't the heart to tell the vendors that, after commission, their precious items would make very little money at all. The single old vase that one customer thought was valuable would probably end up in with a collection of his other pieces and put in as one lot, which would sell for very little. In the afternoon, Terry was sent out with Colin in the van to pick up what John had described as 'a few pieces of furniture'. In reality, this turned out to be the contents of someone's garage, and the two luckless employees spent most of the afternoon loading and subsequently unloading all manner of items. Terry and Colin were exhausted by the time they had loaded the last of the goods into the store. At least John's prior valuation visit meant that they had managed to acquire some good items to guarantee enough commission from their sale to justify the effort.

After the unloading was completed, Terry went straight to the office to check if there had been a call from Janice. Before he could consult her, Julie announced, "Oh! By the way, Terry, your mum phoned. She's at home and said she would make something for dinner to save going out."

Terry felt a mild glow of satisfaction to hear Janice described as his mother. Presumably, she had mentioned their relationship to explain why she was ringing. It still seemed a novelty to Terry, but the more he got to know her, the more comfortable he felt about his mother re-entering his life.

When he arrived home, Terry was met by the enticing aroma of something cooking in the kitchen.

"Hello, love," said Janice as she paused while lifting the lid from a large casserole dish, "how's your day been?"

"Hectic. I feel to have spent my day moving dusty furniture from one place to another. I feel as if I'm encrusted with the dust of centuries, and it was baking hot, so I will have to grab a shower before I can feel human again. What's that you're cooking? It smells gorgeous."

"It's just a chicken casserole; it's quick to prepare and cooks itself. I thought it would be an easy meal, perhaps with a bit of bread."

"I can't wait," said Terry, and he quickly went off for a shower. As he stood under the hot water, he had a chance to ponder his mum's behaviour that day. While many people enjoy the acoustics of the shower cubicle to indulge in a spot of singing, he preferred to take a moment to think. He reflected on the fact that there hadn't been any chicken in the house that morning, and the crusty baguette he had spotted on the work surface wasn't present when he left home either. Janice had obviously spent part of the day shopping, and he was looking forward to the product of her labours. This caused him to draw an early close to his session in the shower. He dried himself vigorously and, splashing on a generous amount of his cologne, he put on fresh clothes and eagerly headed down for dinner.

The dinner table was laid out simply but with what Terry took to be rustic Gallic good taste. There were even serviettes beside each of the large plates. He half recognised the serviettes, but he couldn't remember them having been used for years. Likewise, the small vase holding an arrangement of flowers from the garden was familiar, but he couldn't remember it ever having been displayed. Janice had managed to make the familiar surroundings of a very ordinary kitchen look very welcoming. A large glass mixing bowl doubled as an ice bucket containing what he took to be a bottle of champagne part-submerged in iced water.

"This all looks very special," observed Terry, taking his seat and flamboyantly flourishing his serviette before putting it on his knee. "You must have been working on it for hours."

"On the contrary, I just threw all the ingredients into a casserole dish and let them get on with it. A little bit of wine to bring it all together and it's done. We often have something similar at home. It can be thrown together in a slow cooker in the morning, and when we come home from work it's ready. The wine is one of our favourites and local to our home; Cremant de Loire is quite like some champagnes. It's not our regular tipple, but it can give an occasion that extra something."

"It is rather nice," commented Terry, having taken a sip, "I'm not a regular drinker of fizzy wines, but I could certainly take to this."

"After your performance with the Muscadet on Saturday, I guessed you might cope," she said with a slight smile.

Terry sheepishly nodded and got on with his meal, during which they chatted about their current lives, but as they sat afterwards sipping the last of the wine, there was a lengthy pause before Janice announced, "I saw your Lizzie today. Oh, sorry, I didn't mean that, I know that you're not together."

For once, Janice seemed unsure what to say, and he was keen to know where the conversation was going. He was always keen to hear about Lizzie, but Janice's hesitation hinted at bad news.

"Is she OK? What's the matter?"

"She's fine," Janice placated him. "Obviously, she's been through better times, but there's nothing seriously wrong. As you pointed out, she has been under considerable pressure at work, and for the first time in her life it has got her down. She didn't go into details, but I gather that the big case she has been on for a while was pretty traumatic and involved a very young baby. Unfortunately, she has been involved in a number of such cases in the past, but this one hit her particularly hard."

"And I haven't been much support for her," he admitted.

"We can all see things differently with twenty-twenty hindsight, and we both know that guilt trips are rarely of any use and can become a form of self-indulgence."

"Maybe, but it doesn't make me feel any better. Did she ask about me at all? She did say that we had to get together and talk. Once again, I wasn't there when she turned up. Where did you meet her, by the way?"

"I went for a walk on the bridge after you left me, and I met her on the walkway. I gather she had just gone there to give herself time to think. It is a beautiful spot and there were very few pedestrians about. I recognised her from the funeral, of course, so I stopped to have what I thought would be a brief chat, but when I explained that I was your mother, she seemed keen to discuss a whole range of things. I think she probably saw me as a link with you, and she asked a lot of questions about how you were doing, and she was obviously very pleased to hear that we had got back in touch with each other. She is a very caring girl, and she couldn't hide the fact that she still has strong feelings for you, but she feels that her recent actions have been for the best."

"How could she possibly think that?" protested Terry. "How can splitting up a good relationship be in anyone's best interests?"

"I can't go into details, Terry. You need to discuss it with her. I have my views, but it's not my place to speak on her behalf. We had a very long conversation, during which I grew to like her more and more. There is nothing I would like more than to try and engineer a reconciliation between the pair of you, but my limited experience of parenting has taught me that sometimes it is better to support children rather than to direct them."

"So we still don't know why she acted the way she did and persists in staying away?"

"As I said, we talked for a long time, and she did tell me one or two details, but it's not my place to report it all to you; it's not as if I'm keeping the secrets of the confessional, but you need to hear it from her, in her own words and at a time of her choosing."

"And when will that be?" asked Terry, trying to conceal his frustration.

"She is reluctant to discuss things here and isn't keen on meeting up in a pub with a lot of other people around. I said that Lenin's place might be suitable, but she wasn't keen on that. In the end, she thought it best if you went for a walk down by the river. She suggested that you might want to meet her down in the car park near the bridge after you finish work tomorrow. She thought six o'clock?"

"Of course I'll be there. I've got to admit that I'm worried about what she's going to say, but our situation needs to be sorted out. I can't stand being without her. I know that sounds selfish, but I really feel that we used to get on so well, and can't believe she has suddenly lost all feelings for me."

"I know, love, but you'll just have to see what happens tomorrow."

Recognising that Janice was not going to go in to details about the conversation she'd had with Lizzie, Terry contented himself with general details about his mum's day.

"Was the walk on the bridge as enjoyable as you'd hoped?"

"Absolutely exhilarating! It's almost as if you are hovering above our mundane world. Looking down at the river, so powerful, with only a suggestion of the strong currents making their presence known on the surface as they churn along. It's almost mesmeric. I could stand there for hours."

Terry felt no inclination to mention his recent visit to that very spot and contented himself with a general comment about the view from the bridge.

"After a while the noise of the traffic on the bridge persuaded us to head back for the north bank," continued Janice, "and we went to that café you pointed out this morning. That Lenin's a bit of a character, like someone out of a modern pantomime. He was very attentive, particularly when Lizzie introduced me as your mum. I must admit that I'm quite enjoying such notoriety. He was doing his bit to emphasise your virtues to Lizzie; he would obviously like to see you two back together."

"Yes, I know he's tried to put a good word in for me with her, and so many other people seem to agree that we seem well-suited to each other. I know Lord was disappointed when she left me and, in his last days, expressed a hope that we would patch things up. The only person who seems against the idea is Lizzie's friend Veronica, who has really got it in for me and does all she can to stop Lizzie moving back in with me. Veronica is renting out a room in her place for Lizzie, and at one point I thought that there was a monetary element in Veronica's action. If Lizzie moved back with me, then Veronica loses some rent money, but I don't think that's an issue with her. She has just never liked me."

"It's tempting to assume that if we are generally nice people then everyone will like us," suggested Janice, "but it's just not the case. I always think of the old lady who used to live a few doors away when I was young. As part of a small group of children, I spent some time playing near the old lady's house. We were always respectful and friendly towards her, even running the odd errand and helping her with her garden as best we could. All the other children were treated very well, but the old lady had no time for me at all. When I was known to be pregnant, she took an obvious delight in expressing some rather nasty views about my behaviour. Most people were quite supportive, but Mum and Dad tried to hide my condition as much as possible, and I think they were generally less than understanding, but that's hardly surprising."

A sudden thought struck Terry, and changing the subject somewhat, he commented, "So Lizzie wasn't at work today?"

"No. She's taking a few days off."

"Finally getting the holiday that she was wanting, I expect."

"No, not exactly. Oh dear, this is why I felt you should hear it all from her, but I'm sure she wouldn't mind me telling you that she's on sick leave."

"Sick leave?" queried Terry with more than a suggestion of concern in his voice, "It's not anything serious, is it? She has been looking a bit jaded, nothing like her old sparkling self, but with our split-up followed by Lord's death, I could hardly expect her to look at her best."

"Obviously all that can't have helped, but the truth is she has been told to take a break for a while. She spends a lot of time counselling people who are going through very difficult periods in their lives, and it is not uncommon for people like her to spend so much time trying to sort out other people's problems that they lack the mental energy to examine their own. Lizzie's team get some of the most demanding cases to work on, and burn-out is a strong possibility, that's why all those involved in counselling have access to their own counsellor."

"So the counsellors have their own counsellors?"

"In a nutshell, yes. Many people who are experiencing personal problems in their lives refuse to 'give in'. It's as if they see it as some sort of personal failing, and they have to 'pull themselves together' and just get on with life. Fortunately, Lizzie was aware of the fact that she was experiencing even more stress than usual in her life and had the courage to seek help. She knows, as an insider so to speak, how counsellors work by encouraging people to examine their position and to find their own way to bring about a positive change in their lives. It's not telling people what to do but rather listening and giving the client a bit of thinking time."

For a brief moment, Terry's mind flashed back to his meeting with Michael Lampeter Hodge. Whoever he was obviously had effective skills as some sort of therapist. Perhaps he had been an undercover counsellor? A plain-clothed therapist? He was sharply brought back to the present as Janice continued.

"I was fortunate to have an excellent counsellor who worked with me when I went through a bad patch just after starting at university in Newcastle. It was invaluable to have someone who would listen to me as I tried to come to terms with my position, being away from home and all my friends, parted from you and trying to sort out what was happening with your father."

Terry resisted the temptation to press the issue as to his father's identity as he was far more concerned about Lizzie, and instead he asked, "So why didn't she talk her problems over with me? I could have helped or at least tried."

"I'm sure you would have wanted to, but perhaps she felt reluctant to talk about her work. Much of the time she has to respect client confidentiality, so it would have been against her professional ethics to talk about particular cases. She could disclose more of her situation to a senior colleague, knowing that it would all be kept in house. Anyway, you will have to get the details from her when you meet up tomorrow. I doubt that she will be looking forward to that discussion but she knows it has to happen soon."

At last Terry had a little more information about Lizzie, but it brought him little comfort. He was going to meet her at last, but he feared the news he would receive then would not be welcome.

CHAPTER TWENTY-ONE

As they washed up after dinner, Terry was once again aware how such a routine domestic activity felt to bring a certain sense of normality to his life, but he was still unable to forget how uneasy he felt about his mother's report on her meeting with Lizzie. When the washing up was completed, Terry made them both a cup of tea, which they took into the garden. They sat there for a while before Terry commented, "So you appear to have got on well with Lizzie."

He knew it to be the case, but he felt the need for some positive news from her as he could not shake the feeling of considerable concern as to what Lizzie might disclose the following day.

"Yes, we just seemed to click. It was quite a girly day out in the end, and we chatted about all sorts of relatively trivial things and even had the odd laugh, particularly when we were down at the café. That Lenin is a bit of a character, and he was quite entertaining. Anyway, we couldn't stop around there all day and Lizzie kindly gave me a lift to the shops in Hessle because I wanted to get something in for dinner tonight. She ended up spending the entire afternoon with me and even drove me back here."

"Lizzie was here?"

"Yes, but she wouldn't come in even when I assured her that you would be at work. She obviously felt uneasy about being here. I guess it brought back a lot of memories."

Terry had felt pleased for a while at the news that his mum had got on so well with Lizzie, but the mention of the fact that she didn't want to enter the house reminded him of the detachment she appeared determined to sustain. He was becoming increasingly aware that they had not just had a minor tiff, and once again he started to worry about what Lizzie would say the next day.

Eventually, he determined to change his train of thought, so he turned to Janice and said, "You talked earlier about the problems you had when you started at the university." He paused to let the change of direction of their conversation sink in before continuing. "You mentioned a number of issues you were faced with, one of which was the situation with my father."

It was the first time that he had felt confident enough to bring up the subject, and he was careful not to openly ask who his father was, but Janice had mentioned her issues at university, so he felt he had an opportunity to find out a little about his parentage.

She remained silent for a while but then smiled gently and said, "I had a bit of a rough time when I started up there. For much of my childhood I had dreamt of getting away from the tedium of this place, but the reality of suddenly finding myself in a strange city with none of my old friends around was hard. I even missed Mum and Dad. Home life had been boring, but at least it had a reassuring structure, and I could get out whenever possible to meet my friends. Starting at university can be difficult for many young people. There I was in a strange town, suddenly having to cope with the new domestic arrangements of living in digs and attending lectures where I assumed everybody understood the subject apart from me. Even the natives spoke a different language. For most young people thrown together at that age, it is an opportunity to develop relationships that may go on to last a lifetime, like part of some primeval mass courtship stage in their young lives.

The excitement of the social scene usually kicks in and things get better. I didn't feel that I could get involved with all that because I was committed to my relationship with your father. On top of that, I had to get used to being away from you, and I missed you terribly. Lord told me that Mum and Dad seemed to want to give the impression that I had just abandoned you, and they'd stepped in to make up for my lack of concern. The truth is that Mum, in particular, was more than happy to take over the responsibility of having a baby in the house, and I suspect that she rather regretted that they'd not had any more children. Added to that, I had some trouble bonding with you; nothing extreme, but I didn't seem to have that natural mothering instinct. There was the underlying fact that I cannot deny that I couldn't stand the thought of being trapped in that domestic set-up, and it was selfish to gradually withdraw from your life. It was never my intention to move away completely, but when I saw how settled you were, I convinced myself that it would disrupt your life if I took you from them. Then life happened, and I drifted away. I'm not proud of it, but I wasn't the heartless, uncaring individual that some might have accused me of being."

Janice paused for a while, obviously thinking very carefully about what she was about to say before she continued.

"I know that you must be keen to know who your father was. I have often thought of how best to tell you. It had to be the right moment, but we never met to really discuss things, and it's not the sort of thing to scribble on the back of a postcard. When I met you during my fleeting visits, you never came out and asked me who he was, and I was glad of that because I wouldn't have relished the prospect of disclosing such intimate details to someone I didn't feel I knew. These last couple of days I have started to really get to know you; better late than never, I suppose."

Being conscious of his mother's awkwardness about the matter, Terry interrupted her by protesting, "I can't pretend that the matter hasn't often been on my mind, but my ambition was always to meet up with you again. That's why I tried so hard to get in touch, and now I'm just delighted to have met up and to start really getting to know you."

"That's kind, but you do deserve to know your background. You will have heard the stories about your father having been a big star in a rock band, but that's just not the case. It was a fiction that I originally concocted to imagine myself in a more glamorous world than I actually existed in. Mum and Dad knew the truth, but it was convenient for them to accept it as it left your father's identity a mystery. The fact is that he was a local boy, and Mum and Dad knew his parents and the kind of boy he was. They saw him as a bit wild because he was somewhat unconventional. His name was Martin, he was a very sweet boy, and we had known each other for years before you came along. You look a lot like him, as you might expect. You have his brown eyes and wavy hair and a way of smiling that reminds me of him."

This last comment triggered a faint involuntary smile on Terry's face at this reference to his likeness to his father. He had never tried to imagine that they may have looked alike. He resisted the temptation to press for more details and gave his mum time to collect her thoughts before she continued.

"He was one of the group I would meet on the evenings that I escaped from home. He was a year older than me, and I often felt he was so sophisticated. He wasn't in a group, but he often brought his guitar when we all met up. It was the early seventies when we started going out together, and Martin was still clinging on to what was a kind of hippy lifestyle. It wasn't all free love and drugs, but he was a bit of a nonconformist in his dress and tried to portray a somewhat mystical image.

He enjoyed singing a range of sixties protest songs, a sort of Yorkshire Bob Dylan, but the truth is that he was not the best guitarist in the world, and his singing voice wasn't so good either. It didn't matter to me as we were just so much in love. He smoked a rather expensive brand of cigarettes, and in an attempt to be part of his 'cool' world, I even took up smoking, but fortunately I never enjoyed it. I would just blow smoke around theatrically and try to look like some sort of celebrity."

She paused and gave a short laugh, and Terry found himself joining in with this show of amusement at his mum's recollections of her teenage years.

"As I said, we were very much in love, and if things had been different we would probably have stayed together. People can be quick to dismiss young love as being just some inconsequential fad that will pass in a few months as if the young are just playing at being in love."

"I guess that my arrival split you up very effectively."

"I've told you before that you did not ruin my life, so don't go trying to burden yourself with undeserved guilt. There were so many more important influences on my decision-making at the time. As I said, Martin was a year older than me, and he went on to university in Bath. We were able to see each other very infrequently, and then when it came to my going to university a couple of years later, I unfortunately wasn't accepted for Bath. I had delayed taking my A levels for a year and my results weren't as good as they might have been as my studies had been a bit disrupted, as you can imagine. Mum and Dad could hardly conceal their pleasure that another hurdle was being put up between Martin and me and eventually the strain on our relationship became too much. When Martin graduated, he found a job with good prospects but it was in London. He tried to convince me that if he took it up, he would soon be earning enough to enable us to get married, but it just wasn't going to happen for us. He had changed a lot during our enforced separation. He was no longer the wild young troubadour that I had known. He had become more conventional and even had his hair cut short. His career was obviously more important to him than our love. Perhaps he reasoned that it was important to accumulate a lot of money so he could provide for his family, but I suspect his ambition to succeed was largely driven by his own ego. I guess the separation proved that we weren't really suited to each other, but it was another factor that dictated that we would eventually have to go our own ways. I admit that I was badly shaken by the eventual break-up, but on reflection I see it wasn't so much a break-up as a drifting apart. We kept in touch for a while, but our correspondence became less and less frequent, and Mum and Dad made no secret of the fact that the situation suited them. I think he's still in London somewhere, but it must be nearly 20 years since we last met, and now I'm very happy to be with Greg."

"Did you and Greg ever consider getting married?" asked Terry at the mention of her partner's name.

"We did discuss it, and I think Greg was more for it than I was. His parents are quite elderly, and I get on very well with them. They do tend to see me as a daughter-in-law in all but name, and I know that Greg would like to get married to formalise our little family set-up, though I have never felt under any sort of pressure from anyone. I must admit that, having seen my parents drifting through a somewhat tedious marriage it put me off the idea for a while, but recently we have touched upon the possibility of getting married."

"So, could I put myself forward as a page boy?" quipped Terry.

"I'm not sure we would want such a level of formality, and I couldn't imagine you in short trousers carrying a bouquet, but I would make sure that you got an invitation."

CHAPTER TWENTY-TWO

The following day, after breakfast, Janice announced her intention to take the bus into Hull to do some shopping and to see what the town looked like after what had been some twenty-plus years since she last lived there. She made it clear to Terry that she would have plenty to do to fill her day, and she would not be back until the evening. He appreciated her intention to leave him plenty of time to talk to Lizzie.

Having driven his mum into Hessle to catch her bus, Terry drove on to the auction house, but he found it difficult to develop any enthusiasm for his work as his mind was taken up with thoughts of the meeting he was to have with Lizzie that evening. Even the time shared eating sandwiches for lunch with Colin and Julie was not the cheery exchange of banter that it had been. He had hoped to get away early to prepare for his meeting with Lizzie, but in the afternoon he had to help unload the delivery of items from Jim Bolton's house in Swanland. He couldn't help but notice how the furniture, which had looked very tasteful in the house, now looked just like a very average display of second-hand furniture, and it certainly wouldn't achieve the prices Mr Bolton had initially expected.

Terry became increasingly resentful of the time it was taking to sort the furniture as he saw his plans of a prompt departure after his shift becoming increasingly unlikely. It was past five before he got away, and he knew he had to be at the car park in just under an hour. After a hot, dusty day in the auction house, he was desperately in need of a shower, so his drive home was considerably faster than usual. He had hoped to give himself time to prepare himself fully for his meeting, as it was extremely important to him that he looked his best. It was like preparing for a first date but much more critical. He had laid out his clothes that morning to save some time, but he still felt flustered as he stared at himself in the mirror after he had dressed. He decided that the shirt he had chosen was not really right, but he hadn't got time to change so it would have to do. He splashed on rather too much aftershave, briefly flicked a comb through his hair, grabbed his car keys and ran out to the car. He had only gone a few hundred yards when he realised that he'd left his wallet in his work trousers. The need to retrace his path and collect it meant that it was after six when a rather hassled Terry arrived at the car park.

He soon found Lizzie standing by the entrance but was surprised to notice that her car was not there. He quickly parked up and almost ran to meet her.

"I'm so sorry I'm late," he blurted out when he was still a few feet away. "It's been one of those days when everything seems to have gone wrong. I hope you haven't been waiting long."

"No, only a few minutes, and anyway it's nice to stand here and look out over the river. I've enjoyed the fresh air." There were a few seconds of awkward silence before she continued, "It was lovely to meet your mum yesterday; you must be very happy to have met up with her again."

"Yes, I had begun to think I would never find her, and now I find we actually get on very well, and she really likes you."

They both knew that this stunted conversation was largely small talk to avoid getting on to the reason for their meeting. They set off towards the river bank. Neither of them spoke as they took a path that they had walked together so many times before. They strolled along with both of them ostensibly just taking in the view of the river and making polite but inconsequential comments, but they both knew that at some point they would have to discuss some very important issues. It was Terry who eventually felt he had to meet the problems they had head-on, and without leaving any opportunity for her to interrupt, he started to attempt his rehearsed statement.

"I have missed you more than I could have thought possible. I thought we were so well-suited that I took it for granted that you were as happy as I was. Making such assumptions of your feelings was unforgivable and stupid, as was taking you for granted the way I did. I know now that I was blind to what's important in my life. You were right; I confused monetary value with true value. There are some things you can't put a price on. Lord taught me a lot about what really matters in life. His greatest treasure was his wife, Mary, and he would have given anything to have kept her for a little longer. That's how I feel about you; nothing is more important to me than you. I know you don't want to go back to the way we were, but please don't cut me out of your life altogether."

His outburst had not been exactly what he meant to say, but at least he had prevented her from stopping him in mid flow. She turned away from him and stared out over the river in silence. He felt his outpouring of emotion had not impressed her, but he waited, with diminishing hope, for her response. Eventually, she turned to him.

He was aware that she had tears on her cheek as she declared, "It wasn't your fault, Terry. Yes, we had our disagreements, but nothing we couldn't have sorted out if I'd been able to make the effort. The fact is that I've been under rather a lot of pressure at work, and it's coloured my whole life."

"Yes, Janice told me you'd been off work and had some problems."

"I realised, too late, that I was not coping, so I sought help from my team leader, and she arranged some counselling sessions for me. I know that if I'd been rational, I would have talked it over with you, but in the state I was in at the time everything you did seemed to irritate or annoy me. I began to see you as somehow contributing to my unhappiness. I know it doesn't make sense, but it did at the time."

"Given my insensitivity and selfishness, it makes absolute sense," he said in an attempt to share responsibility for the break-up.

"We are none of us perfect," she continued, "but in this case you were collateral damage. Anyway, my counsellor enabled me to get things in something like true perspective, and I feel a bit better. I have some more sessions over the next couple of weeks, but I'm improving. Identifying the underlying causes of my apparent depression is the first part of getting over it. The counsellor helped me to recognise what I knew was getting me down; I was overwhelmed by the nature of the cases I had been working on and had started to share the trauma experienced by some of the clients. If you're dealing with the tragedies of others, then some of it can wear off on you. I tried to leave the work at the office, but it followed me home."

"And you just let it fester because you couldn't discuss it with me, partly because of client confidentiality and partly because, at the time, I was insensitive and didn't appreciate the strain you were under."

"I should have seen what was happening to me sooner, but it just sort of crept up on me. I knew that I was not sleeping well and my appetite was poor, but the mood swings and irrational behaviour are things that only outsiders see. I'm glad that I acknowledged that I had a problem when I did and talked it through with my team leader, or I could have done something stupid."

"Surely you didn't think of suicide?"

"No, I never formulated any plan, but I have to admit that as I looked down from the bridge there one day, I could see why people found it attractive to just escape all their problems by jumping. I could never do it." She paused for a moment before continuing. "And I certainly couldn't think of doing so now."

Terry allowed himself a moment of hope. Was she implying that things had improved to such an extent that their separation could soon be over? He ventured this tentative suggestion to her.

"If things are getting better, and you feel more settled, does this mean that we can think about getting back together at some time?"

"That isn't what I meant, sorry."

"But why? Everybody who knows us says we are meant for each other, except Veronica, and you apparently. I don't know what she has been saying about me, but all that about me dating some mysterious blonde is rubbish. I had a sandwich and a coffee with my colleague Julie."

"I never listened to her evil gossip, and I knew you would never do anything you considered unfaithful even after I left you. I got fed up with her constant snide remarks and moved out. I'm back with Mum and Dad because I've still got the tenants in my flat. Dad drove me down here this evening."

"I wondered why your car wasn't in the car park when I got here. I can't say I've enjoyed listening to your news, but I was glad to at least try and tell you how I felt. I gather that I have been rather useless at showing my feelings in the past, and even though it's too late, I just had to let you know. I don't think there's anything to be gained from staying here now that we know where we stand, so can I give you a lift home?"

He looked at her and could clearly see that tears were flowing gently down her cheeks. He instinctively moved forward and gave her a gentle hug, and he noticed that she showed no sign of resistance. He took out his handkerchief and gave it to her, and she dried away the tears before declaring, "I'm afraid I haven't told you everything." There was a lengthy pause before she continued, "I'm pregnant; I'm sorry."

This sudden announcement visibly stunned him, and he could only stand for a moment, gazing at her as he tried to take it all in. The message was simple, but the resulting emotional turmoil left him speechless for a while until he could recover enough to ask, "Sorry? What do you mean?"

"I'm pregnant!"

"I got that bit, but why are you sorry? It's the best news I've had in years."

It was Lizzie's turn to be shocked by this revelation, and she explained, "But you never wanted children."

"I know my family could be accused of generally making a pig's ear of raising children as evidenced by my upbringing, but the thought of starting a family with you was more than I could ever have hoped for, if only to prove that the family tradition of screwing up child-rearing could be broken. What on earth made you feel that I didn't want children?"

"You remember when I thought I was pregnant? You made it clear how relieved you were when it proved to be a false alarm."

"I wasn't relieved. On the contrary, I was very disappointed, but I didn't want to let you know that because I thought you were pleased that you wouldn't have the interruption to your career, and I just wanted to react the way I thought you wanted me to. Are you still not keen on having a baby?"

"Of course I want the baby, but being pregnant and dealing with our most recent case involving a mistreated toddler was a contributing factor in the development of my health problems. My doubts about being able to give a child a safe environment and my assumption that you didn't want to be involved just proved too much for me."

"Rest assured that I am madly keen on being a father, and I'm sure you will make a first-rate mother. My only hope now is that we will be able to carry out those roles together somehow."

"I don't know anything any more, Terry. When I have the baby, I would want to give up work for a while. I always used to think that I would miss the job if I ever had to give it up, but now with all its pressures I don't think that I could continue in my present role. I will have to face up to a loss of income for a few years. Our lifestyle would change with less money to enjoy the things we used to do."

"Bugger the money! If there is one lesson that I've learned over the last few weeks, it's that some things are much too valuable to put a price on. Relationships are much more important than mere commercial concerns."

Terry was keen to take up her comments about the fact that giving up work would mean *they* would have less money, so he argued, "We could make it work for us. We've got the house, and I could keep up the auction work and get other part-time employment. Lord, bless him, left me money in his will; it's almost as if he knew we might need it. We could easily get by. I'll do anything to make it work for us."

"You've changed a lot in a very short time, Terry. It's all very confusing. What happened?"

"It's called 'growing up', Lizzie, and It was long overdue, but I'm glad I have at last started the process."

He paused for a moment before he smiled broadly and informed her, "This is really going to shake up Janice; she's just becoming accustomed to being a mother, and she's to become a grandmother."

His attempt to lighten the tone of the conversion were unsuccessful, so he tried once again to explain the depth of his feelings for her.

"I got it all very wrong, darling; my love for you was so intense, so deep, that it never occurred to me that you might not feel exactly the same way about me. Everything seemed so perfect for me, and after being brought up in an undemonstrative home setting, I invested all my emotional eggs in one basket, so to speak. I felt so happy, things were going so well, that I thought you must have shared those feelings. I know now that relationships are high maintenance. They must be monitored, not taken for granted and certainly not allowed to die."

He looked to her for some sort of positive response, but she said nothing for a while. Terry stood in silence, staring at the river. If only everything in life were as constant. He felt that the river never changed but then realised that he was wrong. The river was constantly changing, even when it appeared to be sluggishly moving along, the currents below the surface were in constant conflict with each other. Things can look calm on the surface, the river might look little more than a very large swimming pool, almost enticing on a hot day, but any swimmer who incautiously attempted to enter the water could be in immediate jeopardy. Relationships can be like that; everything seems to be going fine, but nothing must be taken for granted, and he knew he had taken Lizzie and their whole relationship for granted, and he was suffering for it now. He felt deflated. The news of the pregnancy had been like a bright ray of hope, and he had been momentarily elated, but Lizzie's subsequent remarks had shown that she was still unsure of what she wanted from life.

In desperation, he asked, "So you just don't love me anymore?"

"I didn't say that." She paused as she tried to find the words. "I just don't know how I feel. I'm a mess. My time with you was great, the best thing in my life, but I've changed. I feel I have lost control of my life. I want the old times back."

"Then come back," he interjected. "Life can be good again. I don't expect everything to suddenly go back to the way it was, but we can work on it. All my life I've been so stupid not to see that people have to work at relationships. I've been emotionally ignorant, not taking the time to really think what others might want out of life. You've put up with my inability to appreciate what really matters. You lived in a house that I filled with junk because it might make a profit rather than because I liked it. All that time you were employed in a job that repeatedly subjected you to unacceptable stress levels, and I didn't recognise what it was doing to you. You suffered my failings for years, so please let me be around to help you get over your present difficulties."

He looked at her, and the faintest of nervous smiles appeared on her face. He was prompted to press home his plea a little more, and he pointed out, "I want to be around you to help with our baby. Surely we both have to accept that, in what have been bloody awful times, the baby is the only good news?"

"Yes, I know, but it's not how I wanted it to be."

"Reality often doesn't match up to our dreams, but it doesn't mean we have to stop dreaming. You always used to tell me that we didn't have problems; we had challenges. Well, we now have a challenge, and we must face up to it."

For the second time, Lizzie smiled slightly as she realised that her own philosophy was being turned back on her. She turned and stood for some time staring out over the river. Her apparent tranquillity contrasted starkly with Terry's mounting apprehension as he waited for her response.

Eventually, she turned back and said, "I was expecting this meeting to be difficult. I just intended to tell you about the baby and then explain why we couldn't go on together, and you've complicated it all. I admit I was confused, but now you've made it more complicated. I'm sorry if I underestimated you, but I wasn't ready for you to be like this."

"Like what?"

"Understanding, for one, and you haven't tried to pressure me. I got it all wrong about the way you would respond to my being pregnant. In a way, it has added to my confused state, but at the same time it has helped me a lot."

"I want to help you. Call it pay-back time for the years you've carried me. We could still have a great future together, and I think that's something worth working on."

He walked over and took her gently in his arms. The new Terry understood that this was a time for comfort rather than passion, and for once in a long time he knew that she felt relaxed. She needed that hug. They stood together for a while before Terry lifted his head and, looking at her face, said, "There is one thing that I would like you to do if you feel up to it. Could you possibly be the one who tells Janice about the baby? She was really very taken with you, and it would make her day to hear the news from you. There is one problem, or challenge, in that, unfortunately, Mum's due to fly out tomorrow. I know it could be difficult for you but could I give you a lift back to my place now? You could ring your dad to pick you up there, or I could run you home later, whatever you would feel more comfortable with."

Lizzie thought for a while, and Terry regretted putting the idea forward and was visibly relieved when she said, "I'm sure Dad wouldn't mind picking me up from your place, and I must admit it would be lovely to see your mum again before she goes back to France."

Terry couldn't hide his delight at hearing this news and turned to retrace their steps to the car park. The return journey was undertaken at a faster pace in his eagerness to get back to see how Janice would react to the news of the impending baby. In fact, he had to curb his eagerness as Lizzie was in danger of not being able to keep up.

CHAPTER TWENTY-THREE

As they sat in the car before starting up the engine, Terry looked over at Lizzie beside him. On the surface, it might appear that everything was as it had been in their happier times, but he knew that not to be the case. Lizzie lacked her usual vibrant air of self-assurance. The Lizzie who had proven capable of taking on the world now seemed strangely damaged, and he longed to be able to help.

"I was just thinking that you don't look very pregnant," he ventured.

"I only took the test last week. I'd had my suspicions and wondered if it was that causing me to feel so down."

"You still look much the same, no bulges or anything," he commented awkwardly. "Do you know when the baby will be born?"

"I haven't had time to think about it. I'll have to get an appointment at the surgery to do the calculations, but it's going to be some time next spring."

He felt a sense of elation, but he was careful not to display the strength of his excitement at this additional detail of her condition, which offered him a view of what might be domestic normality, but he was making no assumptions about how things might work out. He contented himself by simply observing, "That's a good time of year."

He wanted to ask whether she had a preference for a boy or a girl and to delve more deeply into how she felt and to have all those conversations that expectant parents might have, but he knew it wasn't the right time. Instead, he declared,

"It seems unfair on your dad, dragging him out to pick you up later, so why don't I run you home?"

"Thanks. It might make sense. I'll give him a ring and tell him he's not on stand-by. It's his birthday, and I suspect he might want to celebrate with the odd whisky or two."

In a matter of minutes they were home, and Terry was pleased to find Janice preparing dinner. As he entered the kitchen with Lizzie and before Janice could say anything, he was quick to explain, "No, we aren't back together, but I think it's fair to say we are back on more friendly terms, and Lizzie has some news for you."

Lizzie stood for a moment and, glancing to Terry for some kind of support, imparted her simple message, "I'm pregnant."

"That certainly implies friendly terms," exclaimed Janice before instinctively rushing over to hug Lizzie and saying, "That's wonderful. Congratulations." She paused for a moment and asked, "You are pleased, aren't you?"

"Yes, but things are complicated."

"We both want the baby," interjected Terry, looking to Lizzie for support. "But Lizzie hasn't been too well recently, and we need time to clear our heads over the whole situation."

"If you both want the baby, everything else is relatively insignificant. I'm sorry if I seemed unduly excited, but you seem so suited together. You've both gone through a very rough patch, but at least you haven't started throwing things at each other, and even now there don't appear to be any major recriminations. On a selfish note, I have to declare that I'm absolutely delighted, but having children to please grandparents is hardly a good reason to start a family. Greg will be over the moon, too, to know there's a baby on the way. He loves children, but that should also not be a major consideration.

The important thing is that you want the baby, and that's a pretty good starting point. Why don't the pair of you sit out in the garden, and I'll make us all a pot of tea?"

Terry and Lizzie sat outside together in what was, for a moment, an awkward silence before Terry asked, "You're back with your parents then. How are they keeping these days?"

"Dad's still spending a lot of time in his shed, and Mum's joined a yoga class. They were both asking after you. I think they were a bit surprised to have me back with them, but they are being very supportive."

"And do they know about the baby?"

"No, I wanted to tell you first. It made for some awkward moments at home because I think Mum suspects that I'm pregnant, and I wanted to tell her, but I had to let you know first."

"How do you think they'll react?"

"I'm not sure. They've never been the sort of parents who keep dropping subtle hints about their ambition to become grandparents, but I'm sure they will be pleased. Veronica was in that relationship with Des for years, and her parents took every opportunity to express their eagerness to get a grandchild as if their lives would not be complete without knowing they had added to their family tree. They as much as admitted that they felt 'unfulfilled'. It was rather sad really, and Veronica felt under some pressure to produce; it certainly didn't help her relationship with Des."

Terry couldn't help thinking that the breakdown between Des and Veronica was largely due to her selfish behaviour, but he resisted the temptation to say so, and instead, he commented, "I like your mum and dad. I know they were careful not to interfere, and even though they lived close by, they weren't constantly dropping in to visit. They let us get on with our lives, and so when we saw each other it was always a pleasant experience. I hope you're going to let them know about the baby soon; I'm sure they will be over the moon."

"Yes, they deserve to know what's going on. I had intended to broach the subject this evening when I got back because it's not one of Mum's various classes, and it's Dad's birthday, so they will both be in. I must admit that it's not something I relish; it ought to be such a happy occasion, but I just can't feel that way about it. But I'm sure they will be pleased."

Their conversation was interrupted by Janice bringing out a tray with a pot of tea and assorted mugs, which she set down on the table, declaring, "There we are. I'm sorry, Lizzie, I should have asked, but do you want to join us for supper?"

"That's very kind, but I will need to get back home; Mum and Dad are expecting me to join them for Dad's little birthday do. It won't be a big event, just the three of us, but I think Mum's doing it largely to entice Dad out of his shed."

"I'd forgotten it was his birthday until you mentioned it earlier. I've got a bottle of his favourite whisky in the pantry, but with all that's been going on, I forgot all about it. Perhaps you could give it to him?"

He had hoped that she might suggest that he gave it to her father himself, but she just smiled and agreed to pass it on to him. Having sorted out tea for everyone, Janice smiled at Lizzie and asked, "So, how are you feeling at the moment, love?"

It was question that showed a natural concern rather than being probing, and Terry was quietly impressed at the way his mum was able to display such a genuine interest in Lizzie's state of mind. He waited patiently to hear what Lizzie had to say, and she took a moment before responding to what might have seemed to be just a routine, polite question.

"I don't really know. Things have seemed so bleak for a while now. There wasn't any one thing that seemed to be getting me down. During my first counselling session, he helped me to recognise that my job had become too much for me. I knew it all along. It was a regular item of conversation with my work team. We were working with other people's traumas on a regular basis, and we all knew that we had to keep an emotional distance from their problems. I'd been doing it for two years, and, yes, it was a strain, but I managed to keep my distance from their personal tragedies. As a team, we tried to support each other, but for much of the time we were working on our own on our cases, and we rarely had the luxury of time to talk though them with each other. I convinced myself that I couldn't bring the issues home to talk about because of the confidentiality issues. Of course, I should have known that I could have talked in general terms about me without divulging details of individual cases."

"That's down to me," said Terry. "I should have asked about your work more. I should have seen the pressure you were under and done something to help. At the very least, I should have sorted out a real holiday for you instead of a pathetic overnight trip."

"You're not to blame, Terry. By the time the holiday was planned, I was already aware that I was not thinking clearly; nothing would have lifted that feeling of a dark cloud hanging over me. I felt somehow empty, life held nothing for me to look forward to. I felt hopeless, helpless, worthless, and I turned my negativity against others. I know I was irritable and quick to somehow try and blame others. The obvious symptoms of poor diet and sleep patterns were easy to identify, but trying to understand, let alone explain my mood swings and that ever-present sense of sadness is all but impossible."

Throughout all this, Janice sat listening attentively before asking, "I don't want you to break the confidentiality of your meeting with your counsellor, but did you tell him that you were pregnant?"

"No. I wasn't completely sure that I was pregnant at the time. You and Terry are the only people that I've told so far. Why do you ask?"

"It just reminded me of something my own counsellor discussed with me when I had problems at Newcastle University. It pretty soon became clear to us that my depressive state was induced by a number of issues relating to being away from home, friends and family. A recognition of that fact enabled me to get things into perspective a bit, and I managed to get over the problem. It was in my last session when I was discussing the fact that I was a lot better, that I happened to mention that the feelings I had been experiencing reminded me of what I had experienced at times when I was pregnant. He didn't go into any details, but he told me that it might have been a degree of antenatal depression. I'm not one of those who proclaim themselves as self-taught psychiatrists, but I couldn't help but do a bit of background reading in the university library, and I seemed to fit the pattern. Perhaps you should mention your pregnancy to your counsellor at your next appointment?"

"I've heard about postnatal depression and the 'baby blues', but I didn't know about the antenatal stuff."

"For God's sake, don't take it as a full diagnosis. It's just an observation based on my own experiences, but you've pointed out that you recognised the pressure of your job was a factor, and if you stir in the mixture of hormonal activity your body has been going through, then it might explain some of the problems you are facing. Knowing what might be causing your feelings is not a cure, but it might go some way to explaining your situation and at least lifting the feeling of hopelessness. It is probably no comfort to know that you're far from alone, but if you are willing to talk it through with other people, then there is every probability that you will get over this pretty soon. There are two factors in your favour; you saw the need to seek help, and you have the support of your family around you. Have you thought about seeing your doctor? They may be able to help."

"I did think about seeing Doctor Corbett, but it's hard to motivate myself to arrange an appointment. I know I should see him, but then I ask myself, what's the point? In my more rational moments, I know that what you are saying about this problem getting better eventually is true, but knowing something is true doesn't mean I really believe it. I know that must sound stupid, but everything is confusing at the moment."

Janice leaned over the table and gently held Lizzie's hand. No words were exchanged for some minutes, and Terry looked on at this silent communion. He quietly admired his mother's ability to do the right thing in this way and regretted his own lack of emotional empathy. He wondered if it was exclusively a female trait but had to acknowledge that his upbringing had always made it difficult for him to respond intuitively in such situations.

"You must concentrate on what is good in your life," advised Janice, "think what you have to look forward to. You're going to have a baby soon. You will start your own family, and you have Terry there, who loves you very much. He would relish the chance to prove that he would make a great father. From what I've seen, you have taught him how to love, and he wants the opportunity to develop that love. Your mum and dad will be so happy for you. Life will be good again."

"I haven't had the chance to say this before," added Terry, "but my *mum* is right. I have made a pig's ear of trying to express my feelings for you. I never lacked sincerity but wasn't always able to show it."

"Don't go feeling guilty about it," declared Lizzie, "it's not your fault."

"Feeling guilty is a family failing," interjected Janice, with a knowing look directed at Terry. "We have a tendency to seek culpability for everything that seems to go wrong in the world. What we have to recognise is that looking for someone to blame for many situations is a waste of time. At the moment, we just have to accept how things are, do what we can to ameliorate them and hold on to the belief that things will get better. In the meantime just remember, as the French would say, *Il n'y a qu'un bonheur dans la vie, c'est d'aimer et d'être aimé.*"

"And for those whose French may not quite be up to that?" queried Terry.

"There is only one happiness in life, to love and be loved," replied Janice, "or as the Beatles so succinctly put it, all you need is love. It just seems to sound so much more romantic in French. Whatever ways it's expressed, it is absolutely true, and you, Lizzie, are loved."

Lizzie sat quietly, drying a tear from her eye with Terry's handkerchief and replied, "I know that, I really know that, and it does help a bit, so thank you, both of you."

"And just to give you something else to look forward to, I would love to see you at my wedding to Greg."

Terry couldn't conceal his surprise at this latest bit of news and sat in stunned silence while Lizzie replied, "That sounds lovely, and if I'm feeling better, I would love to try and get there. When are you planning to get married?"

"Whenever you're feeling better."

Lizzie was more than a little surprised at this answer and, resisting the temptation to get some sort of explanation for the unexpected response, she contented herself by asking, "But what about Greg? Doesn't he need to be consulted about the date?"

"He doesn't even know we are getting married. I haven't told him yet. Oh, he won't be annoyed; he's been trying to persuade me to marry him for years. Every time he has a couple of extra glasses of red in the bar, he proposes to me. I know he means it, so I might as well call his bluff. I know he will be a bit surprised when I see him tomorrow, but at the same time he'll be delighted. You do realise that I'm only doing it to get the chance to see you again, Lizzie. It will be a bonus for Greg; he deserves a treat."

Lizzie smiled at Janice's quip, and Terry just sat for a while, impressed by his mother's impetuous wedding announcement, before remarking, "Well, that came out of the blue!"

"Not entirely," replied Janice. "As I told you before, we have been, sort of, considering getting married for quite a while. I just needed an excuse to consider formalising our arrangement. Our discussions over the last few days have reminded me that if you are lucky enough to find the right person, then you should do all you can to keep them. I have never been one of those who contend that marriage is the only way to show commitment, but I've realised that it would make Greg happy, and I want to make him happy."

She paused for a moment as if suddenly becoming aware of what she might be implying and then said, "For God's sake, don't think I'm suggesting that the pair of you get married so you will be able to live happily ever after. You must do what you choose. You know me, Terry, I don't go in for telling people how to run their lives. My track record shows that parental guidance is something I've never been strong on, so I don't feel equipped to start now. What I will say is that my invitation for you to come to our wedding, Lizzie, is absolutely genuine. I've only known you for a few days, but with everything going on and all, I feel that I know you well. By the way, Terry, the invite is extended to you as well, but please don't turn up in short trousers and carrying a bouquet."

It was Lizzie's turn to look confused, but she resisted the temptation to delve into the reasoning behind Janice's remark, and she sat quietly as Janice smiled at Terry before continuing, "I won't pretend that I wouldn't love to see you both turn up together at our wedding, but if that's not part of your future then so be it, but please do come if only as two individuals."

CHAPTER TWENTY-FOUR

They sat together in the garden and talked for a while about largely inconsequential things as if they all felt the need to take some of the emotional intensity out of the evening. Terry found himself looking at Lizzie a lot. He noticed that she was wearing subtle make-up, and it occurred to him that she hadn't been wearing it lately. Perhaps this was a suggestion that she was beginning to take more interest in her appearance. He recognised that it was unlikely to be an attempt to show an interest in him, but he felt slightly reassured that she was beginning to do something that was more like her old self. He watched as she occasionally smiled at some comment. She did not take a major part in the conversation, and Terry scrutinised her behaviour to look for any sign of improvement in her demeanour.

Eventually, Lizzie announced, "Thank you both for this evening, but now I really must be getting home. Is it all right for you to give me a lift home now, Terry?"

"Of course, I'll just go and get that bottle of whisky for your dad, and I'll be right with you."

While Terry was in the house, Lizzie turned to Janice and confided, "I really do appreciate what you are trying to do for me, and it does help. I don't want to cause Terry any more pain. I'm sure I still love him. I know I ought to, but it's all very mixed up."

"I know, love. Believe me, it will get better, but just remember it's always good to talk about such things. Maybe Terry is too close in some bizarre way, but there are others.

It all depends on who you feel comfortable with; your parents or doctor, anyone, as long as you don't bottle it all up. If you want to talk through anything with me, then you can call me on this number or write to this address."

She handed Lizzie a business card she had taken from her purse, announcing, "It all looks very posh, but it's just something I had to have printed for my restoration work over in France. If you phone me, you will have to put 00 33 in front and drop the first zero of my number. Please remember that I'm always willing to have a bit of a chat, if only to finalise wedding plans."

Lizzie put the card in her pocket and stood up. When Terry arrived moments later, his mum was hugging Lizzie reassuringly, and he derived some vicarious comfort from the sight. He was reluctant to break up this special moment, but reluctantly, he had to announce, "I'm ready to go when you are. I've got the whisky, so your dad will be able to party all night."

As they were about to leave, Lizzie turned back to Janice and said, "Thanks again. I will be in touch."

During the car journey to her parents, there was very little conversation, but Terry hoped he wasn't fooling himself when he felt that Lizzie was not quite as distant as she had been. This was not the old Lizzie, but she didn't appear to be quite as irritable as she had been recently. As the car approached her parents' house, she turned to Terry and said, "Thanks for the lift, but please don't be offended if I don't invite you in. I need to let them know about the baby myself."

While he did not understand her reasoning, he knew that she wanted to deal with the situation in her own way, so he explained, "If that's how you want to handle it, then I understand. I admit that I would love to join you in announcing your pregnancy, but I hadn't expected to be welcomed in. You can let me know how things went later."

The last part of the journey was carried out in silence. When they arrived at their destination, Lizzie leant over and kissed him gently on the cheek, and then opened the door to get out. It was at this point that he remembered the bottle of whisky which he had put in the boot, so he retrieved it and was about to hand it to her as she stood by the garden gate when the door of the house opened, and Lizzie's father appeared. She looked at Terry, and her gaze was obviously imploring him not to get involved, but her father was obviously intent upon speaking with him. Lizzie left Terry holding the whisky and made her way into the house with only the briefest of greetings for her dad.

"Hi, Terry, I must say I'm pleased to see you, but it's pretty obvious things are still a bit icy," he said, nodding in the direction of the house. "Megs and I are worried. She's split up with blokes in the past; we had some right weepy dos when she was younger, but this is different."

"Yes, she's going through a bad patch, but I'm sure she'll get over it. She just needs time. Happy birthday, by the way. I thought this would help you pass away the evening," he said, handing over the whisky.

"I ought to say you shouldn't have, but that would be ingenuous, so I'll just say thank you. Lizzie tells me your mother has been staying with you and that she's living in France now."

"Yes, it was a bit of a shock seeing her at Lord's funeral, but even after not seeing her for years, we seem to get on well, but her and Lizzie get on extremely well. Right from the start, they just clicked. It would have been good on all sorts of levels if Lizzie had been living with me, and then they could have had even more time together."

"On the subject of Lizzie's living arrangements, you do know that we don't want her to be living with us, don't you?

That may sound harsh; we love her and like to see her, but she should be with you. When she first announced her decision to move out of your place, she came to us and asked if she could move back in. We didn't refuse, but we made it very clear that we weren't keen on the idea, and that's why she ended up at Veronica's place. Nasty little piece is that one. When that fell through, we took her in here. We probably didn't help her condition by turning her away the first time, but we thought we were acting for the best."

"Rest assured, Mick, I know you and Megs wouldn't want to come between Lizzie and me and, like the rest of us, you've done what you think was best for Lizzie. That's all we can ever be expected to do, and there's no point in beating ourselves up about it if things don't go to plan. I'd better get off now. I don't want Lizzie to think we are conspiring together, even if we are. Give my love to Megs and enjoy the rest of your birthday party, I'm sure it will go well."

His last remark was as near as he wanted to go to suggesting that the evening had at least one more surprise to offer, and he was convinced that Mick and Meg would be thrilled by Lizzie's news. He would have loved to make a joint announcement about the pregnancy, and he even felt cheated to be missing out, but he respected her wish to do it herself.

The drive home on his own gave him time to think, but by the time he got home, he was still at a loss as to how he might help Lizzie get over her present state. He reflected that initially he had wanted her to come back for his sake, but now he was genuinely concerned for her. He had listened to his mother's information about the possibility of Lizzie having some sort of depressive condition, perhaps aggravated by her pregnancy, and he had convinced himself that it was only a temporary problem. He was still worried that in the aftermath of her illness, she might change and not want to get back together with him.

When he arrived home, he found Janice standing by to serve supper for them. He didn't feel very hungry, but as Janice had obviously put herself out to have the meal ready, he felt obliged to try and eat some of it, but after a while he had to admit defeat and, having eaten barely half of the meal he announced, "I'm sorry, but I just don't appear to have much appetite at the moment, it's been a rather demanding day."

"Don't worry about it. As you say there's been a lot going on today; it doesn't do much for the appetite. Never mind, I can put some of the excess food in the fridge, and you can warm it up for yourself tomorrow."

This mention of the following day brought the subject of his mother's leaving back to the forefront of his mind, and he started to formulate his plans for the day. He knew that his mother had booked a flight home for late the following afternoon. He was not a seasoned flier and was not conversant with the check-in time procedures, so he asked, "What time do we have to leave tomorrow to get to the airport on time?"

"You don't have to make any firm plans," she explained. "I've booked a taxi to take me. I arranged it all when I booked the flight."

Terry found it hard to hide his disappointment as he had been looking forward to the opportunity of a lengthy chat with her on the drive to the airport, and he protested, "I told you I would be your taxi while you were here. I've cleared it with John to have the day off tomorrow. Can't you just ring and cancel?"

"I don't like to let people down when I've made a booking and, more importantly, I think you ought to be available tomorrow as I suspect that Lizzie might want to have a word about the conversation she will have had with her parents this evening."

Terry had failed to fully acknowledge that this evening's disclosure about her pregnancy would have had a profound effect on the family. He knew Mick and Megs well enough to know that they would probably be delighted, as his mother had predicted, but he knew that one can never tell how someone might react to such a dramatic bit of news, and he reluctantly had to admit his mother was right to have booked a taxi.

CHAPTER TWENTY-FIVE

Terry woke early the next morning and made his way quietly downstairs so as not to wake Janice, but he needn't have bothered because when he got to the kitchen, he found the back door open, and he went out to find his mum sitting there.

"Morning, love," she greeted him, "there's tea in the pot if you want to grab yourself a cup."

Terry brought himself a cup out, and she poured him a drink. Terry loved being part of this domestic scene; just sitting and sharing a pot of tea with his mother. For the first time in a couple of weeks, the skies were clouded over, and Terry mused that the short mini heatwave they'd been enjoying was coming to an end.

"So what have you got planned for today," she asked him.

"Nothing special. I don't think it's worth planning to go far as it looks like rain. I think you did right to do your bridge walk when the weather was a little more clement the other day. It will be a bit bleak up there later. The clouds are looking particularly dark over Leeds way, and that usually means we will be due for some damp weather. Did you want to do anything special?"

"To be honest, Terry, I'm just enjoying the opportunity to chat with you. It seems that we have a lifetime of experiences to share. I've felt to have discussed more with you in the last few days than in the last 20 odd years. I regret the lack of shared experiences, but there's no point in dwelling on it; we've just got to make the most of what we have now. I would dearly love to go and see Lizzie before I go, but it's probably not the time to intrude."

"I know what you mean," added Terry. "I want to be with her all the time, but crowding her might not be the right thing to do. I must admit I'm intrigued to know how Mick and Meg reacted to the news of the baby. I wish I could have been there, but Lizzie obviously didn't want it. In the normal course of events, I'd be willing to bet they would be over the moon, but with Lizzie's depressive condition I'm not entirely sure, but I still think I ought to have been there to share the experience and to support her."

"We all want to help, but sometimes it's better to just stand back a bit. It's yet another time in life when we realise that there is no instruction manual to indicate what we should do. We just do our best."

The couple set about producing a light breakfast of cereals and toast and spent the rest of the morning sharing details of their lives and generally making up for the time they had been apart. After such an early start to the day, they found they were ready for lunch by half past eleven, and by one they had finished and washed up. A light rain had started to fall by then, so they had eaten in the kitchen. Janice announced that she would have to finish her packing for her trip home and within five minutes, she was back in the kitchen with the same small overnight bag she had brought when she had arrived. Terry was inwardly impressed at the fact that she could have spent a few days away from home with so little baggage. A certain amount of judicious washing over her stay had helped, but Terry knew he would have needed to take much more for even the shortest of stays. It seemed almost indicative of her 'free spirit' that she could just up and go at a moment's notice. Before he could comment on this fact, they were aware of a car pulling up outside. Terry went to check who it was and came back to announce, "It's Lizzie's parents, and I think she's with them."

Trying to appear relaxed, Terry went to the door and, with some trepidation, showed the visitors into the kitchen.

"Well!" started Mick, smiling broadly, "that was certainly some evening we experienced last night. We were sorry you weren't there so we could congratulate you there and then, Terry, but Lizzie explained that she would have felt awkward about it."

Lizzie's father strode over and shook Terry vigorously by the hand, and he was closely followed by Meg, who hugged him enthusiastically for some time and uttered her own congratulations. Terry couldn't help feeling somewhat uncomfortable; not just by what he regarded as the undeserved adulation he was getting from her parents, but by the fact that Lizzie was strangely separate from the celebration. As soon as he was able to free himself, he went over to her and gave her a gentle hug while kissing her gently on the cheek. "This is a bit of a surprise," he said, unnecessarily, "but it's lovely to see you."

"Mum and Dad were very keen to see you after I spoke to them last night, and I wanted to see Janice again before she went home to thank her for all she has done to help."

Lizzie was aware that everyone was listening to her, and she continued, "I may not be showing it, but I am really very grateful for the way you are all trying to help, and I know my attitude hasn't helped, but thanks for persevering. I understand that you've all tried to help in your different ways, and I've been bloody awful in return, to you in particular, Terry. I took your advice about the doctor, Janice, and I rang the surgery this morning. The receptionist explained the lack of appointments, but she was obviously concerned by the few details I gave her and she spoke to Doctor Corbett, and he rang me back almost immediately. I can't help feeling a bit of a fraud, but the outcome is that I have an appointment later today."

"You're not a fraud, love," remarked Janice, "you've been very ill, and it needs sorting. You've been under intolerable pressure that has built up over the weeks, and just soldiering on bravely is not the answer. You need to get yourself sorted out in plenty of time before the baby is due. God knows, having a baby in the house is stressful enough without all you've experienced. Get yourself back in shape and prepare for the baby. Make it the joyful experience it can be, and share that excitement with those around you."

"Thank you," she replied, "I just feel a failure; I've put everyone through so much."

"You are *not* a failure," stated Terry emphatically. "You've gone through more than anyone could reasonably be expected to put up with. It's not your fault. I could legitimately point out that I didn't see what you were going through early enough. It crept up on both of us, but apportioning the blame helps no one. It may not seem so to you right now, but we have moved on. We now recognise the problem, so we can move forward."

There were supportive comments from the others, and Lizzie even managed a suggestion of a smile. The rest of the afternoon was spent in a general chat, with Lizzie's parents taking every opportunity to say how proud they were of their 'clever' daughter. The conversations were eventually curtailed by the sound of a car horn outside.

"That will be my taxi," exclaimed Janice, glancing at her watch. "Could you nip out with my luggage and tell the driver I'll be out in a minute please, Terry?"

Terry dutifully picked up the small case that constituted his mother's luggage and went out to see the driver. Janice took the opportunity to hug Mick and then Meg before turning to Lizzie, whom she embraced for a time before saying, "You take care of yourself and the little one, and let Terry take care of you a bit. Don't forget that you have the invitation to our wedding, as soon as I tell Greg about it. Please let me know when you decide on the date, and I hope to see you both whenever it's convenient."

Leaving Lizzie's bemused parents to make sense of the intriguing wedding invitation, Janice kissed them in turn and then went out to say goodbye to Terry who was chatting to the taxi driver.

"Thanks for the hospitality over the last few days, darling. It's certainly been eventful, but it has proved far more enjoyable than I had dared hope, and it's been marvellous to get to know you and to meet up with Lizzie. She's a lovely woman. Stick with her; she's worth it, and get her to set up my wedding date as soon as she feels up to it."

"You can rely on me not to give up on her. It's bizarre, but it took her illness for me to see just how much she means to me and how I need to show her how much I care."

The taxi driver was obviously eager to get on his way, so Janice gave Terry a final big hug, kissed him and got in the taxi. Terry stood and waved as the taxi went off down the road. Even after it had disappeared from view, Terry stood and looked in the direction it had gone. He was conscious of the fact that, despite the light rain that was still falling, he was deliberately avoiding going back into the house. It had been a reasonably positive afternoon, but there was still a degree of tension in the air, and Lizzie was still obviously uncomfortable with the situation. He need not have worried because he was met by Lizzie, who explained that she would have to be going because of her doctor's appointment. Her parents continued to express how pleased they were with how things were turning out as they got into their car. The prospect of a baby on the way was seen by them as an indication that things were suddenly better, but Terry did not share their optimism.

He busied himself tidying up the assorted crockery from the numerous cups of tea that had been drunk throughout the afternoon. Then, he sat in his usual chair and considered his immediate options. In the past, he would have had Lizzie to talk to, or he could have gone out to the Barge with Lord, but those options were denied him. He didn't have any ongoing restoration work to occupy him since his big clear-out, and it was pointless putting in a late appearance at the auction room when he had taken a day off anyway. He briefly considered going to the pub on his own, but he realised that he probably wouldn't know anyone there. He had only ever gone out with Lord or Lizzie, and anyway it was raining, so it would hardly have been a pleasant stroll to the pub. A quick flick through the TV channels produced nothing that he felt vaguely interested in watching. He could do some washing, but a quick inspection of the laundry basket showed that there was insufficient to justify putting the washing machine on. Terry realised that he was bored; not only that, but he was on his own and bored, and he wondered if this is what it is like to be lonely.

Eventually, he settled for preparing dinner. It would fill a bit of time. Terry quite liked cooking, but it was sometimes difficult to develop any interest in producing complex meals just for himself. The preparation time and all the resulting washing up and cleaning afterwards were much the same for two people as for one. He had found himself gravitating towards supermarket ready-meals recently; by their very nature, they were convenient but didn't compare to the same meals he could produce himself. Today, he prepared lasagne and a salad, which he set aside ready for the evening, and as he looked at the components of the meal, he couldn't help but notice that, once again, he had produced far too much, but he justified that by reasoning that there would be enough for another meal tomorrow. Once the meal had been prepared, he resigned himself to watching the early evening local news on the TV.

The main item the programme reported on was the tragic death of a baby and the subsequent court case in which the parents were accused of involvement in the death. There were clips of other distraught members of the child's family and the local community talking about the dead infant. It was all pretty harrowing, and it occurred to him that these sorts of events cropped up with alarming regularity in Lizzie's field of work. His musings were interrupted by the telephone ringing, but by the time he had gone through to the hall, the ringing had stopped. Terry muttered some mild obscenity at being disturbed for no purpose, and he assumed it was some Asian call centre where they call several numbers at the same time. The first one to answer gets the advertising blurb, while the others have the frustration of being disturbed for no reason. He remembered the way in which Lizzie would occasionally respond to such calls. If she was busy, they got a blunt reply, but if she had nothing pressing to do, she would keep them on the phone for ages with all sorts of preposterous stories. Her quick mind enabled her to make things up as her story progressed. He remembered one particular caller who had informed Lizzie that she had won a family holiday. Lizzie had faked surprise and excitement at this information about a holiday competition she knew she had never entered and proceeded to make up answers to the routine questions that the well-spoken caller put to her. After some time, the caller asked about Lizzie's family at which point she said she had 10 children and proceeded to reel out the names and ages for all her fictitious family along with interesting little details of their particular foibles. When it came to revealing her 'husband's' details, she announced that he drove a snow plough so he would only be free to take up the holiday in the summer months. It was at this point that the caller chose to hang up. Terry had been listening to this conversation and trying to suppress his laughter, but Lizzie carried on the charade right up to the end. He smiled at the memory. That was how 'his' Lizzie used to be; spirited and mischievous, but all that had changed. His contemplation was interrupted by the phone ringing again, and this time he was ready to give the canvasser some free advice, so he picked up the receiver and, in a less than polite tone, demanded, "What?"

There was a moment's delay, and then a quiet voice enquired, "Terry? It's me, Lizzie."

"Sorry, Lizzie, but I think I just had one of those daft phone calls, and I thought they might be ringing back. It's good to hear from you."

Although it was certainly good to hear her voice. It would have been more honest to say that he was surprised to get the call, but he resisted the temptation to put her under any stress by bombarding her with questions.

"Sorry to interrupt your evening, but I just thought it would be a good idea to have another chat on our own."

"You're not interrupting anything at all, and it would be lovely to talk to you."

"Not on the phone," she added. "I thought it would be good to have a walk down by the river. I could do with some fresh air. I've just got back from the doctor and noticed it looks like the rain could set in again, so I'll grab my coat, and I can pick you up in about half an hour if that suits?"

Mention of the doctor focused his mind on Lizzie's condition, and he couldn't stop himself asking, "What did he say? Are you alright? Is the baby fine?"

"Nothing serious, don't worry. I don't want to elaborate now. We can discuss it on our walk. See you soon."

Terry was a little concerned about the possible outcome of the visit to the doctor, but at the same time, he was thrilled at the prospect of seeing Lizzie again so soon. It took only a few minutes to collect his coat and the old shoes he used to wear on their previous walks. Time seemed to drag as he waited, but eventually Lizzie turned up, and he rushed to meet the car as he guessed she might feel uncomfortable about going in the house. Terry was pleased to get in the car to escape the persistent drizzle, and he asked, "Are you sure that you still want to go for a walk? Wouldn't you just rather drop in at the Barge?"

"No, I'd really like to get some fresh air. I haven't been going out much recently, and anyway I feel it's easier to talk away from crowds."

CHAPTER TWENTY-SIX

As they drove off towards the river, it was Lizzie who broke the silence by reporting, "Mum and Dad were pretty pleased about the baby. I was sure they would be, but I hadn't appreciated just how excited they would be. I'm sure that it won't be long before Mum starts knitting, and Dad will be down in his shed making something for the baby. I think he's a bit frustrated because he doesn't know whether to produce something for a boy or a girl. It's embarrassing that he keeps saying how 'clever' I am."

"I guessed that they would be happy, and I would have loved to have been there when you announced it. I wanted to be part of it, but mainly because I wanted to be there to support you."

"Yes, I know and thanks for letting me do it my way. I know it was irrational, but then a lot of my thinking is a bit jumbled at the moment. I wasn't keen to let them drag me over to see you earlier, I didn't feel as if I could cope with such a big gathering, but I'm glad I came."

"It was lovely to see you. I know you've been having problems and I think you did very well. Mum and I were glad to see you. She's really taken a shine to you. I'm so glad to see you get on so well."

The conversation was somewhat strained, but Terry felt happy just to be near her. They drove on to the car park near the bridge and sat in the car for a while, watching the mesmeric sweep of the windscreen wipers as they worked to clear the light rain that interrupted the view of the bridge.

"Are you sure you really want to get out and go for a walk?" asked Terry as he peered through the windscreen. "We could just stay here and talk."

Terry was reminded of the previous times that they had spent together in that very car park in what his grandparents would have called their 'courting' days. Life had been so good then; they had been set on a wonderful future together, and for nearly three years, life had been pretty idyllic. It seemed a very distant memory as he looked at the young woman beside him. What had happened to the vibrant, loving woman he had welcomed into his life? She looked not unlike the Lizzie he had shared some tender romantic moments with in that very car, but her smile that he had loved so much had gone. The fine drizzle that was falling seemed to mirror his mood.

"I really would like to go for a walk, Terry," she replied, opening her door and stepping out of the car.

She stood for a while, zipping up her jacket and looking in the direction of the bridge, and Terry reluctantly joined her. The car seemed a much more attractive location to him, but he was resigned to going along with her wishes. They both stood for a while before Terry asked, "Do you fancy going down to the river walk and heading towards Hessle?"

"If you don't mind, I would rather have a wander onto the bridge. The walkway is unlikely to be full of people in this weather."

Terry buttoned his coat up to the neck and regretted his decision not to bring a hat, let alone an umbrella. He was tempted to point out that no one in their right mind would want to walk on the bridge in that weather, but he resisted the temptation to say anything. Lizzie was already on her way to where he knew they could access the bridge, and he dutifully set off after her. For a while, they walked in silence before Lizzie remarked, "Janice was telling me that she loved the bridge and the fact that it was possible to walk over to Lincolnshire. When we were here, the weather was rather different. It was almost uncomfortably hot but look at it now. I'm glad she was able to see it at its best. The view was breathtaking that day, and you could see for miles. It was so pleasant to just stand and chat that neither of us bothered to complete the walk to the south bank. Your mum is a very bright woman; she seems able to understand why I feel the way I do, even when I'm unsure about what's going on myself. I feel supported in a strange sort of way. She has an uncanny ability to point me in the right direction without actually giving any specific advice. She started me thinking about how exactly I feel about what's going on in my life. I suppose I should have turned to Mum and Dad, but they felt a bit too close. It felt easier to talk things over with a stranger. The obvious person to talk to should have been you. Sorry, but you were also too close. I guess that sounds weird?"

"Not at all," replied Terry. "I felt the same way about talking to someone I met quite near here a couple of weeks ago. We were able to share details with each other that I wouldn't have dreamed of talking about with family, but discussing things makes you examine your own lifestyle. I guess it's a bit like you discussing things with your counsellor; it can start you examining what it actually is that's bothering you."

The couple walked on in silence along the walkway. The drizzle had now turned into steady rain, and the light wind blew it in sporadic waves into their faces. Terry positioned himself to try and protect her from the worst of it, but Lizzie appeared unfazed by the inclement weather. He suddenly became aware that they were near the exact spot where he had the conversation with the mysterious Mr Hodge. Terry couldn't help but think that it was no surprise that Mr Hodge was not there that evening, and he reflected silently on what sort of idiot would turn up on a windswept bridge in such weather. It was at this spot that Lizzie chose to stop and stand for a moment, looking along the river.

"This is where Janice and I had our little chat; well, it was a rather extensive chat, to be honest. She was open about her troubled times when she went to Newcastle and about her regrets over leaving you with your grandparents. She always did what she thought was best for you, Terry; she always loved you."

"I've come to realise that now," he admitted, "and I'm so glad to have this second chance to get to know her. Lord would have been so happy to have known that I'd found her and to know we hadn't split up completely."

"Yes, it's a pity that it took his funeral for you to meet up with your mum again."

Terry was disappointed that Lizzie had not taken up on his oblique reference to the relationship between himself and her not having split up completely, but he chose not to press the idea. They were, after all, as close as they had been for weeks in terms of physical proximity. They were standing together in the same rain, getting steadily wetter together.

"I wanted to tell you about my visit to the doctors this evening."

"Was everything all right?" he asked, trying to hide any trace of alarm in his voice.

"Dr Corbett was very understanding. His diagnosis was pretty much as your mum had suggested in that he thought I probably have antenatal depression compounded by the pressures of my work. It just hadn't occurred to me that my being pregnant could have been a factor in my depression. I convinced myself that I hadn't changed; I was growing a baby, not a second head; I didn't realise that my perfectly natural condition involved hormones racing around my body. Dr Corbett's not the kind to opt for a regime of medication, but he wants the surgery staff to monitor my condition. He's suggested that I stick to a healthy diet and take some specific vitamin supplements. Another necessity is to take plenty of exercise."

"Like walking to the middle of the bridge in the pouring rain?" he asked.

Lizzie smiled, and Terry felt a moment of mild elation. He had missed that smile and its occasional reappearance, and he dared to think that Lizzie might have made a small step back from the darkness of her depression.

"I don't think it's exactly what he had in mind, but I must admit I do think I feel some benefit from trudging over here."

Terry couldn't conceal his concern when he asked, "Did he say anything about the baby?"

"He had a quick feel of my bump, took my blood pressure and said everything appears fine. He's going to arrange some antenatal sessions to monitor how we are both doing, but today's consultation was largely about my moodiness. I thought I was the only woman to have suffered from depression during pregnancy. It was strangely reassuring to learn from the doctor that about 7% of pregnant women suffer from it and that it will pass. He did point out that I had a strong support team among friends and family, and that's a major indicator that things will improve sooner rather than later."

"We will all do what we can to help you through this and with the baby when it arrives. I will do anything to support you and our baby; I just want to be given the chance to do so. I make no secret of the fact that it has been hell to see you suffering and being denied the opportunity to be with you to help. The only redeeming outcome of all this is that it has only served to show me how much I love you, even if you don't want to hear that."

Lizzie looked out over the river in silence for a while. Terry couldn't see if it was tears or rain running down her face, and he waited anxiously for her response. Eventually, she declared, "You remember that I said I felt helpless and hopeless? Well, I still don't feel able to help myself yet, but at least now I have some hope that all this will pass, and the first glimmer of that hope was when you told me that you wanted the baby."

"And I certainly do. I have since regretted that unfortunate misunderstanding when you found that you weren't pregnant, and we both acted as if we were pleased because we thought that was how the other felt. We were both just too stupid to declare our feelings because we didn't want to risk a disagreement. It might have been a noble gesture to feel we were each trying to please the other, but it would appear that openness would have been a better strategy."

They smiled at each other at the recollection of the conversation. It was only a smile, but it was an indication of a shared experience, and Terry gave in to his wish to hug her, and the reluctance she had shown recently was no longer there.

"I'm sorry, Terry. I've been awful to you."

"Don't start apologising, love. One thing I've come to realise over the last few weeks is that there is little to be gained from allocating blame. After all, I could point out that if I'd been more attentive, I would have seen that you were having difficulties and offered help earlier. The important thing to set our minds on is getting you feeling better and arranging the date for my mum's wedding. She wasn't joking when she said she wanted you to select it."

"Janice is a remarkable woman, Terry. She has a real gift for listening, and I felt to get as much support from her as I do from my counsellor. Don't get me wrong, he's great, but I felt more comfortable with your mum; she's been a real help."

"I guess that's what mums often do best, and I've only recently had the opportunity to experience it."

"I know you said it was a waste of time trying to establish who was to blame, but I just wanted to try and explain my actions over the last few weeks. As I've said, my thinking processes have all been mixed up recently, and I'm beginning to accept that it's all to do with the depression. I knew all along that the pressures of my job were getting me down."

"It's a pity that I couldn't see it."

"Please let me finish," she implored him. "The fact is that I knew that I'd changed in terms of how I saw things. I wasn't completely aware of my mood swings, but I knew things were going wrong between us, and I hated that. I clung on somewhere to the fact that I loved you, and yet I was hurting you. I know it makes no sense, but it seemed to at the time. When I found out I was pregnant and believed that you didn't want children, I felt that I couldn't impose that on you. In some perverse way, I reckoned that you had suffered enough, so I withdrew more and more from our relationship. That obviously didn't help my state of mind, and things just went from bad to worse. The initial meeting with my counsellor, the meeting with the doctor and talking things through with Janice all helped, but the thing that has really helped is the fact that you never gave up on me despite the way I treated you."

Terry stood for a moment as the sincerity of her message sunk in before he replied, "You're a very easy person to love even when you try your hardest not to be, and I've recently become increasingly aware of what matters in life. I'm reminded of a conversation I had with a guy a couple of weeks ago just near here. He reckoned that the most important things in life were his wife and young baby. Mum summed it up in that French saying, which I can't for the life of me remember, stating that the best thing in life is to love and be loved."

They stood together in the rain. Lizzie had shown the good sense to wear a coat with a hood, but Terry just stood as the rain flattened his hair before the water was released to run down his face and to trickle secretly down his neck. He could feel the water soaking through the shoulders of what was only a shower-proof coat; he was cold and wet but inexpressibly happy, and he didn't want that moment to end. It was only when Lizzie gave an involuntary shiver that he realised they ought to be getting back to the car. Without saying a word, he gently took her hand, and they set off for the car park.

When they arrived at the car, they both removed their wet coats and threw them onto the back seats. Lizzie started the engine and turned the heater up to full before sitting back. The couple looked at each other; they looked like a couple of drowned rats, and they both had a little laugh at their bedraggled states. Lizzie was laughing! Terry felt such an upsurge of happiness as he saw it as another little sign that things weren't quite as bad as they had been. Their shared openness with each other in their conversation on the bridge had moved them a little further along the path to her recovery, and Terry felt it might be appropriate to discuss other issues.

"I have thoroughly enjoyed this evening, not least because I feel we have a better understanding of each other's experiences, but I have to say that I'm not sure that living with your parents is the best place for you. Perhaps it would be better if you moved back to our home? When you see your mum and dad tonight, you could discuss the possibility of your moving out. I could make up the bed in the spare room for you."

Terry knew he had taken a risk with his suggestion, but he had come to appreciate that hiding his feelings just to avoid the fear of rejection was not going to help him get Lizzie back. Lizzie looked at him and smiled. After what seemed like an age to Terry, she replied, "I'm still trying to cope with my brain fog, but the one certainty in life is that I want to spend it with you, but I don't think that I should discuss the matter with Mum and Dad. I think you should ring them when we get back and tell them that I've decided to move back to our home, where I belong."

Terry was both stunned and elated by this response, and he instinctively leant over and kissed her before his rational brain reminded him that her proposal threw up certain complications, and he asked, "Isn't that going to be a bit of a shock to your parents? Why don't you want to ring them yourself, and what about the fact that you are soaking wet and all your clothes are at your parents' place?"

"Mum and Dad won't be shocked; they will be ecstatic. They've made lots of less-than-subtle hints that I ought to move out; in fact, they have shown that they don't think it helps anybody if I continue to live there. For a while I thought they just wanted to get rid of me, but it's obvious to me now that they were trying to do what they thought was in my best interests. I think it should be you that rings them to give them what I know they will see as good news. You gave me space to tell them about the baby, so you deserve the honour of brightening up their day this time, and I can have a short chat with them after you. Don't worry about my lack of dry clothes because I've got some in the boot. I always carried an emergency overnight bag in case I was involved in something with work that unexpectedly meant that I had to book into a hotel somewhere."

Terry was overwhelmed by a feeling of joy. He instinctively gave her a lengthy kiss, and he was further delighted to see that there was no resistance on her part. He knew his Lizzie was coming back to him.

"I've caused you a lot of problems recently," she started to say, but he cut her short.

"Shush! You've often told me that we never have 'problems'; we have 'opportunities'. Well, it's true. What's happened over the last few weeks has given me the opportunity to think about what I really value in life. Firstly, the things that matter don't always have a price tag, and secondly, if things don't go to plan then attributing culpability to ourselves or others is largely a futile exercise."

Terry began to feel that things were certainly going to get better, so he allowed himself the luxury of looking forward to how he wanted things to be, and he suggested, "Mum will be delighted when we tell her that you are on the road to recovery and no doubt she will be looking forward to her wedding, just as soon as you fix the date. I think it might be a good idea to go over to France to stay with her and Greg to sort the matter out. But rest assured, we will not be going for a paltry one-night visit. We both deserve a proper break. In the meantime, I have a lasagne waiting for us at home, and I could open a bottle of red. Oh! I forgot, you're pregnant, so perhaps a glass of orange juice for you? It's going to take me some time to get used to this parent thing. But I can't wait."

He gently put his arm around her shoulder, and they sat for a moment, staring out towards the bridge, which by now was partly obscured by the rain that was steadily falling from the darkening clouds. Terry smiled contentedly as he realised that the dark cloud that had been hanging over Lizzie was at last starting to break up, and life felt good.

ABOUT THE AUTHOR

Born in Hull in 1949, the oldest of four children I started at Anlaby County Primary School aged four and a half. On my first day mum walked me the quarter of a mile to the school and picked me up later. On subsequent days I was on my own as mum had my other younger siblings to look after. I later went on  to Beverley Grammar School which I chose from a wide range of possible secondary schools in the area for the simple reason that my neighbour already attended the school. I calculated that he would know the way to the bus stop on my first day. On such limited information many of the major decisions in my life have been made. Moving on to Sheffield City College I gained my teaching qualifications, met my future wife Lynne and drifted in to teaching. Having taught at a new Comprehensive school in Grimsby for five years I went in to special education for the rest of my career. Along the way my wife blessed me with three children but unfortunately she died of Alzheimer's in 2024. I now live near Winchester and I never regret my decision to take early retirement from a job that was becoming increasingly tedious.